JEKYLL,
ALIAS HYDE

JEKYLL, ALIAS HYDE

A Variation
by

Donald Thomas

St. Martin's Press
New York

Library of Congress Cataloging-in-Publication Data

Thomas, Donald Serrell.
    Jekyll, alias Hyde.

    Based on the characters in Robert Louis Stevenson's The strange case of Dr. Jekyll and Mr. Hyde.
    "A Thomas Dunne book."
    I. Stevenson, Robert Louis, 1850-1894.   Strange case of Dr. Jekyll and Mr. Hyde. II. Title.
PR6070.H6J4   1989   823'.914   88-30809
ISBN 0-312-02592-0

First published in Great Britain by Macmillan London Limited.

First U.S. Edition
10 9 8 7 6 5 4 3 2 1

For Graeme and Huguette

What binds the better slave to worse
Swindles soul, body, goods and purse
To unlock the secret cells of dark abyss
The power which never does its victim miss.

Richard Dadd,
The Fairy Feller's Master-Stroke,
Broadmoor, 1865

PART 1

1884: A Parliamentary Murder

1

Alfred Swain's pencil followed the graceful line of Romana Utterson's neck on the sketching pad. The motion of his hand was hesitant, almost apologetic. He worked with the air of a novice in medicine or dentistry begging indulgence from his first patient.

'What was your father, Mr Swain?'

Her lips scarcely moved, perhaps for fear of altering the pose. Romana Utterson had turned her profile and bare neck towards him as if timidly and of necessity to the executioner's axe. The dark ellipse of her eyes and the intent seriousness of her gaze were hidden. She was, perhaps unconsciously, imitating the pose of the picture on the wall. It was a drawing of *Proud Maisie* in rust-coloured chalk by Frederick Sandys. Petulant beauty fretted at an end of hair pressed to her lips. Mr Utterson the lawyer had bought prudently from the Art Union exhibitions of the Pre-Raphaelites when he was a young man. But few of his investments had prospered, unless one might count the preliminary sketch for Rossetti's *Beata Beatrix*, which hung in the hallway of the Bayswater villa. The rest were works of accomplishment without genius like his drawing-room centrepiece, *The Bedchamber of Desdemona*, in the colours of Venetian Gothic drama by Henry Wallis.

'The bounder ran off, you know,' Utterson had confided to Swain with a chuckle. 'Eloped, if you prefer it, with the wife of the novelist George Meredith. She being already a widowed daughter of Thomas Love Peacock. So many famous names! The world is a small place in its iniquities, is it not, Mr Swain? And a damned large and empty one to the poor devil in trouble.'

The tragedy of it all had not prevented Gabriel Utterson chuckling again, over his gin and warm water.

'What was your father, Mr Swain?'

Swain's attention was recalled to the present. He frowned a little at his drawing and replied with studied politeness.

'He was a country schoolmaster, Miss Utterson. I fear he died when I was ten and I remember too little of him. He kept a school for the village children at East Knoyle, near Shaftesbury.'

'I do not think I know East Knoyle, Mr Swain.'

'A very small village, Miss Utterson. Sir Christopher Wren was born there.'

'Dear me! How you put one in one's place, Mr Swain. Was that why you became a policeman?'

'To put one in one's place, Miss Utterson?'

'No! You are a goose, Fred Swain! Because your father died?'

There was just a touch of temper in play, a silken whisper of the chestnut hair on satin shoulders as she turned to him. But the laughter shone silently in Romana Utterson's eyes.

'I think I did it from curiosity,' Swain said mildly, 'And then from habit. I don't think I ever did anything in my life, except from curiosity. You should look at the left-hand candlestick on the mantel, Miss Utterson. Or I shall make nothing of this.'

The background would be easy enough. Red damask of the wallpaper. Beyond it, through the arch, the elegant conservatory was secluded from the rumble and clatter of the Bayswater Road. It had been arranged as a romantic bower, through whose leaves the Lady of Shalott or Guinevere might have materialised, as dressed by Lord Tennyson or William Morris. Within its rich green fragrance, during the winter months, there flourished white geranium and heliotrope, fragrant calanthus and blue tree-violets, among the exquisite tracery of hothouse ferns.

Alfred Swain bowed himself to the sensual occupation

10

of caressing the lines of Romana Utterson with his pencil. Seduction *in absentia*, he decided, was the basis of his art. Above him the harsh flare of the gaselier illuminated his sketch. His model sat unnaturally upright and in profile. Her dress was the high-collared silk with the peaked shoulders which had been fashionable since the previous season. Why was it, Swain wondered, that the higher the collar rose and the more she was concealed, the more she revealed herself to him? His features, still youthful, betrayed nothing of his thoughts as he began with loving deliberation to follow the slight inward curve of her back above the waist.

Swain's was the long and gentle face of an intelligent horse. Those who ridiculed him for it were men rather than women. But the ridicule was necessary to some of his colleagues. It gave them a certain self-confidence, tempering the awe provoked by Swain's capacity for learning and memorising, the hunger of his intellectual curiosity.

Mr Utterson's younger daughters were Eugenia, shortened in the family to 'Jenny', who was twenty and Adeline, four years her junior, who was more oddly known as 'Dido'. Swain had not presumed to try these pet-names. Romana Utterson was far too grand to have a nickname. Her two juniors were now at the polished walnut of the Erard piano, Jenny standing or rather leaning over her sister. Dido in a plain day-dress ran her fingers over the keys in easy arpeggios to accompany Jenny's soaring soprano.

'On wings of song beloved, I'll bear thy spirit away. . . .
Far where the Ganges is flowing, where flowers wake bright and gay. . . .'

Effortless and therefore suspect to Alfred Swain, the melodic line of Mendelssohn rose and swooped and rose again in a thousand middle-class drawing-rooms of Bayswater and Highgate, Hampstead and Maida Vale. Not, alas, in the tenements of Cable Street or Southwark where much of his professional life was passed.

'For deep in a beautiful garden, of star and moonlight
fair. . . .
The lotus blossoms are waiting to greet thee fondly there . . .
The lotus blossoms are waiting . . . To – greet – thee –
fond-ly – there . . .'

Few of Swain's people ever saw beautiful gardens. Star
and moonlight revealed to them only a squalor better hid in
darkness. They would go to their mean and narrow communal
graves in Tooting and Hackney, packed down with strangers
for twelve years before their rotted remains were burnt col-
lectively at night, without knowing the difference between a
lotus blossom and a cauliflower or turnip. And without, Swain
thought, caring.

Jenny's voice, a little shrill in the higher register, was
like the rest of her. She was pretty, with the dark hair and
deep slanting eyes of her sisters. But she was not beautiful,
as Romana Utterson was at twenty-four or twenty-five, and
never could be. That was an article of faith with Alfred
Swain.

They had finished *On Wings of Song*. Jenny was now
turning the pages of music for her younger sister, whose quick
fingers skipped and cavorted through the 'Spring Song' from
Songs Without Words. Somewhere there should have been the
figure of Mrs Utterson to complete the family evening. But
the wing-chair with its flower brocade had been empty almost
since the day Adeline-Dido was born. By now, Mr Utterson
had come to look upon himself as a bachelor encumbered with
and ruled by three daughters. It was the great point in common
between the lawyer and the inspector, this bachelorhood. He
and Swain, coming face to face in the Suffolk Galleries and
recognising each other from professional encounters had fallen
into conversation.

Mr Utterson of Maybury, Utterson and Parke, solicitors of
Gaunt Street, St Paul's, had invited Inspector Swain of Scotland
Yard to dinner. The inspector, accepting with reservations,
found himself in a paradise of female beauty where art and

12

music – the easel and the pianoforte – were paramount. To Alfred Swain it was a world of colour and luxury that bordered almost on depravity. All his education had been in books. Historical information and scientific argument, religious debate and travellers' tales occupied him mostly. Poetry sometimes, when it was worthy. *In Memoriam* was worthy. So were the *Idylls of the King*. Swinburne he liked, and rather felt he ought not to. Fiction, never. The key to Alfred Swain, so obvious that it was seldom found, was an urge to self-improvement and a conviction that time was running out. He had once consulted a table of vital statistics. With consternation turning to horror, he read that the average age of the modern man at death was forty-one. It took him a long time after that to see averages in their true perspective.

The Uttersons had taken up Swain in their easy and unprepossessing manner. They did not force sketching or salon music upon him. They merely enjoyed it and allowed him to see their enjoyment.

'Books?' said Mr Utterson cheerfully. 'Reading for pleasure? I believe I have a dozen improper French novels in the house for that and nothing else these last ten years.'

Swain smiled to himself as he remembered this, amused and contented. Then the smile was checked. He had reached a point in his sketch where he must either make it a portrait to the waist or else begin upon the hips and legs. It was impossible that he could avoid showing the sketch to Romana Utterson. To continue below the waist was therefore to offer to her a direct and intimate comment upon what he thought of as her nether limbs. In other circumstances it would verge upon indecency, impoliteness at least. It drew attention to a lecherous musing upon her form. Even among artistic folk of the better sort it was hardly to be risked. The pencil hovered. Dead flesh and naked flesh, of either sex and all ages, was common to Swain's profession. Romana Utterson as a Haymarket draggle-tail would have caused him no hesitation. But now he hesitated.

Mr Utterson saved him, rugged and gruff in the manner of a secretly amiable man, the lines and spouting hairs suggesting

13

an age he had not yet reached. The lawyer entered, putting familiar music-hall words to Mendelssohn's 'Spring Song'.

'Oh, to be on an island where the girls are few. . . .
Oh, to be on an island where there's only me and you-oo. . . .'

A general protest greeted this blasphemy and Adeline stopped playing. Her father scooped up *On Wings of Song* from the top of the piano.

'Don't, father!' said Jenny indignantly.

Utterson turned to Swain.

'The innocent art of mockery, Mr Swain! The good old English nose for the pretentious and the absurd! How out of fashion it is! Will you look at this, Mr Swain. Herr Mendelssohn's publishers warn us: "This song may be sung in public without licence. The public performance of any parodied version is, however, strictly prohibited." So when I am caught yodelling it in the street these three harpies of mine might have me prosecuted. Regina versus Utterson, Mr Swain, in the matter of Herr Mendelssohn's *Wings of Song*. Womankind, sir, lacks an ear for the ridiculous. Come, Mr Swain, you and I will retire to our gin and water.'

'Mr Swain is sketching, papa,' said Romana Utterson, quiet in her reproach.

'Mr Swain is being imposed upon by the pack of you and needs rescue,' said the lawyer scornfully. 'Mr Swain and I have a little business to attend to. Mr Swain has had enough of hysterics and vapours and romantic swoons. And, I daresay, enough of Herr Mendelssohn.'

'I was—' Swain attempted. But Mr Utterson wagged a finger and drew him away.

'Don't encourage 'em, Mr Swain. Your life won't be worth living if you do.'

Gabriel Utterson maintained with Alfred Swain the cheerful fiction that women were created to be the bane of mankind and that unless a united front were presented, all must be lost.

'Woman will be the last thing civilised by man, old George Meredith used to say. Read *Richard Feverel* some

14

day. Ah, but you don't read story-books, do you, Mr Swain?'

Mr Utterson constantly referred to himself as a bachelor and to everything about him as being of a bachelor kind. He lived with his daughters in the protection of a mutual and facetious tolerance.

'Oh, to be on an island where the girls are few,' the lawyer sang murmuringly, tossing the music back on to the piano as he led Swain towards the humid fragrance of the conservatory. 'Regina versus Utterson. I like the sound of it, Mr Swain. I should give them a run for their money, I believe.'

'I believe you would, sir,' said Swain helpfully.

They went through a door from the conservatory into a small reading-room. It was the beginning of what the lawyer liked to call his bachelor house, its walls lined with law reports bound in green and plum-coloured calf, a handsome table and a lectern occupying the room's centre. Beyond that, under a second glass roof, was Utterson's billiard room, the baize immaculate and brightly lit. The room and the lavatory opening off it were tiled in the manner of a sporting club. Utterson opened a final door and they stepped into the smoking room, the deepest male preserve in the whole of the house.

'What vices would the inquiring mind attribute to this place!' Utterson had once said to Swain, 'And what disappointment when they found I practised only the smoking of cigars and the drinking of gin and water. The rage of people who find out that you are not as bad as they supposed, Mr Swain, is never to be underestimated.'

The smoking-room, though visited by the servant every day, had the look of a place seldom cleaned. The cream ceiling and the plaster mouldings were discoloured by breaths of havana. Deep leather chairs had begun to sag under the weight of so many comfortable hours. The linoleum of the floor was frayed and scuffed. Utterson's walls were hung with legal prints and caricatures. Officiating at the table, he poured his gin.

'For you, Mr Swain?'

'Thank you,' said Swain. 'Just half a glass.'

'And no cigar? I will, unless you object.'

Utterson sat down and chuckled again. But now there was no mirth in the sound. Presently he turned to Swain with an enigmatic glance.

'May one speak, Mr Swain, not as to a policeman?'

Swain made a joke of it.

'If not to me, sir, then to whom?'

'A delicate point of interpretation, Mr Swain. I promise you, I shall not compromise you in the least. I will mention no names. I will reveal no secret crimes. It is the principle that concerns me.'

'There can be no objection, sir, to matters of principle.'

'It concerns the client, Mr Swain, of a certain lawyer. An unmarried man who was a long time abroad and is now returned, living alone but for his servants. He comes to the lawyer to draw up a will. You see?'

Swain nodded. Utterson sank further into his chair and resumed.

'The man of whom I speak is distinguished in his profession. He has been known to the attorney in question for many years, though there have been gaps in their acquaintanceship when the testator was overseas. But our distinguished professional man is still in the prime of life. You follow?'

Swain nodded again. Utterson raised a finger and came to the point.

'The will contains a most extraordinary final clause. Indeed, I doubt that it would be held valid in law. It provides that in the event of the death of our friend J all his possessions shall pass into the hands of his friend and benefactor H. That is unexceptional, but that his closest friends have never heard before of H, let alone heard J, mention him. What comes next, however?'

Utterson refreshed himself from the glass and continued.

'The next clause provides – I quote its very words – that in the event of the *disappearance* of J, or his unexplained absence for a period exceeding three calendar months, the man H shall become possessed of the estate as if J really were dead. Disappearance, mark you, not death. Now, Mr Swain, a lawyer cannot be forced to draw up a will where he

16

believes the provisions to be dangerous or unsound. In this case, however, he could not prevent the man himself drawing it up, signing it, and lodging it with him for safekeeping.'

Swain scratched his temple and shook his head, as if to clear it.

'The story is extraordinary. And the man did not die?'

'No, sir.'

'Nor disappear?'

'No,' said Utterson. 'My understanding is that the case stands just as I have described it.'

Swain relaxed, as if with relief that there was nothing in this to embarrass either of them. It was plain to him that Utterson in referring to an attorney was talking about himself. But he had the good sense not to make it specific.

'I believe,' Swain said, 'that the lawyer might confront his client with the will. He might argue the unwisdom of such a provision. He might point out that it is legally unenforceable and therefore pointless.'

Utterson rubbed his chin.

'Possibly, Mr Swain. Not certainly. I confess to doubts because the courts have never tried precisely this issue. A man may disappear and be presumed dead. He may go off to the jungles of Africa and not be heard of again. After a time the courts would presume him dead but not after three months. But there is a worse case. It might be argued that the will attempts to convey a power of attorney from J to H. The means used would be irregular but someone must sooner or later administer the estate of the missing testator. You see? I do not think there could be any validity in it. But the waters are muddy, Mr Swain.'

'Then, sir, ought not counsel's opinion to be sought for the sake of all concerned? I am no lawyer, Mr Utterson, heaven knows.'

Utterson wagged a finger again, chuckling as if he had caught Swain at last.

'You are no lawyer, my friend. You are better than a lawyer. You are a policeman. The question I would put is to Scotland Yard, not to the Middle Temple. It is this. Suppose

17

circumstances arose in which such a man as J were to go missing, and suppose he had made such provision as this. What would you think?'

Swain looked almost blankly ahead of him.

'That he was dead in suspicious circumstances and the body not found for some reason.'

'Right.' Utterson approved it.

'Or that he had gone into hiding for reasons which might be innocent or not. They do not sound innocent, on the face of it.'

'They do not, Mr Swain.'

'Or, since no one has ever seen or heard of H, that H is merely a disguise for J. That, at the least, suggests the intention to deceive.'

'Indeed, it does. My own comment upon the matter, after long consideration, was precisely that. At first I thought it was madness. And now I begin to fear it is disgrace.'

'It might, of course, be madness,' Swain conceded. 'I had assumed, though, that the soundness of mind was not in question. Madness would explain everything.'

'It would, sir,' Utterson said. 'I doubt, however, if it does.'

The two men sat in silence until Swain judged it time to ask the most delicate question of all.

'Does the story have an ending, sir?'

Utterson shook his head.

'It stands just there. J and H where they always were, if H ever was. The will in safekeeping and the legal brotherhood awaiting the great event.'

'Then,' said Alfred Swain with a desire not to sound priggish, 'it is perhaps best that I should know no more of it at present.'

Utterson's large head lolled round towards him, the mouth gaping slightly in a humorous reprimand.

'There is no danger of that, Mr Swain. No danger of that whatever. You have heard from me upon the subject all that I propose you ever shall hear.'

And yet, Swain thought, a man of pertinacity need only find a list of Utterson's clients whose names began with J.

18

Those who had no distinction might be eliminated and among the handful of names remaining the maker of the curious will might be identified.

That night Alfred Swain thought a good deal about the story and cast his vote for madness. It was far and away the safest choice. And then, soon after that, he was walking in Kensington gardens on a summer afternoon with Romana Utterson on his arm. They were talking *tête-à-tête* in a manner that hinted at far greater intimacy. Behind them, within hearing, walked the Utterson's maid Lizzie with a friz of auburn hair that was the beauty of Rossetti's *Beata Beatrix*. And Alfred Swain stepped back, begging Lizzie not to eavesdrop on them, growing quite cross when she laughed and would not promise. And then he marched Lizzie behind the laurel bushes, hidden from the world, and found to his dismay that he and she were both naked. And Lizzie said, 'It's not disgrace, Mr Swain, only madness.' He looked for Romana, remembering that he must not keep her waiting alone on the path. But Romana had gone and he was at his wits' end to think what to tell her father. And at last, to his great relief, Alfred Swain woke up.

The comfort of his rooms in Pimlico, the gas popping and the glow of the fire in the wintry dawn, were profoundly reassuring. All the same, Swain was wary of the dream-dramas that came to him at such times. Romana Utterson was embedded in his thoughts and fancies. She was too much in his mind. And that, Inspector Swain thought, would not do at present. It would not do at all.

2

The evening after Alfred Swain's homage to the drawing-room elegance of Romana Utterson, Sergeant Oliver Lumley paced solemnly along the river walk in sight of London Bridge. His private-clothes frock-coat and rusty trousers advertised his profession as plainly as any uniform.

At this hour on an October night, the docks and wharves were deserted. Only the portly deliberation of Lumley's own footsteps hung in the frosted air. Other men of the division shunned the night watches. Lumley preferred them. London by dark was a quiet and contemplative city, the moon and shadows evoking the troubled ghosts of a distant past. Crime, at such an hour, struck with brutal and dramatic rapidity. But in Lumley's experience it struck rarely. A man was far more likely to have his pocket picked or his throat slit in the sunlight.

Glancing either way to make sure there was no inspector on patrol, the sergeant drew from his pocket a veal slice, folded in a cabbage leaf and wrapped in turn by an old playbill: 'Lyceum Theatre, Manager Mr Henry Irving – FAUST – Mephistopheles played by Mr Irving – Every evening at a quarter to eight – Carriages at eleven.' Sergeant Lumley shook his head, as if it were all beyond him. He crumpled the paper and threw it down. Then, with a little groan of plump satisfaction, he sank his teeth into the veal slice.

All around him the great warehouses were closed, the long wall of the Custom House huge and dead, full of blind windows. The damp wharves were securely gated and barred. Yet even in the night air he breathed the suffocating odour of secondhand fish, vegetables and fruit, potato sacks and coal-dust, the sulphurous reek of the adjacent gas-works.

As Lumley poked the last of the veal slice into his capacious mouth, the church bells began to chime the hour in the thin dank air. The deep note of St Paul's was joined by the lighter peals of St Clement Danes and Bow Church, followed by the distant trebles from evangelical Hackney and Puseyite Pimlico. Sergeant Lumley, with the contentment of food inside him, resumed his steady magisterial pace.

It was not so much a beat as a sweep, this plain-clothes sentry-go. He was to begin at London Bridge and end at Marlborough Street lock-up, trespassing on the territory of several Metropolitan Police Divisions, before meeting Inspector Swain at Regent Circus. He followed the dark by-ways of the City and Holborn, where the faces of the hoardings smiled down on behalf of Rowlands' Macassar Oil, The Louis Velveteen from all Drapers throughout the Kingdom, White Enamelled Bedroom Suites from Hamptons of Pall Mall East. A print from the *Illustrated London News* showed General Prendergast ordering the King of Burma to abdicate at ten minutes' notice.

Oliver Lumley sang softly to himself as he followed the quiet streets beyond the Charing Cross Road into the courts and alleys of Soho. Here there was a different London, shops open and brightly lit at all hours. Round the coffee stall, men in corduroys and thick jackets clutched their blue-and-white earthenware mugs. What came from the tall steaming cans behind the counter had no claim to be anything but hot and sweet, despite its boasted pedigree in tall red letters of 'Coffee as in France'. Sergeant Lumley had not the least idea of how things were in France. He supposed them to be 'flash and bounce' but did not greatly care.

He felt in his pocket, counted the value of the coins by touch, and decided against further indulgence.

The next corner marked the beginning of Trim Street. The little shops at this end boasted a prosperity of fresh-painted shutters. Those at the other had a look of antique decay. At all hours of day and night, it seemed to Lumley, small children tumbled between the legs of passers-by, sprawled and howled and beseeched assistance. Their elder brothers and

21

sisters chalked the pavement for hopscotch and fly-the-garter, thread-the-needle and shove-halfpenny. The footway was a gamut of hopping, swaying, galloping, kicking infancy.

The neat eighteenth-century shopfronts of the French patisserie and the Italian grocer, the German clockmaker and English tailor ended. Another Trim Street began. The children still skipped and lurched on the chalked pavement. But the houserails were occupied by men in slouch hats, who picked their teeth to pass the time, and women in tight silks and shabby furs. That some of the children belonged to these families was not in doubt.

A round bold-faced urchin with a younger brother behind him confronted Sergeant Lumley in his private clothes.

'Got sixpence?' said the elder child holding out a hand with an air of impatience.

'You'd better 'ave,' said the infant behind him, 'supposin' you know what's good for you.'

The rage of authority seized Oliver Lumley and lured him uncharacteristically into a trap. He snatched at the collars of the two boys and began to lift them with a pleasant fantasy of bringing their heads together in a splendid crack. At that moment another pair of arms bound him from behind. A disembodied hand entered his waistcoat pocket and withdrew his watch. A deft tug wrenched it from its button fastening. Lumley, weighed down by the two small boys and unable to free his arms to which they now clung, went sprawling from a powerful shove in the back. He got to his knees, then his feet, in time to see the two infant beggars disappearing round the near corner of the street. Sprinting the other way was a youthful footpad. Lumley recognised him at once as Carlo Beamer, known in the trade as Waistcoat Charlie for the embroidered silk spanning his narrow chest.

The audacity of such an attack on an officer of the law left him incredulous with rage. But the street was in an uproar. Several of the children joined in the race with Lumley. Most of the others darted about trying to impede him.

'Come back here, Waistcoat!' Lumley bellowed. 'That's

police property! Hand that watch over or I'll see you crucified for it!'

Beamer, looking round, seemed to realise for the first time the identity of his victim. There was dismay in his glance but the sight of Lumley pounding after him merely caused the boy to run faster still. The watch was tossed among his friends.

'Stop him!' roared Lumley to anyone who would listen. 'Stop him! He's a thief!'

The inhabitants of Trim Street stood back, allowing the two contestants to decide it for themselves. Beamer had reached the shabbier end of the street where, almost at the corner, there was a low entrance to a court with a door in a blank wall. A hundred years earlier a dictionary writer had lived and died in poverty there. The curiosity of the neighbourhood had given the place the local name of Terminology House. That name had stuck.

Lumley knew that he was not going to catch the juvenile thief. Charlie Beamer's legs seemed to twinkle in the lamplight with the speed and grace of their action. Lumley heard his own breath rasping. The weight of his boots thumped on the slippery paving with a deliberate and cumbersome beat. The veal slice had done its worst. He might as well have tried to outpace a swallow or a pigeon.

More bitter than the loss of the watch was the prospect of having to explain to Inspector Swain or even Colonel Mayne how he had been taken for a gull by a couple of infants. But Waistcoat Charlie with his oiled locks and neat-cut suiting was striding away like a champion, opening up the distance effortlessly.

Resigning himself to the loss of the police regulation-issue watch as Beamer approached the corner, Lumley slackened his pace. Somewhere behind him, he could hear a group of drunken voices raised in derisive song.

'Ev'ry member of the force 'as a watch and chain, o'course.
If you want ter know the time ask a p'liceman . . .'

Then there occurred what he could only think of as a miracle. A man turned the corner, coming the other way.

He was a short and possibly slight figure, though the black cloak and tall hat gave him an air of greater bulk. He carried a silver-knobbed stick and it seemed that he was stamping rather than walking along the pavement at the shabbier end of the street. Pale and dwarfish, he might have been the victim of some deformity or other, though there was no deformity that Lumley could see. The stranger appeared to be talking to himself, drawing his breath in a sudden hiss from time to time as if at the complexity or the horror of the problem he confronted.

His hand had just drawn a latch-key from his pocket when Waistcoat Charlie sprinted at him, evidently expecting that the man would step aside. Instead, there was a collision. But it was not of the kind that usually occurs between pedestrians. At the last moment, the dwarfish man prepared for the impact by a short lunge at the boy with the knob of his stick. The fugitive checked and swerved, trying to get round the other on the outside edge of the pavement. At which the pale figure in the cloak and hat darted the stick between the young thief's speeding legs and tripped him irretrievably. Waistcoat Charlie rose like a swimmer taking a plunge and came down on the cobbles. He rolled and sat up, hugging one leg to himself with an expression of agonised concentration. He was still rocking to and fro with the pain of the injury when Lumley seized him by the arm.

'Right, Waistcoat!' said the sergeant with plump satisfaction, 'that's the last of your little game for the next eighteen months or so. I shouldn't wonder if you ain't catted as well for once. Just to pass the time.'

Waistcoat Charlie set up an appealing wail, pleading to the bystanders for rescue. But Lumley was the victor now, Beamer's hands locked in the metal cuffs behind his back. Trim Street opinion changed sides and supported the law. There was only one little girl, a mite of six or seven and a worshipper of Carlo Beamer, who could not endure her young hero's downfall. She ran hard at the stranger in the cloak and hat, now approaching the door in the plain and windowless wall, the low and narrow entrance to Terminology House.

24

What she intended was by no means clear. But with her little fists raised, she flew towards him.

She might have beaten him about the knees and thighs but he gave her no opportunity. As with Waistcoat Charlie, he anticipated the impact and sent the child flying with a peremptory shove. She fell motionless, though only stunned, on the pavement before him. Lumley, being behind the dwarfish man, could not quite see the sequel. He thought at first the man had merely put his foot on her as a gesture of contempt. Then it seemed that he had trampled her. And last of all he kicked or at least moved her body aside with his boot.

What Lumley saw most clearly was the way in which the man turned his face aside to the onlookers and favoured them with a smile of murderous timidity. He was a poor thing, he seemed to suggest. Yet had he not got the better of this little trull and her miserable companion in the most dexterous manner? It would teach them to look out for the future.

Lumley, his hand still clutching the collar of Waistcoat Charlie, watched in dismay. The tenant of Terminology House showed no further interest in the little girl than if she had been a discarded sack. In the space of a minute he had, without the least compunction, proved himself willing to inflict lifelong injury on a pair of children. Lumley recalled for the first time that Waistcoat Charlie, despite his fame as an operator upon fob-pockets and purses – even despite his oiled hair and romantic looks – was little more than twelve or thirteen years old.

Clutching his prisoner, Sergeant Lumley tried at the same time to control the row that was boiling up among the witnesses of the event.

'Kick him down, the brute!' screamed one of the street-girls from the railings of Trim Street's shabby north. 'Snatch his stick away and give him a good kicking!'

Lumley shouted without avail. To intervene, before intervention was needed, would mean to lose his prisoner. To delay might be to see injury or murder done. A pair of tramps sat huddled together on the doorstep of Terminology House as if

to deny its tenant a way in. The children who had been playing
shops upon it gathered up their wares and drew back in alarm.
They took shelter among the full skirts of adult womanhood,
one or two holding the hands of the street-women by the
railings to whom they belonged.

The little girl who had been knocked down was sufficiently
recovered to begin screaming with fright and shock. Lumley
felt a profound relief. Shock and indignation rather than the
low misery of a true injury coloured her cries. In a moment
more her screams were overlaid by those of her mother and
sisters coming out of one of the poorer houses. The sight
of the child on the ground was reinforced by the cold and
Satanic indifference of the man with the cloak and stick who
slunk back against the chipped brick of the street wall with a
foolish and yet malevolent smile. He seemed to suggest that it
was nothing but a misunderstanding. And if it were not, then
they might go to the devil for all he cared.

It was the women who were to the front of the crowd that
formed in a semi-circle round him, imprisoning him with his
back to the blank wall. If they paused, it was only because
they could not yet envisage street justice cruel enough to
reward him. The mother and an older sister lifted the child
and carried her back a few yards. At least, when they set her
down, she was able to stand and walk. Her tears were checked
as she lost herself in the adventure of the street quarrel that
was now developing.

'Break his head!' screeched one of the girls by the railings.

'Hold him,' said the middle-aged woman next to her. 'Hold
him and I'll use a razor. I ain't shy of that. See if he ever
shows his face in the light again.'

Lumley had almost resigned himself to letting go of his
prisoner and intervening when he heard another voice beyond
the crowd.

'I beg you will do no such thing,' the voice said with calm
command to the plump and fresh-faced woman who had offered
to do the cutting. 'You will compound his crime by committing
a worse.'

'Then I'll compound it with pleasure, Mr Enfield, sir.'

But the arrival of this tall and smoothly dressed young man, who might have been a fashionable clergyman with the looks and voice of an actor, changed the situation at once. Lumley tightened his hold on Waistcoat Charlie again.

Enfield looked about him, the slope of the brow noble in the lamplight and the sweep of dark hair suggesting elevated thought. The aquiline features added a patrician quality to his bearing. It was not hard to imagine that women would love him easily. All eyes turned to him as a leader of decency against the deformed foulness of the creature trapped by the blank wall.

'Where is the child's mother?' he asked.

She stepped forward, one arm still cuddling the youngster to her skirts.

'I'm here, sir. I'm Mrs Warren.'

Enfield squatted down.

'And who is this, Mrs Warren?'

'She's Ellen, sir. The youngest of the four.'

Whatever the girl might have suffered was forgotten now in being the centre of attention and having such a handsome and benevolent face close to her own.

'And what does Ellen say?' he asked with a smile.

She put one hand over her face and turned to her mother's skirts.

'She's not as bad as she might be,' Mrs Warren confided, still with tone of one reluctant to let the matter drop.

Enfield stood up.

'And there is no reason, Mrs Warren, why she should be bad at all. Poor little soul.'

From the wall by the pavement came a voice that quivered with contempt rather than fear.

'Pass the child round the crowd and take up a collection for her, why don't you, if you feel so tenderly?'

Enfield answered without turning round.

'I have not finished with you, sir. Indeed, I have not yet begun.'

He turned again to the mother.

'If the child is not hurt, you will perhaps allow me to settle the matter. I cannot believe that a police court charge and the

27

ordeal of examination would be to Ellen's advantage.'

The woman nodded, eager but not yet understanding. Enfield turned, the nobility of the profile seen again to advantage. The crowd drew back so that he might confront the stunted Satan in cloak and hat. As the others fell silent, Enfield's quiet voice carried to where Lumley stood and listened.

'You, sir, are a cowardly brute—'

'A father, if she had one, would keep such a brat in order and out of the way of honest folks.'

'—and a cruel devil. Every man should be the father of every child, sir. If you have not learnt that already, you shall be taught. You may face the police court and the ruin of your reputation, if you choose. Or you may make amends to this child and her mother here and now.'

'Amends?'

The word was half question and half sneer.

'One hundred pounds is less than you deserve to pay.'

'One hundred pounds? Be damned to the pack of you!'

'A penny less,' said Enfield simply, 'and I shall walk away to find a policeman. I shall not hurry. When I return with a constable, so that you may be given in charge, you will be a sorrier sight than you now are.'

The tenant of Terminology House looked about him at the fierce grins of some of the street women.

'Hold him for me,' begged the fattest of them again. 'I'll razor him a treat!'

'Where the devil should I get a hundred pounds this time of night?' he asked sourly.

Enfield had foreseen the difficulty.

'You shall pay gold with what you have and give a cheque for what you have not. Let there be no deceit. The dishonouring of the cheque will be as nothing to the dishonouring of your own reputation. I promise you that. I will prosecute myself, if the law does not.'

There followed a good deal of muttering between the two, most of which Lumley failed to hear. But Enfield had the matter so well planned that the sergeant would not have interfered for the world. At last the assailant of little Ellen Warren said,

'You may have ten sovereigns specie. For the rest you shall have a cheque to cash. It is drawn on Coutts, so I suppose you will not question that!'

'If questions are to be asked,' said Enfield evenly, 'we shall know where to find you, sir.'

'Then you must permit me to go indoors and fetch it.'

One of the women at the railings screamed for Enfield's information:

'There's no other way out of that court, sir. Only one door to the dictionary house. Let the brute try going to ground now. I'll smoke and burn him out if no one else will.'

'I fancy we shall find him too sensible for that,' Enfield said, never taking his own gaze from the fire of hatred in the other man's eyes. 'I fancy our gentleman knows when the game is up.'

With mounting expectation the crowd saw the door of Terminology House open and the man go inside. He appeared after two or three minutes and handed Enfield the ten gold coins and the cheque for ninety pounds. Enfield glanced at it and then looked up at the little man with a start.

'How does a man of your sort possess himself of such a cheque as this?'

'I am not a robber!' hissed the dwarfish man. 'I am not a thief as you and your gang of harlots prove to be! May the gold choke you all!'

Lumley heard the door slammed and bolted. Enfield turned to the woman and the child.

'The cheque is made to cash, Mrs Warren. It is not drawn by the man himself but the name upon it is known to me. I assure you it is guarantee enough. Unless it be forged. I do not think our man would dare that. Tomorrow we shall go together to the bank in Piccadilly and the money shall be placed where you may always get it when you need. I hope that it will be prudently drawn upon for little Ellen and that she shall grow up beautiful and good.'

There was not a woman there, Lumley thought, from the

29

shopkeepers' wives to the street-girls who did not love Mr
Enfield just then. But the benefactor was still troubled.

'Tell me,' he said, 'who is the man that lives in Terminology
House?'

They murmured together but could not decide.

'He is, at any rate, not Dr Henry Jekyll?'

That amused them a little.

'No sort of a doctor, you may be sure of that, sir.'

Enfield nodded.

'I thought not,' he said. 'All the same, I hope there is no
villainy hidden in this.'

He led the woman and child away. The bell of St Anne's
began to strike three. Sergeant Lumley, in a luxury of self-
righteousness, tightened his grip on Waistcoat Charlie's collar.
He was about to pronounce judgment, witty and menacing,
truculent and vengeful, when a voice behind him spoke first.

'Mr Lumley! Where the deuce have you been?'

Alfred Swain's mild face had an air of injury rather than
anger.

'Detained, sir, in apprehending a criminal.'

Swain wrinkled his nose and looked closer.

'Waistcoat Charlie? We could find him any time we wanted,
Mr Lumley.'

Lumley swelled out a little.

'Apprehended in the committing of a felony, Mr Swain.'

'Meaning, Mr Lumley?'

' 'E stole me watch!' The sergeant spoke with offended
pride. Swain looked at him, baffled.

'Have I, Mr Lumley, been standing and freezing at Regent
Circus the past hour or more for one miserable tin police-issue
watch?'

'I'm accountable, Mr Swain.'

'By God you are, Mr Lumley! By God you are! And first
of all you shall be accountable to me!'

With the sergeant's hand still on the prisoner's collar, the
three of them set off, Lumley exuding a warmth of offended
propriety. The eyes of Waistcoat Charlie flicked from one to
the other of his captors, ever hopeful of evasion.

3

'Who is he?' said Swain irritably. At seven in the morning he was light-headed from lack of sleep. The long intelligent face looked pale and tight-skinned. 'There's a uniformed man under arrest in the receiving-room. A police officer, Mr Lumley, sitting with the other charges. What, in hell's name, is going on in this place?'

Lumley, in the half-windowed little cubby-hole leading off the room was filling the details of the charge sheet for Waist-coat Charlie.

'You don't want to worry about him, Mr Swain. That's only Billy.'

'Billy?'

Alfred Swain opened the door again cautiously and looked out into the busy receiving-room where the newly-arrested from the night's disturbances were being charged and documented. Billy sat opposite him, the dark blue serge tight and creased on his muscular figure, wearing his helmet. The face was round and ruddy, suggesting to Swain the outdoor complexion of a comfortable farmer.

The uniformed prisoner performed a sitting bow in Swain's direction.

'Good morning,' he said with an enthusiastic grin. 'Good morning, old fellow. Had a busy time last night?'

The casualness of such insubordination was breathtaking. Swain walked across and stood over the prisoner. His voice was quiet but there was a discernible tremor of exasperation.

'I am an inspector in this division. You will conduct your-self accordingly in my presence. Remove your helmet in this building. And stand up when you address a superior officer!'

31

Billy grinned sheepishly, as if apologising for having got the better of Alfred Swain.

'You ain't superior to me, old boy. Not in any way that you could name. My old guv'nor could buy you up every day of the week and not even need the change in his pocket to do it. I'm Billington.'

Swain almost winced at the easy slangy manner of the speech. It reeked of heavy swells and racing men, the 'Pink 'un' and dinners at Romano's. With a parting glare at the insolence of the man, he went back to Lumley.

'I want that man charged with disciplinary offences, Mr Lumley. Failure to obey a superior officer and improper behaviour in a police office.'

Sergeant Lumley did not even bother to look up.

'You can't discipline him. That's Mad Billy.'

'Who the devil may that be?'

The sergeant put down his pen and looked up.

'Harry Smith-Billington. His family owns a stretch of land bordering on Essex and Yorkshire, 'f you see what I mean. Rich as Croesus. He's not got his hands on it yet, but he will once he's of age. Six months or so.'

'He's not a policeman?'

Lumley, having picked the pen up again, put it down once more.

'No, Mr Swain, he's not a policeman. He likes the uniform. That's all.'

Swain nodded. Now he knew where he was.

'Impersonating a policeman, Mr Lumley. I want him so charged. We'll put an end to his game.'

'He's been charged,' said Lumley patiently, 'for all the good it'll do. That's why he's here.'

'Why won't it do good?'

'Mr Swain!' Lumley's voice approached a pitch of exasperation, 'he's Mad Billy. He don't care. And in any case he's harmless. He likes dressing up as a policeman to go up and down Haymarket talking to the girls there, pretending to arrest them and all that.'

'And all what, Mr Lumley?'

'You know,' Lumley said with a sigh.

'I've never heard the like of it—'

He opened the door and shouted into the babel of voices in the receiving-room.

'Be quiet! I want Mr Smith-Billington in here. At once!'

Mad Billy, his helmet now removed, got to his feet and lumbered across. He was a giant with a grin of pure amiability.

'Shut the door,' said Swain crossly, 'and tell me exactly what all this is about. Why are you masquerading as a police officer?'

Billy gave him a puzzled smile.

'I like it, old fellow. It's smart. I'd never wear ordinary clothes like you, if I was on the force. I'd wear a uniform. The girls like it too. Not half they don't.'

'A man with a criminal record,' said Swain severely, 'is debarred from joining the Metropolitan Police.'

Billy knew it and was prepared.

'That's why I thought of the trains, sir. You wear a uniform as well and there's the fun of driving the engines. I've always liked engines.'

'But not driven them,' said Swain scornfully.

Billy favoured him with a good-natured confidential smile.

'Last Monday they let me take the 10.30 passenger express out of Euston to Crewe. In railway livery. That was prime. By Jove, it was! There was another fellow on the footplate, of course. But I was the one who let rip with the levers.'

'Then the Railway Company Board shall be informed.'

Billy pulled a mouth and waved the objection aside.

'I don't know all about that, sir. My people are the board, more or less. They think I'm cracked. Perhaps I am. But I ain't silly, by jingo I ain't. I'm up to a trick or two with the young ladies. How they love a policeman in uniform. I met Aggie like that.'

'Aggie?'

'Miss York,' said Billy with fatuous solemnity. 'My fiancée.'

Swain sat down and stared at the height of the young man. For some reason, about which he must ask Lumley, he had never before heard of Mad Billy. But Aggie York had been notorious up and down the pavements of the Haymarket for ten or fifteen years past. She was known variously and unflatteringly as a trout and a bloater.

'You are engaged to marry Aggie York?'

Billy gave a proud chuckle.

'It wasn't easy, sir. She had a beau that was with me at Eton. Josh Butter. I made it all right with him, though.'

'You can't marry Aggie York,' Swain said, the horror of the thought plain in his face.

Billy grinned.

'I know,' he said reasonably. 'I know I can't. I ain't of age yet. But I'll be of age in August and I'll marry her then. I'll have enough to settle a fortune on her and still be rich.'

'She's older than you,' said Swain evasively.

Billy looked concerned on the inspector's behalf.

'You're wrong there, old fellow. And even if she was a bit, she don't act it.'

'She might be twice your age,' Swain said furiously. 'Apart from that, there's her profession. The way she makes a living.'

Billy smiled at his own ingenuity.

'When she's Mrs Harry Smith-Billington, she won't need to make a living. Will she? Mind you, I can't say my old guv'nor and the family care much for the idea. They still think I'm cracked. Perhaps I am. But the money don't belong to their side of the tribe. It's from a sister of mama's and it goes straight to me when I'm of age. And that's all about that.'

Swain turned to Lumley.

'Leave that charge sheet, Mr Lumley. Go and see what arrangements have been made for Mr Smith-Billington's bail and recognizances. I don't see the use of the charge going before the justices this morning. Police bail, I think.'

Lumley laid down his pen on the incomplete charge sheet of Waistcoat Charlie. With a careful display of ill-temper he went out into the receiving-room. Swain heard him begin to shout.

'Who's here for Smith-Billington? Anyone here for Mad Billy?'

'They call me that,' said Billy to the inspector. 'Only in fun, though. I'm a bit mad sometimes, I suppose. No one in the family really minds except Uncle Weightman that led the Guards at the Redan. Still, he's a rummy cove all round. Showing himself to ladies in the park and that.'

'You can't marry Aggie York,' said Swain, desperate on behalf of the young man he had not known half an hour before. 'To marry her and settle money—'

'Don't you start, old fellow,' said Billy plaintively. 'It's bad enough with the old guv'nor and the rest of them. I know Aggie and they don't. And nor do you.'

Alfred Swain sighed and sat down in Lumley's chair behind the little desk. His eyes had begun to ache with fatigue. Mad Billy brightened up.

'I say, that was a bit of all right in Trim Street last night. Was it you that nabbed old Terminology?'

'Term-in-what?'

Billy nodded vigorously.

'An old master of mine that lives in Terminology House. There's a story round the village this morning that he was nabbed for attacking a girl. He's a brute when crossed, but he can get a club or an introducing-house roaring.'

'And he lives in Trim Street?'

'That's right!' Mad Billy's mouth hung open in expectation of the sequel.

'No one arrested him. The man is not known to the police. Whereas you are. A damn sight too well known.'

'Here, I say!' protested Smith-Billington. 'Stop a bit. I don't see there's a call for that sort of thing!'

Swain ignored him. Behind the mask of the intelligent horse-face the fragments of Lumley's story and the intriguing inconsistencies began to form a pattern of speculation. A man with a cheque signed in another man's name for a precise amount. . . . A certain reek of fraud, Swain thought.

But just then, Lumley returned with a quiet-looking man in a well-pressed frock-coat and sponge-bag trousers.

35

'Mr Nathaniel Carpenter,' said Lumley, 'of Carpenter and Rowe, solicitor to the Smith-Billington estates. Mr Carpenter was in the commissioner's office, discussing certain aspects of the present case.'

Mad Billy stood up, beaming at Swain over the heads of the other two.

'The commissioner suggests,' said Carpenter pedantically, 'and I agree, that too much need not be made of this matter. Certain undertakings are required and shall be given. Mr Smith-Billington is not yet of age, though certainly above that of criminal responsibility. However, it is my understanding that charges will not be pressed.'

Swain nodded.

'Mr Lumley, have the goodness to show Mr Smith-Billington out, while I complete the formalities of release with Mr Carpenter.'

When Mad Billy and the sergeant had gone into the chatter and shouting of the receiving-room, the door was closed. Carpenter said,

'I am not aware of the need for further formalities, Mr Swain.'

'It's not that,' Swain said. 'It's your client. Mr Smith-Billington has undertaken to marry a woman called Aggie York as soon as he is of age.'

Carpenter nodded and seemed unconcerned.

'I have been instructed in that sense, Mr Swain.'

'He can't!' Swain shouted. 'That woman is a brass-faced villain who probably won't see forty again. Smith-Billington says he bought her from a man called Josh Butter whom we know to have been her keeper for about five years. She was convicted for running a disorderly house about fifteen years ago. She has convictions for wounding and receiving stolen goods. I can't count the number of times she's been fined for soliciting. The fines she's paid would almost pay the entire naval estimates. She hasn't gone to prison. The reason is to be mentioned only in this room. A certain metropolitan magistrate has cause to fear Aggie York and what she might tell about him, if she would. That is the future bride of young Mr Smith-Billington.'

'I am aware of the lady's reputation, Mr Swain. So are the young gentleman's family. I know something of the rumours concerning a certain justice. Not, I imagine, as much as you.'

And that, Mr Carpenter seemed to suggest, was the end of the matter.

'Look,' said Swain, 'he has given his word. Either he will marry her in August and the wretched woman will rob him blind. Or he will refuse to marry her and be sued for breach of promise in the most enormous sum. Whichever the outcome, his family will be the centre of disgrace and scandal. As for the estates, they will be at the mercy of the most predatory harlot that ever plagued the streets of the West End.'

Carpenter favoured him with a slight, bleak smile.

'Mr Swain, I am fully aware of all this. I am also fully aware that once Mr Smith-Billington is of age he is free to commit folly if he chooses.'

'And nothing will be done to save him?'

The lawyer rolled the answer round his mouth for a moment before delivering it fully judged.

'You are a discreet man by reputation, Mr Swain. Therefore, I will say to you what I would not say to many people under these circumstances. Whether a man is of age or not signifies nothing should his mental faculties fail him. There is a point, Mr Swain, where a man's actions and the need to protect him from himself draw upon him the attentions of the Commissioners in Lunacy.'

'Then Mad Billy is truly insane?'

Judicious in the extreme, Mr Carpenter would not have it.

'He may or may not be, Mr Swain. It is not for a lawyer or a policeman to say. But it is for his family to choose whether the matter be put to the test of medical opinion. And that is a defence against the worst that Miss Agnes York may do.'

'A man who could bear to breathe the same air as Aggie York must be cracked,' Swain said savagely.

'Yet, Mr Swain, think how many pay for the privilege of breathing it in the closest proximity. And now, if you will excuse me, I have another matter to attend to.'

37

Repressing a shudder at the image that Carpenter evoked, Swain saw him off the premises in company with the beaming amiability of Mad Billy. He went back to Lumley.

'Oblige me, Mr Lumley, by repeating the matter of Terminology House.'

Lumley shrugged.

'I was holding on to Waistcoat Charlie. There was a row got up about the man knocking down the little girl. Looked as if he might be set upon until that Mr Enfield arrived. The one that used to be so wild. Now sings hymns at Exeter Hall. Mr Enfield made it up between them. The fellow that lived in the house was to pay a hundred pounds to the girl's family. I could hardly believe it, Mr Swain. A hundred pounds! More than the poor devils saw in their lives. Anyhow, he went in and came out with ten gold sovs and a cheque for the balance on Coutts Bank.'

'A cheque made out for cash and drawn on the account of Henry Jekyll?'

'So Enfield says.'

Swain picked up Waistcoat Charlie's charge-sheet and glanced at it.

'Did it not strike you as odd, Mr Lumley, that a cheque made out to cash for the precise amount of the balance should have been lying in the house just then?'

Lumley looked at him with suspicion.

'Not necessarily. Whoever wrote the cheque could have been in the house. Or the cove who knocked the girl down might have been called Jekyll. I was holding on to Waistcoat Charlie, Mr Swain. There was no other crime committed or complained of. Not that I wanted the little mite knocked over by the fellow but she was doing her level best to help Waistcoat do a bunk. See?'

'But the man who lives in that house is surely not Dr Jekyll, if Mr Enfield is right,' Swain persisted.

Lumley shrugged.

'I don't see it signifies what he's called, Mr Swain. That's an incident we don't need. Waistcoat Charlie we've got here. Ready to be charged. And that's more like it.'

Swain refused to let it drop.

'Mad Billy talks of the man who lives there. Not Henry Jekyll, you may be sure. When Enfield puts it to him, this man says he's only got ten pounds and they'll have to trust the rest as a cheque. He goes in and comes out in a few minutes with a cheque for the exact amount. It's made out for the balance in cash and it's signed with another man's name.'

'A dud,' Lumley said wearily. 'A fake. The bank won't cash it. What about Waistcoat?'

Swain tore the charge-sheet across.

'I'm not spending a morning in court, Mr Lumley, waiting to prefer charges over a miserable tin watch. I've got a matter to see to.'

'That was my regulation-issue,' said Lumley furiously.

'Indent for a replacement, Mr Lumley, and they'll dock it from your next wage. It's not expensive. Indeed, as a lesson in the need for constabulary vigilance at all times, I'd say it comes very cheap. He took your watch, Sergeant Lumley. With your arms held as they were, he could as easily have cut your throat. All right?'

The bitterness of the defeat was a taste that lingered for Sergeant Lumley. Carlo Beamer, alias Waistcoat Charlie, left the receiving-room to be welcomed into the arms of his mother outside as a lost and inoffensive lamb. Lumley was still meditating solitary confinement, the treadmill and the lash when Swain returned.

'I'll have that little swine one day!' Lumley stared ambiguously at Swain.

'Never mind that, Mr Lumley. I went to see Mr Enfield in the Strand.'

'Oh, yes?' said Lumley without interest.

'That cheque was cashed at Coutts in Piccadilly without a murmur. Ninety pounds without a question. And what man in his senses writes a cheque for so much cash and then hands it round Soho? And why was it for just the right amount?'

'Because the fellow was waiting there in Terminology House,' Lumley said.

'The fellow who drew that cheque, Mr Lumley, lives in the better part of the West End. You'd be as likely to find him in

39

Trim Street after midnight as to find you at church on Sunday. All right?'

Lumley began to sulk.

'Ask him about it.'

'I shan't do anything of the kind,' Swain said. 'I'm two hours overdue for relief now. And if I was you, Mr Lumley, I should get on home to bed. You look properly whacked.'

4

Since returning from the Zulu war, and inheriting his title, Sir Danvers Carew had become an awkward companion in politics. His 'Damascus Road' conversion from military ambition to liberal beliefs caused a disagreeable fluttering on both sides of opinion. Such spiritual and moral honesty had made him more admired by a few enlightened friends and more loathed by the rest of the world than any other figure in the House of Commons. Duty to conscience, not party allegiance, governed him. Consequently, he was regarded as a most unreliable colleague. Though not long a member of the House, he had easily held Repton for the Liberals in the general election of April 1880.

In less than a year after that, his unpredictability was notorious. Having served on the staff of Lord Chelmsford during the Zulu war, Sir Danvers now declared his support for the Boer farmers in their rebellion against British imperial oppression. When the British army was defeated at Majuba Hill, a crowd of Tory cabmen smashed the windows of his town house in Cheyne Walk.

He was rich and he was righteous, a combination rarely appealing to the poor and the prejudiced. Sir Danvers, once the head of school at Rugby, had also inherited the great Thomas Arnold's dangerous passion for religious honesty. But this led him far from Dr Arnold's pattern of the Christian Gentleman. In middle age, the troublesome politician concluded that he could not continue to subscribe to the basic tenets of the Christian religion. The new light of science had put faith quite out of the question. He would not, indeed he could not, take the required oath as a member of parliament.

With increasing gentleness and determination, he protested that it would be offensive to belief and unbelief alike to swear

41

by a God he did not believe in. He made common cause in the matter with Charles Bradlaugh. Like Mr Bradlaugh, Sir Danvers was rejected by parliament and re-elected by his constituents. In the end, the House of Commons let such troublesome consciences have their way. All the same, it did so with ill grace. Had Sir Danvers been born a sceptic and an anti-imperialist, he might have been tolerable. But a man cannot have his parliamentary cake and eat it. To serve on the staff at Isandhlwana and preach the gospel according to Rugby – then to renounce such things in a fit of self-righteousness – had a certain flavour of humbug.

In the lobbies and the refreshment rooms of the House of Commons, it was generally thought a pity that Sir Danvers Carew had not been cut up small by the Zulu tribesmen – or else by his own party. But his constituents admired him and his majority at Repton was not in peril.

In all this, his critics were blind to the quality that had led him such a dance. Sir Danvers Carew had the pitiless incorruptibility of a Brutus or a Robespierre. If a thing was right, he did it without compunction. If a belief was false, he discarded it. The House of Commons looked aghast at such intellectual anarchy.

The constituents of Repton saw other virtues in their representative. He had a head that a sculptor would have paid a fortune to reproduce in stone. None had ever done so. Jacques Louis David and the heroic painters of revolutionary France would have courted him a century before. But they, like George Frederic Watts and William Powell Frith in his own day, would have been sent packing. Posing and art seemed to Sir Danvers an inexcusable frivolity. He prided himself that he was free of such vanity. In truth, he was the victim of a greater vanity still, which lay in moral arrogance and quiet self-righteousness.

Yet the young face and the silver hair, which put him any-where between thirty-five and fifty-five, made him the most individually handsome of all those on the Liberal benches. In a profession where his humourless dedication offered a road to success, it was not impossible to imagine Sir Danvers Carew on the Treasury Bench in a few more years. Had he been able to keep his private opinions to himself, he must have been a candidate for Downing Street.

Still, he would have been the first to concede that he was neither a clubbable nor a sociable man. He had no small-talk and he had no wit. The ridiculous was to him contemptible and no subject for amusement. That being so, he avoided the company of heavy men. When those of his own party and the few agreeable Tories withdrew to smoke and discuss, to drink brandy or seltzer and talk through the night, Sir Danvers preferred the cool air of darkness or starlight.

Seen in the moonlight on the House of Commons terrace, or pacing the embankment towards Cheyne Walk, he appeared beautiful. The fine silver of his hair and the smooth elegance of his face gave him the look of an angelic messenger in an opera cloak and silk hat.

It was a milder October night than a week before with no breath of wind upon the river. A hunter's moon cut the ripples of the Thames in a pale beaten gold. Here and there the first mist had begun to gather, just on the surface of the water like steam rising from a warm bath. Sir Danvers Carew had left the House of Commons after a long debate on the clauses affecting redistribution of seats in the British Franchise Bill. He had no confidence that the extension of the franchise would make for a wiser electorate or a nobler parliament. But the thing was right and he had supported it.

The reward for his day's work was a two-mile walk to the house in Chelsea where he lived during the parliamentary sessions. What other men found in the companionship of malt or brandy and Flor Rothschild, Sir Danvers Carew sought alone, walking beside the river from Westminster to Cheyne Walk. As the grim fronts of Millbank and its penitentiary gave way to the handsome town-houses of Chelsea Reach, he felt the luxury of solitude. The moon's light glared with such cold intensity that he could see almost as well as by day.

At length he had passed Chelsea Bridge. He was level with the open green across which the handsome bulk of Wren's Royal Hospital dominated the view. He was nearing the corner

43

of Tite Street when he first heard the other man's footsteps. There was no one else in sight and Sir Danvers' attention was drawn at once to the sound.

In the darkness, with little else but the quiet chuckle and ripple of the river along the embankment, the footsteps were a positive distraction from thought. They clicked and plopped and echoed in a manner never heard in the London streets except during the quiet coolness of the night. Sir Danvers puzzled over them a little. They were not true footsteps after all. Footstamps, he would call them. A man stamping along. A large and weighty fellow to judge by the noise of him. And the click was the tip of his stick upon the pavement. The sound perhaps of someone who was lame? Yet what energy or anger there seemed to be in their weight! A man in a temper, then. But men in tempers, Sir Danvers thought, seldom produced quite that kind of noise for more than a minute or two.

He felt a curiosity to see his man. The figure was coming down Tite Street beyond the railings, hurrying as if to be at the corner before him. For the first time Sir Danvers felt a pang of unease. It was absurd, though, to think that anyone should want to follow him or cut off his route forward to Cheyne Walk. He was close to home. No one would waylay him here for an evil purpose.

Even before he reached the corner he saw the stamping man quite clearly. Not a giant or a portly fellow, after all! An odd creature, to be sure. Either very bent or rather stunted in figure. The beat of the feet on the pavement, the rap of the stick, and the scuttling urgency were a characterisation in themselves.

This curious individual turned the corner eastwards, walking along Chelsea Embankment towards him. Sir Danvers drew himself up and took firmer hold of his own stick. There was no harm in being on the safe side.

The little man came hurrying on, looking up presently with what was decidedly a grin on his face. It was a grin rather than a smile and there was nothing engaging about it. The line of the mouth and the squint of the eyes suggested a bitterness towards the world. A quick and unpleasant wit, Sir Danvers concluded. He gave a slight, involuntary shudder.

The dwarfish figure confronted him. There was a look of the jig-dancing peasant about such busy movements.

'If you please, sir! The way to Cremorne Lane.'

Sir Danvers smiled but the younger man was too impatient for pleasantry.

'Cremorne Lane!' he repeated more loudly.

'Where you were walking just now. See the turning across the other side of Tite Street.'

Sir Danvers lifted his stick and indicated the gap between the houses. The two men walked forward together for fifty yards or so. The stamping man showed no inclination to go ahead until he was sure that Sir Danvers had directed him accurately. They came presently to the turning, where the mews lane began. In a gesture of casual parting, they faced one another. Sir Danvers tipped his hat, as if to indicate that their acquaintanceship was at an end.

'I am obliged, sir,' the dwarfish man said, 'the more so because I recognise in you a man of public fame. Sir Danvers Carew?'

Sir Danvers acknowledged this with a half-bow of the head and a self-conscious smile. All such recognition was a plague to him. He liked best to walk alone or else in the anonymity of crowds.

'I am obliged the more, sir,' said the smaller man. And he raised his stick, as if in salute. Then with a contortion of his features, he brought it down in a manic blow across the side of Sir Danvers' face. Carew stumbled back with a dumb and foolish expression of shock. But the stamping-man allowed him no respite. With grunts of savage energy, he smashed him about the head with the heavy stick, this way and that, and this way again. Sir Danvers Carew went down backwards but somehow fell on his knees, the silk hat tumbling and rolling away. Left and right! Crack and thump! The stout polished wood with its metal ferule beat him viciously about the skull.

Sir Danvers did not so much as raise his hands to protect himself. The first damage of the assault had wrought such injury to his brain that he no longer seemed able to register the pain of the blows. He knelt upright on the pavement, swaying a little as if with drink. His breath came in a gurgle and his lips bubbled with blood. Then the dwarfish man, with the strength of a navvy, smashed him down with all the vigour that he could put behind the stick. So mad was the power of the attack that in a final blow the stick itself broke in half and the lower section bounced across the pavement with a hollow clatter.

If Sir Danvers Carew was not already dead, the injuries to his head were sufficient to ensure death before any help could reach him. But the other man was not at all satisfied. With the stick broken, he stood on one foot, the other raised as high as the knee would bend. Down came the boot on the hand of the motionless victim. Down again and again, until the fine bonework could be heard splintering under the fury.

Then it was the other hand, and then with a terrible sideways kick the ribcage was broken in. That Sir Danvers Carew would never rise from the pavement again, except to be lifted into the municipal coffin, was beyond doubt. But the dwarfish man, in a frenzy that was like rejoicing, broke and smashed the bone-tree of the corpse. Terrible though the damage might be, it was all over in a couple of minutes. He tumbled the body about with his foot until it rolled into the shadow of Cremorne Lane. Then he turned round, shook himself down like a dog, and stamped off towards Cheyne Walk. In his hand he held the upper half of his stick. The broken lower half lay in the gutter and he did not so much as give it a look.

During the whole of the assault, no cab had passed and no footstep had been heard. The precise corner was not directly overlooked by any window. As the stamping footsteps grew fainter, the clocks of the churches began to strike eleven. And then, from a window that gave a view of the spot only if someone were to lean out and look sideways, there came a sound. It was not a scream of fright but rather a low and fainting moan of terror.

There was no sequel to the sound. No cry for help or raising of an alarm. The moon shone full on the swifter flowing river as the tide from the estuary slackened. A rat slid and slithered through the shadows of Cremorne Lane. From time to time a carriage rattled or a cab clopped by along Chelsea Embankment. Once a uniformed policeman with a rolling gait passed on the far side of the road. But for three hours there was no alarm and no disturbance. It was as if the world had rewarded Sir Danvers Carew's life of moral concern with a display of utter indifference.

5

By the following afternoon, the *Standard* and the *Globe* had
gone to press with the first accounts of the Carew murder case.
Now that the modern Robespierre was dead, it was agreed
on all sides that he had been no less than the St Francis of a
secular age.

'Mr Lumley!' Swain's head appeared round the doorpost of
his room. 'Have the goodness to bring that statement in here
again. The one from the witness, Mary Smith.'

The discovery of the body, soon after 2 a.m., had brought
Swain out of bed and into the centre of the case. It was
curious, though not necessarily sinister, that no card or paper
identifying the victim was found in the pockets of the clothes.
A purse and a gold watch had been left, which suggested that
Sir Danvers could scarcely have been the victim of robbery.
In any case, what robber would have stopped to subject the
body to such ferocity as this? The key to his identity had been
a sealed letter addressed to Mr Utterson at his chambers in
Gaunt Street.

Swain had at first hoped for some magnificent revelation
from the sealed envelope. But he was disappointed. In the
small world of society, as Utterson called it, Sir Danvers
Carew was the lawyer's brother-in-law. Even the promise of a
family feud withered when the envelope was opened. Gabriel
Utterson and Danvers Carew had not the least interest in one
another. It was hard to imagine two men of more different
temperaments or consciences. They met rarely. The only
bond between them was a small legal duty over the entailing
of some family land. The money involved was so little that it
was more than Sir Danvers' dignity was worth to notice it and
more than Gabriel Utterson's time was worth to count it. The

lawyer managed the affair and Carew was distantly grateful to him.

But that night there was a dead man to identify. Mr Utterson had been woken at six and brought to a cell in the 'A' Division lock-up. There he confirmed the body as being that of Sir Danvers Carew, younger brother of the late Amelia Utterson.

Chief Inspector Newcomen, handing the immediate investigation to Swain, had almost glittered with professional ambition.

'A case like this makes a good deal of noise, Mr Swain.'

'Unfortunately it does, Mr Newcomen.'

'And you and Sir Danvers both knowing, Mr Utterson! Mr Utterson might have in mind something that would help us find our man.'

It had taken Swain a while to get rid of Newcomen's assistance and devote himself to the solitary witness of the murder. Mary Smith, a maidservant, was living in the house adjacent to Sir Danvers Carew in Cheyne Walk, the premises having been leased several years before to the widowed Lady Carew, Sir Danvers' mother. For the past twelvemonth she had spent her time in the country, leaving her London home in the care of the servants and under the supervision of her son. It was unfortunate that Newcomen had taken the girl's statement and sent her to the waiting-room in the company of a police-matron. Swain had read the statement.

'To me, Mr Lumley,' he said quietly, 'it has a stink riper than last week's kippers. Listen to this. Mary Smith is described as seeing the assault upon the victim from her bedroom. She was at the window, looking out at the river and the moonlight. "It seems she was romantically given," it says in the notes.'

Lumley sniffed.

'Young persons is apt to be romantic, Mr Swain. There's nothing in that.'

'Not the point, Mr Lumley. Did you read the next part? Mary Smith, the only witness to see the murder, says that "At the horror of these sights and sounds she fainted."'

'Likewise, Mr Swain, young persons is apt to go off into a swoon on these occasions.'

Swain glared him into silence.

' "It was two o'clock when she came to herself and called the police." *That* is the point, Mr Lumley. Young ladies, under the pressure of such sights, may swoon. They may swoon for two minutes or five minutes, even ten or twenty minutes. They do not swoon for three hours. Miss Mary Smith is damnably lucky not to be charged as accessory after the fact. She saw a man brutally done to death. On the pretext of not coming to herself, she said nothing about it to a living soul for three hours. Three hours! By which time the murderer of Sir Danvers Carew could be at Dover or Folkestone and perhaps on the boat for France.'

Lumley looked plump and discomfited.

'If you put it like that, Mr Swain.'

'How else should I put it, Mr Lumley?'

Sergeant Lumley stood in the doorway, exuding his familiar air of offended worthiness. Swain slapped at the paper with the back of his hand.

'She thinks that she recognised the murderer as some-one who once visited a house where she was previously employed. That needs following up. Though, quite frankly, Mr Lumley, a witness who delayed reporting the murder or the evidence for three hours is more use to the defence than the prosecution. Three hours isn't a swoon, it's a good sound sleep.'

'It's what she says.'

'Then she's lying, Mr Lumley, and I mean to know why. First things first. I shall ask for permission to check Sir Danvers Carew's papers. Here and in the country.'

'They could be tampered with by now,' Lumley said sceptically, 'all except the House of Commons. When a member dies, the sergeant-at-arms seals up his room. Something to do with documents being privileged and all that.'

'I'll start with an inventory of the papers there.'

'That's what you think.' Lumley's plump face glowed with a subversive satisfaction. 'You're not even allowed on the premises. The Palace of Westminster is holy ground. You can't even pass the door without their permission.'

Swain threw the paper down.

'I mean to have the truth of this, Mr Lumley. Go to the receiving-room and fetch her here. The girl and the matron. We may have a short answer to this whole business.'

'You be careful, Mr Swain. She's the only witness you've got. Frighten her off, and that's the end of that.'

'Just send her in, Mr Lumley!'

Mary Smith in her brown holland cloak, comforted by the matron, was a pitiful sight. She was a plain but not unattractive girl of eighteen or nineteen with dark hair and a firm profile. But her nose was red and her eyes streaming, for all the world as if with hay fever or influenza. She held a moist ball of a handkerchief in her hand, with which she dabbed her eyes and nose alternately.

'Sit down, Mary,' said Swain gently, the mild horse-face concerned and hopeful for her well-being. 'In a moment you shall go home. First I want to ask you two questions about your statement. Whatever the answers, I promise you that you have nothing to fear. They shall not be repeated outside this room. Isn't that so, Mrs Handley?'

The police-matron nodded and Mary Smith looked up as if with hope renewed.

'First of all, Mary, the man you saw. The one who attacked Sir Danvers Carew. He looked like a man that once visited a house where you were employed a few years ago? Is that right?'

'Yes, sir.' A sniff and a dab of the handkerchief got her through.

'And you remembered that on that occasion you didn't like him? And that was all? You had never seen him again until at some distance last night, at about eleven o'clock?'

'No, sir. How could I have done?'

'A man you had only seen once before, some years ago, and hadn't liked. Now you saw him again, eleven o'clock at night, looking down the road from your window. And you knew him at once?'

'I did!' she sobbed. 'Oh, I did!'

51

Swain made a placating gesture.

'We'll say no more about that, Mary, for the moment. But to see the end of Cremorne Lane from your window, you must have leant out a little, I think. You would not see it otherwise?'

The tears stopped.

'I might not,' she said warily. 'I can't say I recall.'

Swain made another gesture to indicate that it was of no consequence.

'Last of all, Mary, you called for the police at two in the morning.'

'I did, sir.'

'Three hours after you had seen the murder?'

Tears brightened the blue eyes again.

'I fainted dead away, sir. I did! It was so horrible. It was! I – hoo-hoo-hoo!'

Swain waited.

'No, Mary,' he said presently, 'you probably did not faint at all. Certainly not for three hours. But you were frightened. Very frightened. Not only by the murder.'

She looked at him, dry-eyed now and expectant.

'Who was with you in your room, Mary? Who was it with whom you discussed what you had both seen? Who was it that had to leave the house quietly before you could call the police?'

The tears came again easily.

'You have a young man, Mary. He was with you in your room. Why else would you have delayed so long?'

There was not the least doubt in Swain's mind. It was the classic predicament of the servant-girl with a visitor to smuggle down the back stairs.

'Noooo! I never! I was aloooone!'

'You had to wait until the others were safely in bed before you could see him out, Mary.'

Mrs Handley the police-matron looked at him hard.

'She's in the house alone, sir, except for two male servants in the other part. The mistress is in the country. Lady Carew's house, sir. The dead gentleman's mother.'

52

Swain looked at her blankly and then gritted his teeth.

'Then see this young woman taken to her own family or to safe refuge. Stay with her, if need be. But make sure we know where she is.'

In his vexation, he glowered at the pair of them as the matron shepherded Mary Smith to the door. When it had closed, he allowed himself the luxury of bringing his fist down on the varnished oak of the desk.

'Damn and blast it!' he said savagely. And then Alfred Swain felt a little ashamed of himself, knowing that the misjudgment of Mary Smith had been entirely his own. He could swear that a man was the explanation of her three-hour swoon. But persuading the girl to admit it was another matter. She was in all probability more terrified now of Alfred Swain and his revelations than she had been of the murderer of Sir Danvers Carew.

It was almost five o'clock when Sergeant Lumley knocked at his door.

'You was lucky,' he said grudgingly. 'The commissioner spoke to the sergeant-at-arms and the Speaker of the House. You can have a look through Sir Danvers Carew's parliamentary papers any time you want. More or less. Only you aren't to bring any away. That's privilege or something. See the commissioner's secretary, the commissioner says.'

Whatever gratitude Swain felt was deftly concealed.

'Mary Smith had got a man in her room,' he said wearily. 'The house half empty and only servants looking after it. She wouldn't call the police until she'd got him out.'

Lumley was unimpressed.

'Only thing,' he said, 'when that happens, it's generally one of the other servants. In that case, she wouldn't need to get him out.'

Swain grunted.

'If I'm wanted, I'll be with the commissioner's secretary. And after that at Westminster.'

He had spared Oliver Lumley nothing of his scorn. And yet he knew, by instinct and experience, that in the matter of

Mary Smith's lover being another servant, Sergeant Lumley was very probably right. Alfred Swain felt a little ashamed of himself for the second time that day. For one who had aspired to a world of culture and enlightenment a few evenings ago, he was behaving very badly indeed.

6

The Gothic door, whose architraves were filled by clear glass, swung open to admit Inspector Swain. He stepped into a vestibule which was partly like a Plantagenet choir but mostly like a gentleman's club. The sergeant-at-arms, who was not a sergeant at all but a brigadier of the Household Guard, was too occupied about the business of parliament to attend in person. He had sent Mr Learman to supervise the inventory of Sir Danvers Carew's papers on behalf of the Palace of Westminster.

Mr Learman was a round ball of a little man, cheerful and pugnacious. Energy shone from his dark eyes and animated the snub features. The starch was so sleek upon his collar that the linen looked like freshly enamelled tin.

'Mr Alfred Swain?' he said jubilantly. 'Mr Alfred Swain of Scotland Yard? You are almost late, Mr Swain. By which I mean to say that you come precisely at the time arranged. That is almost to be late, is it not? *En retard*, as they say.'

Turning about, Mr Learman led the way down corridors and up stairways. There were pale stone arches of Plantagenet design that had not yet been built fifty years. Sprays of fan-vaulting graced the tall ceilings above the tracery of Norman windows. An abbey cloister had been turned into a closed passageway. Fretwork and gilding embellished the doors. Upon the walls in bright blue and red, the murals showed King James throwing the Great Seal into the Thames and King William finding it again. Cardinal Wolsey presented the demands of Henry VIII to Sir Thomas More, Speaker of the House. King Charles bowed before the headsman's axe on a cold January morning in Whitehall.

'He nothing common did nor mean,' Swain said appreciatively, 'Upon that memorable scene.'

'What was that, Mr Swain?' Mr Learman turned his head, beaming. 'What was that, sir?'

'A poem,' said Swain, 'about King Charles I.' Mr Learman chuckled, as if his visitor would be the death of him with such pleasantries.

It was, Swain thought, like being Alice down the rabbit-hole. The floor-tiles, diamonds of blue and yellow and brown by Pugin and his pupils, were all patterned with clubs and spades, hearts and diamonds. The officials who passed in their red livery and buckled shoes had the appearance of kings and knaves in a pack of cards. The very titles upon the brass-furnished oak of the doors suggested a world of logic gone mad. In one room there lived 'Motions' and in another 'Questions'. Here there was the 'Court Postmaster' and there the 'Table Office'. At any moment, a white rabbit in a Tudor jacket and tights would appear round the corner and fall into conversation with Mr Learman.

'Here we are,' Mr Learman said. 'Sir Danvers Carew's room. A tidy and methodical gentleman. Much respected here, Mr Swain. Much respected.'

The door he unlocked opened on to a large room that might have belonged to the fifteenth century. But it was the late Middle Ages recreated by the bright colours and comfortable furnishings of the Industrial Revolution. The ceiling lozenges were by Sir Charles Barry and the upright furniture with its Tudor carving and red leather was by Mr Pugin himself. The pointed elegance of the windows looked out across the terrace to the river. A mantelpiece in grey marble and chairs of padded leather belonged to St James's clubland rather than the age of chivalry.

'A moment,' said Mr Learman. 'We shall need a key to the desk.'

He disappeared again, leaving the door ajar. Alfred Swain made a tour of the room and came back to the desk, its top inlaid with green leather. A cylindrical ruler and a blotter, a calendar and a glass pen-holder made up the desk furniture. Tidy and methodical, as Mr Learman said.

What Swain would have called a search, the sergeant-at-arms had prudently termed an inventory. For the Metropolitan Police to search the House of Commons would have contravened privilege. For the officer of the sergeant-at-arms to make an inventory in the presence of a policeman was another matter.

In the gaslight, Swain tipped the woven rush of the wastepaper basket and heard the stirring of discarded scraps. He glanced at the doorway to see that the coast remained clear. Then he stooped down and retrieved three crumpled leaves.

Two were false starts to a letter. The third was the same letter in rough with alterations in several places.

It has come to the notice of Sir Danvers Carew that Dr Henry Jekyll will be proposed as a governor of the Hospital for Military Incurables. Sir Danvers believes that Dr Jekyll will, upon reflection, realise the extreme inappropriateness of this proposal. It is evident that he must further realise the nature of the public discussion which would be bound to result were he to accede to that suggestion. Sir Danvers Carew is therefore obliged to insist that Dr Jekyll must find another avenue for his philanthropy. Sir Danvers is himself a governor of the institution and would be compelled to raise the matter at the next meeting in very specific terms, were the proposal presented.

Swain had not the least doubt that this was the rough copy of a note sent, by post or hand, the previous day or late the night before. The excitement of it quite put from his mind the wasted opportunity with Mary Smith.

'The key,' said Mr Learman happily in the doorway.

He unlocked the desk and took from its drawers two small piles of papers, a notebook, and a tin box decorated with a painting of Turner's *Ulysses Deriding Polyphemus*, opposite a royal patent for Cadbury's Chocolate which it had once contained.

'Very little for you there, Mr Swain,' said Learman sympathetically. 'Depend upon it, the evidence is elsewhere.'

But he obligingly turned his back, walked to the window, and stared out across the lamplit river while he sang softly and patiently to himself.

Swain drew the chair to the desk and began to go quickly through the papers. Whether it was proper to open and read the diary with its red leather spine was a delicate question. But Mr Learman kept his back turned and sang quietly, as if to reassure his visitor. Swain opened the cover and began to skim the pages, each covered in a sloping script with Sir Danvers' *aides-mémoires* of meetings and social encounters.

As he read, names and places were noted and filed in the long intelligent head. Whether he would again have access to the diary was doubtful. It was now or never. A brief note made in the previous June caught his eye.

A man whom I should have known immediately, even after long absence, as Henry Jekyll was pointed out to me at Lady Moira's party. Seen across the room while he was talking to Sir Philip Ashmore. I do not think he knew me, though I stared so long that our eyes met. I fancy something went cold in him then to judge from his look.

Swain turned the pages with greater deliberation. He found no further mention of the proposed new governor for the Military Incurables. However, there were several references to 'J' in the previous September and October.

J was at Burlington House this afternoon. We did not speak. I think he did not see me. The poor devil is broken and nothing would come of making a row about him. C was right, after all. The sickness of his soul is in his face. I shall not reveal him so long as he keeps low – himself to himself.

There was a third entry which Swain read with greater care.

Sir Henry Giles at supper, talking to me afterwards about illnesses of the Grand Old Man and other matters. A strange tale of J. After his fall from grace, he continued to write on medical topics without putting his true name to

58

them. The oddity is that Samuel Parr was still his favoured incarnation! Had he no shame, after the business in Africa? Or had he begun to believe himself possessed of this identity? Giles had something for the *Lancet* by Parr. Hopeless theory. Madness no sickness but devil's alchemy, so Giles reads it! The hand and the provenance so obviously J's that he tackles him on being Parr. Whereupon extreme agitation and denial – and no further papers. None will touch his work which is all about a second life in dreams and mirrors. He has now stopped. No more writing of any kind. His last unscientific balderdash, 'Dreams of Men Awake', appeared in a journal of spiritualism! It is as if, Giles says, he would deny there exists such a person as Henry J. Were superstition credited in our time, he might be one who had sold his soul to the devil. But then, where is his Mephistopheles? There is none, Giles says. Only J himself. Like so many who profess the science of madness, J has become the victim of his own enthusiasms. I kept my word to C and said nothing of 'Samuel Parr's' conduct that dreadful day when all our poor friends died. Was there a real Parr, by-the-by? If there was, what became of him?

Mr Learman hummed loudly and stirred himself to give ample warning that he was about to turn round. Swain closed the book and picked up the tin box.

'You won't mind, Mr Learman, if I look inside?'

'An inventory stretches to that, Mr Swain. In a tragedy of this kind, there is always the danger that something might otherwise be passed to a widow or daughter which would be better destroyed. If you catch my meaning, sir.'

'Perfectly, Mr Learman.'

Swain eased open the painted tin. Its interior was packed with photographic prints. They were of young women. He was familiar with the belief that the most virtuous public figure has his private vices. But Sir Danvers Carew would surely not be ensnared by the camera studies of Holywell Street or Soho.

'Oh dear,' said Mr Learman over his shoulder. 'Nothing scandalous, I trust?'

Swain eased the glossy cards apart. He frowned at what he saw.

'No, Mr Learman. Not scandalous. Damnably curious, though.'

There were about thirty half-plates, packed into the tin chocolate-box. Not one could have been objected to by the strictest moralist. And yet, as Swain put it, they were damnably curious. Who had taken the pictures for Sir Danvers Carew? Was it possible that he had developed them himself? Surely it was the late member of parliament for Repton who had been the photographer in each case.

The first studies showed several young women whose sex was scarcely recognisable in a costume of boots, patched trousers and jerkins. Their heads and hair had been covered by triangular kerchiefs. They were hefty in build and grimy in appearance, their faces dusty and smeared. One was leaning forward to use a shovel and, at the same time, smiling sideways at the camera.

Under these was another set of half-plate prints, showing a housemaid at work. In several pictures she was lying on her hip as she washed a tiled floor. She was also seen at the mangle and brushing a pair of boots. There was a milk-girl with a wooden yoke round her neck and across her shoulders, from which hung two large pails. The subjects were nothing, Swain thought. It was the obsessive and selective passion of the photographer that gave them an almost sensual and erotic suggestiveness. Two or three were of a young female acrobat in blouse and fleshings at the Surrey Music Hall. Last, there were the collier girls again in their shabby and shapeless cotton trousers and jerkins, the head-coverings and boots that robbed them of all grace and femininity.

'Very keen he was, Mr Swain, on improving the lot of working women.'

Swain nodded. He noticed that even the collier-girls with their sieves and shovels had been photographed in the tiled hall of a gentleman's house or in a photographer's studio. There was a loving and caressing attention to detail that reminded him uncomfortably of sketching Romana Utterson. He did not doubt that he had discovered the secret world of Sir Danvers Carew. It was characteristic of the man that the concealed passion was not vicious in the least. His private obsession was indistinguishable from his public virtue. He himself could not have told which was which.

'Will that do? Will it, Mr Swain?' asked Mr Learman hopefully.

'Just nicely, Mr Learman,' said Alfred Swain courteously, closing the tin. 'Just nicely for now.'

He allowed himself to be escorted back through the medieval Alice-in-Wonderland palace and out into the raw breath-clouded evening of the Westminster riverside.

In his mind, the first small mystery of Sir Danvers Carew's murder had been resolved.

7

'It only means being sensible,' Swain said gently. 'Now, where can be the harm in that?'

Mary Smith looked at him, dry-eyed but doubtful, from the edge of the bed on which she sat. Swain's chair squeaked on the floor as he drew it a little closer and became confidential. Behind him Mrs Handley the police-matron shifted with the uneasy weight of chaperonage.

He would lose her again in a minute, Swain thought. There would be tears or panic and he would lose her for good.

'All I want,' he said, fighting grimly with the mangled ghost of Sir Danvers Carew, 'is to start all over again. To tear up the statement you made first. To start again. Now, where's the harm in that?'

She tucked her chin down defensively.

'Don't know, sir.'

Swain smiled at her.

'There's none, Mary. None at all. Look.'

From his inner pocket he drew a small photographic portrait. It had been coaxed from the Horse Guards after a good deal of patience from Lumley and an intervention by the commissioner. The portrait was of a large, well-made, smooth-faced man. He might have been forty-five when the photograph was taken. There was something a little sly about the mouth, perhaps. But the eyes showed kindness. He would do no deliberate evil. Swain handed the picture to the girl.

'Do you know this man, Mary? Have you ever seen him or anyone who might be him? Take your time and look carefully. The photograph was done several years ago, so he may look a little different now.'

She frowned, shook her head, and at last handed the picture back to him.

'He could not have been the man?' Swain inquired. 'The man you saw attacking Sir Danvers Carew?'

'Oh no, sir. He was not a bit like the gentleman in the picture. Not a bit like at all.'

It came too easily and naturally from her to be a lie. There was too much relief in it. Swain had dealt with liars of all shapes and sizes. He knew that Mary Smith was telling the truth. There was one more matter between them. Alfred Swain, conscious of the police-matron at his back, felt a scrupulous embarrassment. He turned in his chair.

'Mrs Handley, be so kind as to go down to Mr Lumley in the cab outside. My compliments to Mr Lumley and I'll be finished in ten minutes. He will have the goodness to wait until then.'

The burly matron looked uneasy.

'It's all right, Mrs Handley,' Swain insisted. 'There's nothing irregular in that.'

Alone with Mary Smith, he leant forward in his chair.

'There's one more thing, Mary. However hard you may try, you will never make people believe that you fainted away for three hours when Sir Danvers was killed. Perhaps you might have swooned with horror at the sight for half an hour. But I believe you knew he was dead, that perhaps you even went out and saw for yourself. And still you hesitated to call the police.'

Worry and fear began to crumple her face again. Swain held up his hand.

'I mean you no harm, Mary. You are a good girl and, I think, an innocent one. I know a little more about Sir Danvers now and I believe I understand why you behaved as you did.'

She looked at him, dreading what might follow.

'He was coming to you, Mary,' Swain said.

The collapse of her composure proved him right.

'Sir Danvers Carew was your young man, was he not? An honourable man who meant to take no mean advantage of his mother's maid but to make her his wife before all the world.'

Swain had not quite believed it himself, despite the chronicle of Carew's strange and secret ambitions. But he was right. He knew he was right.

'I can understand, Mary,' he said in the same gentle and encouraging tone, 'when that dreadful thing happened, what confusion there must have been in your mind! Would your secret be discovered? If it was, what would the world say? Might you not be taken as the murderer of your lover because he had disgraced you? Would it not be thought, at least, that he was coming here that night to dishonour you under a cloak of propriety?'

'He was to marry me!' she cried, despair overcoming all.

Swain dropped his voice.

'And so he would, Mary. He was a fine and honourable gentleman who saw in you what he could never find in Mayfair or St James's. You must be proud for the future. Proud to have shared with him such love and honour.'

The girl looked up at him, surprised, as if there might be a consolation she had not so far realised.

'It would have been so wonderful,' she said helplessly. 'I never meant it. It was he who wished it so.'

Swain nodded and stood up. Before he could turn away, Mary Smith clutched his sleeve.

'There was another reason,' she said. 'When I saw the man hit him, I thought it might be my father. That something had been said – dishonourable. That he'd heard it and was in such anger with the master, for my sake.'

All Swain's gentleness evaporated.

'Did the man look like your father?'

'He was not unlike,' she whispered. 'I feared it might be he.'

'And so you told a story about the attacker looking like a man who once visited your employers several years ago?'

'To see a lover killed and a father hanged for it!' she said piteously.

'Where is your father now?'

Her doubt cleared at once.

'It can't have been he, sir. They sent this morning to say that old Lady Carew is gone to Switzerland and that Coachman

64

Smith is with her. Poor soul! She's that weak that father must lift her from the carriage and carry her up the steps. What the news of the young master's death will do to her, I daren't think.'

And in her pity for the older woman, Mary Smith began to lose some of that reserved for herself. Swain took her hand. Despite the red nose and the running eyes of their first encounter, she seemed a healthy and passionate girl. In a year or two there might be a young man of her own class and a servants' wedding. Mary Smith would be a good wife to him and would, in all probability, carry to her grave the secret of a far stranger love. And yet Swain wondered, as he went down the stairs alone, whether the crime of Sir Danvers Carew himself had not been to unfit the girl for all such hope.

Lumley's impatience was evident.

'Well, Mr Swain?'

'A sensible young woman, Mr Lumley. Sensible and, I believe, honourable.'

'Oh, yes?' Sergeant Lumley's scepticism lay between them like an odour in the cab. 'How's that then?'

'She feared only for her reputation.'

'And she never twigged Jekyll's picture?'

'Never did, Mr Lumley.'

'Lot of use that was, then,' the sergeant said, grievance heavy as grief in his voice, 'fat lot! There's nothing whatsoever against anyone! He might have beat hisself to death for all the good Mary Smith done us!'

Sergeant Lumley concluded the exchange with an expressive sniff, a nasal suggestion of disbelief and contempt.

8

Henry Jekyll's house was the second in Caleb Square, a fine ensemble in the later Georgian style of the 1830s with mews buildings at the rear to accommodate the servants and horses. For many years the houses had been divided up, one by one, and the little mews cottages had become homes in their own right. It seemed to Alfred Swain that Dr Jekyll was the only tenant in the square who still retained a house intact. With its tall windows looking out upon the plane trees and shrubberies of the central gardens, it had previously been the property of Sir Willoughby Denman. Sir Willoughby's sole distinction was to have been briefly surgeon-in-ordinary to her late majesty Queen Adelaide, the dumpy consort of William IV with her corkscrew ringlets and the noble earnestness of Saxe-Meiningen in her brow.

Swain arrived by appointment on a bright autumn morning. Fallen leaves were already slippery on the smooth York paving.

'Inspector Swain to see Dr Jekyll?'

The butler who answered the door echoed the request as a question. Poole was a tall and grey-haired stalwart with a long chin and a mobile humorous jaw. He led the way through the hall, where a fire sputtered in the grate, and across a paved courtyard at the rear. The mews building at the end of this yard had been Sir Willoughby Denman's anatomy theatre, attended by groups of favoured students. There was a private study on the floor above. The lower level still bore witness to its former use, housing the dissecting table and a lumber of crates and bottles. But the table had long been sheeted over and the bottles bore a patina of dust. Henry Jekyll was no anatomist.

The wooden staircase led up to a door covered by red baize

and studded in brass. Poole knocked and was admitted.

'Inspector Swain of Scotland Yard, sir,' he said portentously.

Swain entered and found himself in a room whose comforts far exceeded those of Gabriel Utterson's 'bachelor' quarters. There was an Afghan carpet patterned with the Tree of Life and hangings upon which exotic birds and strange flowers had been woven. The firelight danced in the glass fronts of medical cabinets and upon blue phials or bottles. The plain red damask of the walls had been hung here and there with devil-masks that suggested heathen rituals in the darker corners of the globe.

Henry Jekyll, tall and benign in appearance but with a hint of doubt in his eyes, gestured his visitor to a chair.

'I trust you have not been kept waiting, Mr Swain. I think there is little I can tell you. What little there is you shall have at once.'

Swain studied the round and somewhat effeminate face without, he hoped, appearing to do so. It bore an expression of intelligence and scruple. It lacked malevolence and yet, by the same token, it lacked strength. It was the face of a man who might love but not defy. More directly, Swain thought, here was one who could hate but not fight. The violent passions he might control, but the softer ones would have their way with him. In the inspector's mind, he did not look at all like the murderer of Sir Danvers Carew.

'It was the dreadful business on Chelsea Embankment, Mr Swain? It was that upon which you sought an interview? I am not in the best of health at present. But I will do my utmost to answer your questions as fully as I can.'

'I am sorry to find you unwell, sir,' Swain said. 'I shall keep you no longer than I need. Indeed, it is the matter of Sir Danvers Carew.'

'To be sure, Mr Swain. To be sure.'

Swain looked again at the round soft-featured face and thought that it showed no physical illness. There was an animal worry and apprehension. He caught a tremor of profound disturbance at the prospect of their conversation. But not illness.

'As a matter of routine, sir, it is my duty to visit all those who were friends of Sir Danvers Carew. Those who might know of some association that led to his death.'

Henry Jekyll smiled, as if to reassure himself rather than Swain.

'I was no friend of his, Mr Swain. Nor enemy neither. I was scarcely even his acquaintance. Our paths crossed once, some years ago, when I was travelling abroad.'

'His journal records an encounter at an evening party, this very summer.'

Light filled Henry Jekyll's eyes with an attempt at honest recollection.

'I believe he was pointed out to me as the Liberal Member for Repton. I cannot think we were introduced.'

But even as he spoke, the head of the victim went through the noose of the snare the inspector had laid. Beyond doubt, Jekyll was J in Carew's journal.

'I wondered, sir,' asked Swain helpfully, 'why, in that case, Sir Danvers would have written to you the day before his death. A formal note, pointing out the impossibility that you should become a governor of the Royal Military Incurables Hospital without a scandal.'

There was much greater disturbance now, but it was deep and hardly glimpsed. It lay in Jekyll's soul like a glimmer on water at the bottom of the deepest well. In Swain's experience, the man who controlled his fear so profoundly was one who confronted it day by day and hour by hour. Henry Jekyll had not murdered Sir Danvers Carew but he had done things that were far worse in his own mind. The doctor managed a bewildered smile.

'I received no communication, Mr Swain. It is true that I was nominated as a governor of the hospital. But I had not decided on acceptance. If I decline, I assure you it will be health and not scandal that prompts me.'

'I have every reason to believe, sir, that he wrote in those terms.'

'Then he did not write them to me, Mr Swain.' Jekyll had dropped his head to study his hand in his lap. He muttered the final words. When he spoke again, it was more quietly still with an intense neurotic precision.

'I daresay I have done wrong, Mr Swain. Which of us has not? But I am no murderer. I have done nothing that a court of law has business with. When I was younger the worst of my faults was a certain gaiety of disposition. If I felt guilt, it was merely that I found it hard to reconcile such frivolity with a wish to carry my head high.'

'Hardly an uncommon fault, sir.'

'But one that troubled me, Mr Swain, more than it would commonly do. I concealed my pleasures and so stood committed to a life of duplicity. Many a man would have blazoned such casual irregularities. I hid them with a morbid sense of shame. From causes that would seem innocent to many young fellows, I became committed to a double life. I was no hypocrite, mind you. Both sides of me were in dead earnest. Can you understand that, Mr Swain?'

Henry Jekyll stared into the fire, coals like burning mountains in the toy landscape of hell.

'Yes,' said Swain, 'I can understand very easily.'

'*Video meliora proboque, deteriora sequor*. The story in five words. Perhaps you do not follow me, however.'

'Horace, I think, sir. I see what is good and better, but I follow what is worse. My father was a country schoolmaster. I learnt Latin tags by rote at six years old.'

Jekyll nodded, showing no surprise that a policeman should remember so much of his education.

'Then you know all that there is to know about my past, Mr Swain. Two natures contended in the field of my consciousness. I was both. It was like a perennial war between my limbs. But I was a doctor and a man of science. Could I not therefore put my disturbance to some good purpose? My scientific studies had always led towards the mystic and the transcendental. Very well, I would make my own disease my study. My predecessors had believed in the primacy of reason. But not I, Mr Swain. I came to believe profoundly in the duality of the psyche. Those are provinces of good and evil which divide and compound man's dual nature. And so I wrote, often under names other than my own. And so I was disbelieved and rejected.'

The firelight played upon the violet and crimson bottles in the glass cabinets. Swain thought the story might be over.

'There can be no shame in that, sir.'

'I daresay not.' Henry Jekyll's face assumed a grimace that was almost a smile of self-mockery. 'But then I did a wrong so grievous that I could no longer bear the faces of those I knew and who thought me innocent. At that time my life still held promise. I had degrees and honours. I was one of the youngest Fellows of the Royal Society. But I could only think of the need to redeem the past by the future. Henry Jekyll should die. Like Frankenstein, I must create a better man. And so I took another name and went abroad to lose myself in work.'

'There is no crime in that either, sir,' said Swain quietly. 'As for the matter of the Zulu battle, I know the story of it. I have heard nothing the least dishonourable spoken against you.'

Jekyll shook his head and looked up, surprised at the inspector's slowness.

'Then you know nothing, after all. I had forgotten Isandhlwana. It is not of that I speak. I went up from brigade to the battalion that morning. Surgeon-Major Shepherd was already there, and no work for him to do. The attack and the massacre came two or three hours later. No one expected it. By then I had returned to the brigade camp, where I might be more use. That I escaped butchery with the rest was the merest fluke.'

'Then I am right,' said Swain. 'You have no need of self-reproach.'

But Henry Jekyll looked at him, as if in despair at the inspector's scepticism.

'You do not know why I went abroad in the first place, Mr Swain. Nor shall you ever hear it from me. I will only say that I chose exile because I killed where I would have loved. Natural causes, to be sure. No crime that you could name. Yet, Mr Swain, I sit here and I know that Henry Jekyll's name is blotted from the book of nature and the book of life.'

'You can't know that, sir,' Swain said quietly. 'No one can.'

It happened from time to time that Alfred Swain, the anonymous policeman, became the repository of such personal confessions. He saw in Henry Jekyll a wild and familiar quest for absolution, where he could offer none.

Jekyll turned to the fire again and said nothing for a moment.

'You are right in one thing, Mr Swain. Isandhlwana put an end to the philanthropist I had created as a refuge from myself. It brought me home.'

'And then, sir?'

'Then there came a man,' said Jekyll softly, 'who taught a clever creed. Is a pagan evil who makes human sacrifices to his gods, when he has been brought up since a baby to believe these practices are virtuous? Is a man who eats beef or pork unclean because other nations than his abhor the practice? Is a man guilty of lust or murder in his dreams when he has no control upon his thoughts? Is a man, who has been brutally treated as a child, to be wholly responsible for the marks of cruelty in his own conduct? Can a man help how he is born? Is not passion as indelible as the colour of the eyes?'

Swain watched him as Jekyll studied the fire again.

'All this, Mr Swain, my philosopher taught me. I could, I daresay, have repudiated such moral logic. I laughed at it. But I welcomed it too, for it set me free where I wished to be free. The human race, I concluded, lived in a state of merry cant. Every man will compound for the sin he is inclined to, by damning those he has no mind to. I was no worse than my neighbours, for my evil was offset by my active goodwill. Surely I was better than those who avoided acts of indulgence but saw no wrong in the lazy cruelty of their neglect of others? I found my excuse and stamped my passport into hell. You see?'

'I begin to, sir. It is not my business but I begin to.'

'And when the ground was truly laid, Mr Swain, there was such merriment. My philosopher had made me like himself. He came at a time when I was low and offered me amusement in my misery. He brought companions and entertainment to numb my brain in its grief. I was exhilarated by pleasures to outrage love and nature. Cold commons it seems now, Mr

71

Swain. Stale and cold. But the bill is to be paid. And paid again. The worst of it is, I hate him and I am like him. I hate him because I am like him. There are those who would tell you we two are one. We are not, Mr Swain. But we are like as twins in our minds.'

'I think not, sir,' said the inspector softly, 'for you have rejected your philosopher's teaching.'

Jekyll looked up, drew breath and shook his head. There was a brightness in his eyes which had the suggestion of tears.

'One is not permitted to reject, Mr Swain. It is not allowed. There are what holy men call sins. They glitter and entice. Perhaps they do not, for you. In that case, you cannot imagine the excitement of anticipation. How they prick and thrill the soul! Today I shall have my heart's desire! I shall do with someone what I always longed and never dared! And so the poor dupe does. Again and again until his mind is whored and his reputation lies in the hands of the worst of men and women. They might blast him with a word to the world. And the glitter wears off the sins. The acts that once blazed for him are so dull after all! They are so damnably dull, sir, that you would avoid them if you could. They are chores, nothing less. But you go to them. You must. The worst of it is that such sins require companions, Mr Swain. A man does not commit them without associates. The hooks of those companions are into him.'

'There is a crime of blackmail, sir,' Swain said.

But Henry Jekyll shook his head.

'Those of whom I speak, Mr Swain, want more than a man's money. It is his soul they mean to have. And they get it. His courage is worm-eaten by them and his resolve is lost. At last he struggles no more, as I have ceased to struggle. I do not go to them, Mr Swain. But neither can I defy them.'

Swain stared for a moment at the firelight dancing in the glass panes of the cabinet. He recalled a line of Sir Danvers Carew's journal, referring to Henry Jekyll. The doctor might be a modern Faust, Carew had thought. 'But then, where is his Mephistopheles?' No more than Carew could Swain answer the question. But, unlike Carew, he knew that the question had an answer.

'I am no alienist, Dr Jekyll,' he said tentatively, 'nor am I a theologian. Least of all am I qualified to offer advice to a man of your standing. But I should be greatly surprised, when things are as you describe them, if criminal pressure were not brought upon you. If that is so, I beg you will call upon me to assist you. For the rest, if you have faith either in the alienists or the clergy, they may help you more than I.'

Henry Jekyll shook his head again. When he looked at Swain, however, there was a slight reminiscent smile upon his lips.

'I have a comfort, Mr Swain, drawn from an observation of my own. Written many years ago. I think because I know my mind is hurt that it cannot be hurt as terribly as I fear. I am like a man that knows he is mad – and therefore cannot be quite mad after all.'

'You are surely distressed, sir,' Swain said, 'not mad.'

The encounter was not at all what he envisaged. The inspector was no closer to the truth of Dr Jekyll's secret. He had supposed it to be the drama of some involuntary and uncharacteristic act of cowardice at Isandhlwana. And yet, from what was said, it appeared to be a more ancient and more terrible act of destruction by this gentle-seeming man upon a beloved victim.

By no stretch of the imagination could Henry Jekyll be the murderer of Sir Danvers Carew.

'Come back, Mr Swain, when you have the answer to your riddle,' said Jekyll vaguely, as if he could not quite remember what that riddle was. Sir Danvers Carew had gone from his mind already.

'To be sure, sir,' said Swain, taking the outstretched hand in his and feeling it cold as ice. They walked together towards the red baize door.

'See how he treats me,' Jekyll said suddenly, taking from a shelf a book bound in gold-stamped calf. He opened it and showed Swain a finely printed title-page of Tonson's *Lucretius*, 1712: the dragon of disease slayed by the power of science at the Temple of Reason. The simple beauty of the antique design had been scrawled across and across with the freshly-inked obscenities and profanities of the Victorian gutter.

Swain was more profoundly shocked by this destruction of art and learning than by anything else that Jekyll had told him. Jekyll opened a cupboard door. On its back was framed an oil portrait of an Edinburgh gentleman in the high collar, blue coat and silk bow of the Regency. Beneath it had been inset an identifying slip of brass: 'William Tooke Jekyll, Esq., by Thomas Lawrence R.A.'

Swain looked, about to admire, and was surprised to see the darkened canvas cut across in two precise diagonals.

'My father's portrait!' Henry Jekyll's voice betrayed the catch of tears for the first time. 'See how he has defaced it!'

Swain's indignation prompted him to demand the name of the desecrator. But Jekyll opened before him a fine medical quarto of Galen's *Commentaries on Hippocrates*, published by the Elzevir Press at Amsterdam in 1665. Gold on vellum and printed with studied opulence, it seemed to Swain more a work of art than a book.

'See!' whimpered Henry Jekyll. 'See how he treats me!'

Across the figures and landscape of the frontispiece ran the freshly-inked scorn and indecencies. Alfred Swain stared in dismay. But this time he recognised the hand that had written them, for they were more careful and precise than the previous scrawl. He had, the day before, received a confirmation by note of the present appointment. From that he knew the desecrations of Galen and Lucretius to be the work of Henry Jekyll himself.

Either the man before him was a victim of the cruellest insanity or else he was in thrall to a modern devil.

That afternoon, by arrangement, Swain attended the reading-room of the Phrenological Society in Bedford Square. It was such a room as he had dreamed of but never occupied, a sanctuary of tall shelves and galleries with their winding metal stairs. There was a hush of leather chairs and deep red carpets. He sat at a table and waited, while a leather-bound volume of the society's transactions was fetched and laid before him.

'Not strictly orthodox, Mr Swain, you understand,' murmured the librarian. 'But in those days the editors would not lightly dismiss the views of a Fellow of the Royal Society.'

And so Alfred Swain found the page and began to read 'The Thorough and Primitive Duality of Mind', by Henry Jekyll, M.D., F.R.S. It had been the last statement of the case before the creation of Samuel Parr.

The terms of this debate are as old and commonplace as man. I must speak here by theory alone, saying not that which I know, but that which I suppose to be most probable. Man is not truly one, but truly two. I say two, because the state of my knowledge does not pass beyond that point. Others will follow, others will outstrip me on the same lines. I hazard the guess that man will be ultimately known for a mere polity of multifarious, incongruous and independent denizens. If each could but be housed in separate entities, life would be relieved of all that was unbearable.

It was the curse of mankind that these incongruous faggots were thus bound together – that in the agonised womb of consciousness, these polar twins should be continuously struggling. But the doom and burden of our life is bound for ever on man's shoulders. When the attempt is made to cut it off, it but returns again upon us with more unfamiliar and more awful pressure. . . .

He read with care to the end of the article and then closed the heavy volume. Its contents had been issued fifteen years previously. Though having no claim to be a man of science, the inspector had not the least difficulty in seeing why the paper had been refused by all but an eclectic and eccentric journal of this kind. So far as he could determine, there was no science in it. Henry Jekyll's learned theory was a compound of assertion and whimsy, delusion and self-indulgence.

The sage of Caleb Square had indeed made his own disease his study. In the pages of the learned paper, the soul of a weak and unhappy man was revealed to the world. What so-called evil deed of his own might have driven him abroad and tortured him by remorse it was impossible to guess. But Alfred Swain was first and last a policeman, only in his spare time did he become a dabbler in modern thought and its theories. For all the reassurances received that morning, he knew that Henry Jekyll's hurt mind offered meat and drink to some unknown trader in blackmail and extortion.

9

Firelight cast a shadow-play on four Gothic panels of the scrapbook screen. Its pointed arches made a pair of right-angles to conceal the artist and his model from the tawny-carpeted expanse of the lamplit drawing-room. The summer green and golden petals of its design had been cut from magazine-plates and pasted into the tall panels of the screen by the Utterson sisters on winter days long past. Through this frieze of wild flowers lay glimpses of arcadian fields, thatch and cottage gardens. Swain recognised a Birket Foster landscape of John Milton's towers and battlements in lofty trees.

His own preference was for the Pre-Raphaelite cut-outs that glowed in the colours of jewels. Burne-Jones's beggar maid before King Cophetua had the thin-clad sensuality of a languid and neurasthenic seamstress unveiling herself to a first customer. The little girls sledging in muffs and fur hats were perversely and disturbingly adult. Young women in the satin fashions of the 1870s posed as knowingly as children. Erotic goddesses of mid-century mused and fretted among the pasted foliage. They were velvet dressed and silken haired, ribboned and brushed, blood-warm with promise. The scrapbook screen was an apt shrine for the beauty of Miss Utterson.

Alfred Swain called his thoughts to order, reprimanded by the public faces of the panels. The Poet Laureate, bearded and anxious. Field-Marshal Lord Napier of Magdala victorious on the rocky hilltops of Abyssinia. General Sir Garnet Wolseley sharp and imperious among the submissive leaders of the Ashanti. But it was on the translucent-clad vision of King Cophetua's beggar maid that his eyes had joined Romana Utterson's with such meaning.

The screen secluded them like an intimate drawing-room

bower. Swain resumed his second sketch of Romana on the maroon velveteen ottoman. Her neck was bare, the chestnut hair drawn back in a dark blue ribbon. A shawl of Indian reds and saffron, yellowed ivory and crimson, was pulled about her. She looked to Swain like a captive princess or a Roman bride.

'Is it not curious, Alfred Swain? If I were to pose for you *nuda veritas*, and you were to call me Truth or Venus, the world would applaud your finer sensibility. Were you to call me Miss Utterson, they would howl you down for a cad.'

Swain scowled at his sketch with concentration. It was not the first time that Romana Utterson had matched his thoughts by her own.

'No doubt,' he said with a sigh of dissatisfaction at his work, 'and so I should be. Truth is anonymous. Miss Utterson is a name in Bayswater.'

'I hope, at any rate,' she said, squinting at the sketch, 'not to be anonymous.'

He had caught the tilt of her chin and the angle of the nose rather well, it seemed to him. The softness of the chestnut hair as it parted on her forehead was better suggested this time. The eyes defeated him still. They were a little tight-lidded in the manner of all three Utterson sisters. He could get that. There was a slight enigmatic slant to them. And he could almost get that. What he could not capture on paper was the light in her eyes, the hint of the uncanny and the edgy. It was laughter and suggestion. It was also madcap and dangerous. He thought it was not precisely dissolute or immoral but it was unprincipled and sensual. How the devil could anyone draw that?

To one side, he heard Jenny and Dido chattering over a pattern-book at the far end of the handsome room. Mr Utterson was away from home, attending to some matter involving his late and distant relative, Danvers Carew. As she sat in thoughtful profile on the maroon velveteen, Romana held a morocco-bound album. Swain had wanted a book to occupy the hands. She had chosen this.

'There you see us,' she said softly, opening the volume.

'May I look?'

Securing the shawl with one hand, she passed the album to him. The photograph was done in sepia. It showed a group of two men, a woman, and a pair of little girls whose hats and laces, full skirts and pantalets gave them the elegance of beribboned kites.

She did not need to identify the women for him. The eyes of the little girls had not changed in twenty years. Romana and Jenny, for Dido could not yet have been born, had that elusive and suggestive cast which baffled Alfred Swain in the present sketch. The image of the woman beside them confirmed what he had guessed. It was from Amelia Utterson, the long-dead wife, that the girls inherited such looks. In the picture she appeared about Romana's present age, standing in her tight-waisted, full-skirted, polka-dot promenade dress. Behind her a range of low and sandy cliffs enclosed a bay of hazy sparkling water. The photograph caught the pale heat of a forgotten summer as no painter could.

'Father you will recognise despite the improvements of time,' Romana said dismissively, 'and no doubt his companion who is now your own subject of concern. You need not gape so at my deductions, Alfred Swain. I do not spy upon you. Father heard from Henry Jekyll as soon as you had made your visit. It is legal etiquette between a lawyer and his client.'

'This is Henry Jekyll and that your father?' Swain stared at the two young men in the photograph, patterns of all that seemed handsome and humane.

She took the album back and twisted it round to look at the picture.

'It was taken at Tenby the year before Mama was ill. Henry Jekyll had been in Ireland and stopped for the day on his way home. He was a man for children, you see. For children but not for marriage. I was ten or eleven when he went away – went abroad that is – and hardly saw him afterwards. Last year, when we were taken to see Irving's Hamlet at the Lyceum, I knew that Henry Jekyll must have been my Yorick. He hath borne me on his back a thousand times, Alfred Swain. Playing horses with Dr Jekyll is my memory of that summer. As for infinite jest and excellent fancy, he was full of stories that make me think of summer evenings when he told them. The garden still light as one lay in bed and clutched so firm a hand for safety, and listened to the tale. To fall asleep with him there was far the best thing then.'

Swain frowned to himself.

'And did Henry Jekyll set the table on a roar with his merriment?'

'Dear Alfred, for God's sake try not to look so solemn about it! Of course he did! Twenty years ago, when they were all young men, the shouts of laughter from the dinner-table carried even to the children's bedrooms at the top of the house. It was not always as you see it now.'

Swain checked his reply. Without the least warning, Romana Utterson had become irritated by him. When that happened one could feel it like thunder in the air. But unlike thunder it was more immediately dangerous, malevolent, exhilarating. The eyes were impossible now. No pencil would capture their quickness and irregularity. She talked calmly again but more rapidly than before.

'It was quite understood between us that he was twenty-one and that when I grew up I should marry him. I suppose I must have been thirteen or fourteen before I knew absolutely that I should not marry him – that it had been all in game. You see? Or rather you don't see, do you? Under that inquisitive face, poor Alfred Swain, you have an imperceptive mind.'

He glanced up from the sketch and gave her an automatic smile of acceptance for her criticism.

'It amuses you, this little girl's game,' she said softly. 'And yet I cannot think I shall ever love any other man quite so freely as I loved Henry Jekyll at seven years old.'

'But he was not twenty-one nor anything like it.'

The light caught the sleekness of the Indian silk and he saw beneath it the frail fin-like beauty of her shoulder-blades and the narrowing to her waist.

'No,' said Romana Utterson. 'He was about thirty, I think. Already honoured for his medical researches on diseases of the soul. Already a Fellow of the Royal Society. But there was never a man more willing to spend his evenings telling stories to little girls of how the animals lived together in the wild wood. How the crows debated together and the badgers built their homes. How the kittens would tease the cats and the wild bears steal honey from the bees.'

'Had he no family of his own to tell stories to?'

'Does it matter?' Romana Utterson turned her head a little more and smiled. 'He had a family wherever he went. It seemed so natural at the time. Now I see him as a sort of man that appears at all such gatherings. The man who is gentle and loved by little girls with eager hearts and sticky fingers. But he does not belong to anyone. And no one belongs to him. He is the unmarried brother or uncle with whom no one knows quite what to do.'

'It would be better,' Swain said, 'if you let the folds of the shawl lie as they will, instead of holding them.'

A scream of laughter from the younger sisters, unchecked in Mr Utterson's absence, distracted him for a moment. He put down the sketching board, which he had been holding on his knee, and got up. The india rubber and the sharpening knife lay on a music-stool by the piano.

'But still,' he said with his back turned as he whittled the pencil into a china dish, 'you do not see Henry Jekyll now.'

'Not more than two or three times since his return,' she said, 'and in any case you do not come here to talk to me of him.'

Swain turned round again and walked towards the screen. Only within its shelter, hidden from the rest of the richly-furnished room, did he see that Romana Utterson had let the shawl drop so that it lay diagonally across her thighs. He had supposed her to be wearing a dress beneath it. She was wearing nothing at all. The skin was a perfect pallor and the shape of her body from the shoulders to the knees was a paragon of beauty such as he had seen only in sculpture and never believed. He could argue that, sitting as she was three-quarters turned from him, there was nothing improper. He

81

knew, however, that it was the situation and not her nudity that made for impropriety.

'And now, Alfred Swain,' she murmured, inaudible to Jenny and Dido far off beyond the piano and the fern in its gold-rimmed pot, 'you shall be King Cophetua and I your beggar maid.'

'You must not. It will not do,' he said ambiguously, aware of the sisters' giggling over the pattern-book at the other end of the room. One of them might get up and walk across at any moment. Mr Utterson himself might return.

Romana made no movement.

'Is it not curious, Mr Swain?' she murmured. 'You will walk through the galleries and feast your eyes on drawings of the female nude. You would attend life classes at the Royal Academy Schools or at Kensington and spend a day copying the nakedness of a young woman who was a total stranger to you and for whom you cared nothing. But when she who is a friend offers you the same study, it will not do. When she tells you that she would like you to honour her by your talent and attention as you honour the stranger, you say she must not. Or is it you that must not, Mr Swain?'

Swain remained standing.

'It is a question of what is judicious and injudicious,' he said, at a disadvantage.

'A policeman's answer!' She teased him openly for the first time. 'But if you continue in this manner, Alfred Swain, I shall think it is the answer of a prig.'

Her face was a mask of pretended scorn. She was likely at any moment to break into the giggles of a child that has been caught at mischief and whose defence is to hint at its parent's grown-up guilt.

'Your father—'

'My father would not mind. He would not like to be told because then he would feel that convention required him to disapprove. If he knew but were not told, he would not mind. When you understand that, you know all there is to know about my father.'

'If he were not told, he would not know.'

But Romana Utterson, more potently naked in the dangerous seclusion of the scrapbook screen, had had enough of
this.

'If you are to continue the sketch, Mr Swain, I wish you
would sit down and do so. A person may not pose all night,
after all.'

With mingled feelings of misgiving and the absurdity of his
own scruples, Swain sat down.

'You have an eye for a line, have you not, Mr Inspector
Swain?' Romana said presently. She turned her head and,
Swain thought, if there was such a thing as malevolent laughter it was what illuminated her beauty and filled her eyes
just then.

'It is not at all what I intended,' he said doubtfully and this
time she laughed out loud.

For almost half an hour, Swain sketched the lines of
Romana Utterson's figure, adding them to the head he had
already completed. At last he put down the pencil.

'It will make a beginning,' he said self-consciously.

She stood up with the shawl about her and took a step
forward from the maroon velveteen of the ottoman.

'King Cophetua has honoured the beggar maid and she is
obliged.'

She knelt at the stool where he was still perched and
took his hand. The eyes that troubled Swain were lowered in
uncharacteristic submission. With a stirring of excitement, he
felt her lift the hand and press it to her lips. He was about to
lean forward over her when with a sudden and savage energy,
Romana Utterson drew back her lips and sank her teeth hard
into the back of his hand at the fleshy base of thumb and
forefinger.

The shock was worse than the pain and he managed to re-
strain himself to a sharp intake of breath. As he tried to draw
his hand back, Romana still kneeling held it in both of hers.

'You witch!' he said, letting the breath out again.

'That's better!' she said gently. 'The real Alfred Swain is
emerging.'

The eyes slanted with a passion that might have been hatred

or hunger. Swain could not, without wrestling her, draw his hand away. Romana Utterson held it and menaced him.

'I have risked the edge of the precipice for you, Alfred Swain. And will you not do the same for me?'

When he remained silent, she seemed to lose all interest in him at once. She let the hand go. Swain bound his handkerchief round it and stood up.

'Your hand!' cried Jenny, as he appeared from the arbour of the screen, the blood showing through the linen.

'I caught it on the sharpening knife,' Swain said foolishly.

'And what a clumsy thing that was to do.'

Dido's scepticism was evident in the quizzical movement of her eyes.

Then Romana Utterson stepped from behind the screen in the decency of the shawl.

'I bit him,' she explained. 'Very hard. And he's ashamed. He makes a story of it instead!'

Dido's expression cleared at once.

'If she bites you, Mr Swain, that's more than she does for her other sweethearts. She wishes to be remembered by you and a little discomfort will be far the best keepsake.'

The older sister slipped an arm about the younger and hugged her.

'I don't think, darling, that Mr Swain would like to be my sweetheart. I don't think he would like that at all.'

'And what does Mr Swain think?' Dido inquired.

The sisters stood round him like the Furies of ancient drama. Three pairs of eyes alike in the sensual tight-lidded mockery that they had inherited from Amelia Utterson. Romana echoed Dido.

'And what does Mr Swain think?'

Swain thought only that he wished himself out from the pack of them and back in Pimlico. To his relief, he heard the front door slam as Mr Utterson returned. The vindictive light died in their eyes. Dido snatched up her sewing and Jenny sat down with a book. Romana walked with even steps towards the door and went up to her room to change. For all their witch-eyed mockery, the frown of Mr Utterson abashed them.

84

They were like little children interrupted in naughtiness who scampered to put on a display of earnest employment.

Utterson was not the least inclined to tease or argue that evening. The immobility of his face as he came into the room was not so much a mood of grief as one of detachment. Matters had gone beyond his control. He could do no more. Swain, observing him on such occasions, saw a numbness of shock or distress that was like the appearance of drink in other men.

'Mr Swain, if you please. We will retire to my bachelor quarters. I have a matter to discuss with you.'

The lawyer said no more as he led the way through the small reading-room and past the billiard table. Not until they were seated in the chairs of his smoking-room and the gin and water had been poured did he explain what was in his mind.

'I have just come from Henry Jekyll, Mr Swain. What passed between us was between lawyer and client. Except for one thing. It is something that I am obliged to tell you because you are a policeman. But I would not do so until I had warned Jekyll of my intention. As a witness identifying the body of Sir Danvers Carew and not as a lawyer, I thought I recognised the stick with which we suppose the poor fellow was beaten to death. Or, rather, I believed I recognised that half of it which was found lying in the gutter beside the body. It is made of an unusual wood. South American. Dark and very hard, bound with a silver band at the bottom. If you will look at the base of the stick there is a very small half-circle burnt on the wood. It is not truly a half-circle but a letter U. This afternoon, in your superintendent's office, I asked to be shown it again and I have no doubt of seeing it before. I gave that stick to Henry Jekyll many years ago. Long before he went abroad. This evening I put the question to him. He no longer has it. How it passed from his possession I cannot tell you. I believe him innocent by his nature of the crime – and innocent by the circumstances. But Carew was killed with Jekyll's stick. Of that there can be no question in my mind.'

Swain looked at Utterson but could not catch his eye. The time had come to advance with special care.

'But is the upper half of the stick not to be found?'

'He thinks that he has not seen the stick for more than a year,' Utterson said. 'If he did not kill Carew, there is no reason for him to have the missing portion.'

Swain nodded.

'I shall have to ask him about it, as well as about other matters. So far as the murder is concerned, we have one description of the assailant. A maidservant witnessed the attack. If her account is at all accurate, the attacker could not possibly be Dr Jekyll. I had not seen him, except in a photograph, when I took her statement. Now I have met him and I know that the man she describes cannot be he.'

Utterson seemed to relax with the warmth of the gin and Swain's reassurance. He treated his guest to a show of mock-solemnity.

'You shall do as you please, Mr Swain. Or rather, you shall do what you must. But though Carew was my brother-in-law, I tell you in confidence that I should not thank you for proving Henry Jekyll his murderer. Henry Jekyll, for all his faults, used to be a companionable fellow. I owe him the memory of a hundred delightful evenings. Danvers Carew was an admirable man in every way. The conscience of the patrician order. But he was not agreeable, Mr Swain. A cold fish – but a virtuous fish. You would applaud Danvers Carew from a distance. You would not wish for him as a companion. He and I were civil enough to one another. I am sure we wished one another well. But we were both too sensible to believe that we could endure much of one another's company. I do not think I care greatly for such admirable people, Mr Swain. On the other hand, I assure you that I do not go round murdering them.'

Alfred Swain gave a wan, indulgent smile. He withheld his request until the second glass.

'A little while ago, sir, you asked if you might speak to me not as a policeman. I should like to ask a similar favour. May one speak, Mr Utterson, not as to a lawyer?'

Utterson laughed.

'I am a lawyer with decreasing frequency, Mr Swain.'

'What I would ask, sir, may help to clear Dr Jekyll's name. It is on the very matter where you first asked my advice. The strange provision of a will, whereby if J were to disappear for three months or more, H must assume possession and control of his affairs.'

Utterson frowned into his glass, shifted in his chair, and looked uneasy.

'I must be prudent, Mr Swain.'

Swain turned to the lawyer, benevolent and well-intentioned.

'I would not have you otherwise, Mr Utterson. At that time, sir, you had no need to disguise the initial letters of the names. There was no inquiry over the death of Sir Danvers Carew. There were no murmurs as to how easily another man possesses himself of cheques signed by Dr Jekyll. Cheques that hardly can have been signed by him for such exact amounts at such short notice. Were you to tell the story of the will now, sir, you might call the men X and Y rather than J and H. And still it would not need the wisdom of Solomon to guess that one of them is Dr Henry Jekyll.'

Utterson made a disapproving clearance of his throat.

'Solomon, Mr Swain, had the advantage of not being answerable to the Law Society for professional misconduct.'

'Sir,' said Swain earnestly, 'I do not ask about J. It is H who concerns me. You smelt villainy yourself. I think there is villainy now. But I shall save Henry Jekyll more easily if I know where to look for it. Who is H?'

Utterson looked doubtful.

'It is hardly proper, Mr Swain, for a lawyer to disclose who may benefit under a will. Indeed, it is grossly improper.'

'Only, sir, if I know whose will it may be. I do not ask that. I ask only H and not J.'

Utterson rolled his mouth and fought temptation. Swain persisted.

'How will it help, sir, if a good man is destroyed?'

The lawyer sat upright in his chair and put the glass down.

'I cannot tell you that Henry Jekyll is a saint. I think it very likely that he is anything but that. I will say only this, Mr Swain. If you would find the fellow you want, you must play at hide-and-seek with him.'

'That will do, sir. Indeed, I think that will do very well.'

'And what else do you think, Mr Swain?'

'That it may be blackmail, sir. That it must be blackmail, indeed. And forgery. A cheque was demanded from a certain villain after a quarrel in Soho. He was not Dr Jekyll and nothing like him. He came back in a moment with a cheque for the exact money, the ink still wet. I cannot think Dr Jekyll was there to write it. Imagine, Mr Utterson, a blackmailer that has a grasp upon his victim so fatal as that! He may forge the man's name to cheques, safe in the knowledge that there shall be no complaint. Might he not forge a will?'

'If it were blackmail, I should have heard,' Utterson said. 'And I doubt he would forge a will, where a witness is required.'

'Say the cause of the blackmail were too dreadful for your ears, sir?'

Swain looked at the lawyer's face and saw it harden at the thought. Then the hardness went and the eyes faded a little as if with despair for a friend. He shook his head and would not talk of it. Utterson got up, turned his back and refilled the glasses. When he swung round again he was the self-possessed and unaffected attorney of Gaunt Street.

'You have had an accident to your hand, Mr Swain.'

Swain smiled.

'It was a slip with the sharpening knife for the sketching pencils.'

'Curious, Mr Swain.'

'Sir?'

'Curious that a right-handed man should cut himself just there in sharpening pencils. On the right hand itself. You are right-handed, I believe, Mr Swain?'

'Yes, sir.'

'Then I beg you, Mr Swain, to take more care. You flirt, as they say, with danger. I ask you to believe me in that.'

The lawyer thought for a moment more. Then he smiled and looked again at the injury to Swain's hand, still concealed by the bound handkerchief.

'You must deal more prudently with your muse, my friend. Like the vampire, she has been dead many times and

88

learned the secrets of the grave. Do you read Walter Pater, Mr Swain?'

'A little, sir. I hope to read further when I have leisure.'

'You should read him on Leonardo. La Gioconda with her famous smile and the enigma of her eyes. It would help you in your art. She is not the object of love, Pater believes. She is what in a thousand years men had come to desire of women. Set her beside the goddesses of pagan Greece, he says, and how troubled they would be by her beauty. Beauty into which the maladies of the soul have passed. You are still too Greek, I believe, Mr Swain. Young ladies will take advantage of you for that.'

Alfred Swain met the kindness and understanding in Utterson's eyes. He knew that many a man or woman in the witness-box had been deceived by the look, not knowing the doom that lurked behind it. On this occasion the lawyer was merciful to his subject. The name of Romana Utterson lay in the air between them, almost more potent than her presence. But it was not spoken.

10

'A pretty pickle, mister! A pretty pickle y'have here, by God!'

Superintendent Toplady, a spry bow-legged gnome, seemed about to dance round from behind his desk and box Alfred Swain, man to man. The inspector could never encounter Toplady without wondering what freak of genealogy had given a name suggesting feminine elegance to so incongruous a figure. Montague Toplady was the great-nephew of a more famous namesake who had fought for Calvinism against free-will and written some of the most famous lines in the English hymnal, 'Rock of Ages, cleft for me'.

The size of the superintendent's head, by comparison with the stunted body, was a pantomime disproportion. The grizzled hair was cut short as a 'Newgate fringe'. It stood stiff and upright with an appearance of comic fright. Indeed, Toplady seemed to improve upon his naturally grotesque appearance. He favoured collars that were high and starched with exaggerated points. At every turn of his head they scraped his cheeks in a slight razoring sound. Swain looked on with an apprehension that a sudden downward glance by Toplady would cause the cruelly-starched collar-point to pierce the superintendent's eyeball.

Toplady slapped one hand into the other behind his back. He paced up and down before the broad windows which looked out across the embankment to the rusty sails of the barges and the black funnels of the penny steamboats between Westminster and Blackfriars.

'This is what comes, mister, of an officer that goes skulking away from duty to bury his head in schoolmiss nonsense.'

'With respect, sir—'

'Schoolmiss nonsense, mister! Have the goodness to listen when I talk! Schoolmiss nonsense and Mary-Ann poetry-books, mister! What sort of pastime is that for an inspector of constabulary?'

'With respect, sir, a man may choose his own private reading.'

'Think so, mister? Think that, eh? I'll be damned if he shall in this division! May I be damned if he does so under my command, sir! A man may go home and rot his brains and his commander must have no say in it? A man may fill his mind with Mr Rossetti's lilies, or Mr Swinburne and Greek indecency and no harm done? Why, mister, if you'd spend your time in drink or with a common strumpet on each arm, you should do better. And now you tell me of sketching? Sketching! Are you so great a fool, Mr Swain, that you do not know sketching is milky stuff for schoolgirls to be taught by governesses?'

'Neither Lord Leighton nor Sir John Millais think sketching beneath them, sir.'

Superintendent Toplady swung round on his victim with a mad grin of triumph.

'And tell me, mister, how many murderers have his lordship and Sir John brought to justice? Eh? Tell me that, if you please.'

'With respect again, sir—'

'Answer my question, Mr Swain, if you value your place here! How many?'

'None that I am aware of, sir.'

'None that you are aware of, mister!'

Toplady rolled the saliva round his mouth as if he might expel it in a jet upon Swain. But he walked up and down a few minutes more. Then he came back to his grand preoccupation.

'And so, Mr Swain, this imposing fellow, Jekyll, shows you a picture cut up and nastiness scrawled in his books in his own hand. And he tells you that someone else did it, though you see his own script before your eyes, and you believe him! And he tells you what a miserable wretch he is, and you believe that too. Well, you may, I suppose. A villain is often a miserable wretch. And he says he is so mad he cannot tell what he does in his dreams and what he does awake.'

'It was not just like that, sir.'

'Was it not?' A sneer of glee began to gather on Toplady's lips. 'But you come back here, mister, and write in your diary that we must all bleed a little from our hearts for the poor devil. He cannot have beaten Sir Danvers Carew to death. Oh, he cannot, for he is such a sensitive and ill-used fellow. He has something of the schoolmiss and the poetry-book about him, has he not?'

'I will stand by what I reported, sir.'

Superintendent Toplady swelled with ironic admiration of such courage.

'Oh, will you, mister? Then you may also stand by the fact that the lower half of Jekyll's stick with which Sir Danvers Carew was clubbed to death lay in the gutter beside the body. You may stand by the fact that it is identified by an independent witness. You may stand by the fact that every conclusion points to your friend, Dr Jekyll, being there and having done the bloody deed. And a pretty pickle you have made of it all, mister! A pretty pickle!'

'There is only one witness, sir. She has already said positively that Dr Jekyll bore no resemblance to the man.'

Toplady worried this round his mouth for a moment or two, staring out across the river scene under a bright cold sky.

'You are wrong, mister. There is a witness that will put such tales to shame. The dead, Mr Swain. The dead are witnesses against him.'

'Sir?'

Toplady grew calmer with the assurance of a man who has won the argument.

'Samuel Parr, mister. The name the fellow goes by from time to time. He was a surgeon-major with Lord Chelmsford and the expedition to the Zulus. He was at Isandhlwana. Two thousand brave men stood to their arms and died rather than desert, mister. All except Samuel Parr or Jekyll, call him what you will. Thought himself too good to die like the poor fellows all about him. When he saw the spears of the tribes rip up

92

the first few bellies of the riflemen, it was all mewl and puke
with such a sensitive soul. Too strong in the imagination for
that. He bolted, mister. Left the sick and the wounded – and
all his comrades. Left them to die. Every man-jack of them.
Stole a horse and rode blubbering away.'

Superintendent Toplady had been Lieutenant of Horse Ar-
tillery at Inkerman. In the blind and bloody skirmish of that
battle, the position had been overrun. Toplady had fought
hand to hand with the advancing Russian troops in the terrible
hour that followed. However grotesque his constabulary role,
he knew something of the slaughterhouse of war. But some of
his private information from the Horse Guards was no longer
of the best.

Swain's silence pleased him.

'Yes, mister! We understand a little of Jekyll or Parr, call
him as you will. And you may ask why he was ashamed of his
own name even before that. Why was he Parr and not Jekyll
in the day of battle? Eh?'

Swain drew a deep breath.

'Because it was Sir Danvers Carew he feared meeting
more than he feared the Zulus. Because he never knew till he
reached the camp that Sir Danvers was riding there with Lord
Chelmsford's patrol. The man who rode away to the brigade
camp with Henry Jekyll swears that it was the mention of the
name Carew that set him trembling.'

Toplady's lips were drawn back in a rictus of contempt.

'Then if he's an honest man, why does he fear meeting
a man of honour? Why must he do a skulk as Samuel Parr?
Answer me that, sir!'

'As yet I have not the least idea, sir. I mean to uncover
the reason.'

'Not the least idea, sir?' Toplady turned mimic with evident relish. 'By God you don't, mister. And without my boot
behind you, y'd never find out. I'll tell you this, however. He
was an unlucky fellow, for he could only hide and not get
clean away. No doubt he hoped to be the only survivor who
struggled to Rorke's Drift. A hero, perhaps. Well, mister,
Lord Chelmsford's column came back. They found him doing

a skulk among the rocks. Hid himself there to watch his comrades butchered and never fired a shot to help them. Then it
was that Sir Danvers Carew, on Lord Chelmsford's staff, got
the full story.'

'I understand that far, sir.'

'I doubt that you do, mister. I doubt it mightily. I have spoke
to Lord Chelmsford. For the honour of the dead, it was agreed
between he and Sir Danvers that the scandal should never be
spoken. Nor was it, that we know of. Some whispers perhaps
among a few scoundrels. But no public scandal. And then Sir
Danvers sees Jekyll by chance a few months ago. Recognises
him as Parr. He realises that the man whose name might be
printed far and wide as a patron of hospitals and causes, is the
wretch that ran from the Zulu fight. When he is announced as
a patron of military incurables, Sir Danvers can stomach it no
more. He composes a note – sends it no doubt. Jekyll must
withdraw his name or be exposed for what he is.'

Reluctantly, like a man compelled to walk the plank, Swain
followed the logic of Toplady's account.

'Deny it, mister? Deny it, do you?'

'No, sir.' Swain shook his head.

'Well then, mister. No sooner is the challenge issued,
than the next night Sir Danvers Carew is set upon and
beaten to death. The stick that beats him is used with
such force that it breaks in two and one half is left behind.
And that stick, mister, is recognised by Lawyer Utterson as
belonging to the fellow Jekyll. Deny any of that, mister?
Eh?'

'No, sir,' said Swain humbly.

'And yet, mister, y'come whimpering back here on the
scoundrel's behalf and bleeding from the heart for him.
He's been wicked and he's sorry for it, he says! His mind
is that deranged he can't tell dream from wake, he says!
He writes nastiness across his own books and can't see
his own signature in it! He writes cheques to cash for
the riff-raff of Soho to pay for his pleasures! What sort of
man? Eh?'

Swain endured the storm in silence.

'And I want to know, mister, why the fellow has not been arrested and charged.'

'With respect, sir, the girl who saw the attack on Sir Danvers swears the man looked nothing like Dr Jekyll.'

'And you did not find out what cause she has to lie and who may have put her up to it. You did not, while you had the chance. This comes to Jekyll's door, mister. Unless there was a fellow loved him so much that he did his murder for him.'

The scorn with which Toplady suggested the last possibility was emphasised by a bravura sniff.

'With respect, sir, Sir Danvers Carew may have died for quite different reasons. The malice may have arisen from other causes.'

'With respect, sir!' Toplady relished the phrase like a fine vintage. The sneer that accompanied the exclamation was not reserved exclusively for Swain. The superintendent treated him better, in general, than the rest of his subordinates. 'Who the devil else used Jekyll's stick, d'ye suppose?'

'A man that was younger, and slighter in build, and a good deal more villainous in his expression, according to the witness, sir.'

'Very convenient, mister! Yes, I shouldn't wonder if it wasn't convenient! No one else ever saw him and the witness might make him anything she chose. She might be Jekyll's bastard daughter protecting her father, for all you know. She might have a grudge against such a man as she described. Why, you poor fool, there may be a hundred reasons she would tell such a story!'

There was only one way forward.

'I'll go to Dr Jekyll, sir, and try to clear up the matter of the stick.'

Toplady moved to and fro on his toes, as if about to begin sparring.

'See that you do, mister! And see that you come back with more sense and less slop than last time. I don't stand for being made to look ridiculous, mister. The man that thinks to make a fool of me shall drink a bitter broth!'

'And Mary Smith, the maid, shall be questioned again,' said Swain placatingly.

'Shall she indeed?' Toplady assumed a wild and humourless grin. 'Have the goodness to read the public prints, sir. If you please!'

Swain went back down the stairs. He tried to imagine the man who had leapt upon Sir Danvers Carew and beaten him to death with such savage and irrational glee. As he turned into the lower corridor, it occurred to him that he had only met one such freak of human nature in his life. It was an aberration that precisely corresponded with the character of Superintendent Toplady.

Alfred Swain's rest-day and his immediate summons from Toplady had kept him from his office for almost forty-eight hours. Sergeant Lumley was waiting for him, ready to follow him in.

'There wasn't much point, Mr Swain, looking for you yesterday. You wasn't home and, in any case, there's nothing you could have done. And anyway it's in the papers today.'

The public prints. Toplady's instruction returned to him. As it did so, a cold apprehension spread through Swain's entrails. Sergeant Lumley reserved his lugubrious tone for the more monstrous misfortunes of police investigation.

'What the devil are you on about, Mr Lumley?'

'Mr Newcomen went to see about it,' Lumley said. 'Being your day off, it seemed best. Bottom of the page. First column. There's a report on its way but it don't say much that's not there.'

Swain took *The Times* and sat down.

DOMESTIC TRAGEDY IN CHEYNE WALK. – Mary Smith, a maidservant in the employment of Lady Carew, was found hanged in her room yesterday morning. The victim of the tragedy had been several years in domestic service and it is supposed that the late melancholy death of Sir Danvers Carew or some personal disappointment was the motive for so desperate an act. Her Ladyship was not in London at the time. An inquest will be opened by Dr Galt the Chelsea coroner next week.

Alfred Swain looked up with a face like a tragic mask.

'The poor soul,' he said, as if pitying himself. 'Why, Mr Lumley? Why?'

Lumley shrugged.

'She never left a note. Put the room tidy. Packed up her things. And then did it. There wasn't no point getting you over there with Mr Newcomen on duty.'

Swain stared at him, a first glint of anger pricking his eyes.

'I was talking to Toplady just now. About her. About her evidence. He never said anything about this. But he knew, Mr Lumley. Even told me to read the public prints. And all he did was make rubbish of the poor girl! Almost laughed at her!'

'That's old Toplady,' said Lumley philosophically.

'That man is a brute, Mr Lumley! An unregenerate brute!'

Lumley shrugged again.

'If you only just twigged that, Mr Swain, then you're a lot slower than most round here. Swine, we reckon mostly though, rather than brute.'

Swain grunted, as if to dismiss his sergeant. But Lumley held his ground.

'There's another thing you aren't going to like, Mr Swain. About old Toplady's notion that Jekyll or Parr did a bunk at the Zulu battle and Carew was there and vowed never to let him hold his head up again. Didn't happen.'

'Toplady talks as if it's true.'

'Well, it ain't,' Lumley said simply. 'They never saw one another that day. I had a long talk yesterday with Corporal Vickers that was medical orderly with Jekyll, so-called Dr Parr. They rode up from brigade to the forward camp that morning. Carew was out scouting with Chelmsford's staff. Never got back till the fight was over and they were all dead.'

'What about Jekyll?'

'According to Vickers, he behaved quite normally at first. Then there was talk about who was out on patrol and so

97

forth. Then Jekyll starts getting more and more worked up. In the end, he says that they've already got Surgeon-Major Shepherd to look after the camp. He's only a supernumerary himself and he really must be getting back to brigade. Duties there and so forth.'

'Did Vickers think it odd?'

'Not half he didn't,' Lumley said. 'But Jekyll or Parr never bolted from the fight. When he and Vickers rode out again, no one knew there was going to be a fight. But if you believe Vickers, old Jekyll certainly acted like a man doing a bunk from something.'

'From Carew, before the scouting party got back?'

Lumley shrugged.

'Could be. He never said. And Vickers never knew. But just riding back like that wouldn't be much for Carew to hold over him, would it?'

Swain turned and stared from the window across the smoking chimney-pots of Northumberland Avenue towards the cold gleam of the river.

'Carew had a very precise view of duty, Mr Lumley. It might have been enough for him.'

Lumley smirked.

'But not enough for old Jekyll or most other people. There's no disgrace in not happening to be there to be killed. Not enough to threaten a man with for the rest of his life.'

'Henry Jekyll has a morbidly sensitive conscience,' Swain said thoughtfully. 'A diseased conscience, you might call it. There's no telling what that might do to him.'

'Gammon!' said Lumley with casual scorn. 'He never rode away from the enemy and that's all there is to it.'

Swain shook his head as if to clear it.

'No, Mr Lumley. He rode away from someone, perhaps Carew, or he rode away from something. Whatever it was, the poor devil was in greater terror of it than he was of being ripped open on the blades of those native spears. And he lives in the same terror to this day.'

Lumley sniggered again.

'You let old Toplady hear you talking like that, Mr Swain, and you could end up patrolling a beat down the Waterloo Road in a tall hat with a badge on it.'

Swain glared at him, discomfited by the knowledge that Lumley was right.

11

A bardic preacher. That was the answer to the riddle
of John Poole, Henry Jekyll's manservant. Swain had not
seen it before but as Poole led him towards the curve
of the elegant staircase it was plain at once. The shock
of white hair and the deep-set eyes, of course. But the
voice with its baritone resonance and slight reverberation
of laconic menace rang bardic and evangelical at the same
time.

'Your master,' Swain said, as Poole took his hat and coat,
'I hope he is better than I saw him last?'

Poole turned away towards the mirrored mahogany of the
hall-stand.

'Dream and wake are more and more the same to him. I
pray to God, sir, there comes not a day when they are all the
same for ever.'

He drew a deep breath and turned upon Swain, drawing
himself up as if defying the inspector to improve upon such
rhetoric as his.

It was not to be Henry Jekyll's study this time. Swain was
shown into the saloon on the first floor. The largest room in
a large house, it seemed wider and longer by virtue of empti-
ness. The floor was of polished parquet-wood. Honey-coloured
blocks bound in squares and oblongs caught a liquid sheen of
light from tall windows that overlooked the square. Each pale
green wall was inset with a large panel, painted as a wide border
and a flower-pattern circle. The room was curiously bare of
furniture. There was an Egyptian settee, its frame gold-painted
and scrolled at either end, its feet carved to represent four
dolphins diving. Upholstered in silk of broad-striped green and
gold, equipped with two large and pale pink cushions of silk,

it showed another side of Henry Jekyll's nature. The cabinet had revealed Jekyll the victim of adventures in dark science and mental pathology. The saloon suggested what Superintendent Toplady still called by the old-fashioned title of an amorist.

Apart from the settee there was a crimson and gold silk screen in three scrolling but diminishing panels. Unlike the Gothic propriety of the Uttersons' creation, the crimson and gold frivolity suggested that it was intended to conceal the rituals of wardrobe and coiffure. In the rest of the room there was nothing but a deep pink camellia in a bulbous pot of dark green glaze upon a stand of ornamental iron. The settee had been disordered. One pale pink cushion lay upon the floor by a gilt dolphin-foot. Upon it reposed a mandolin.

Had Swain entered such a room and been asked to name its owner, Henry Jekyll's name would have been almost the last to come to mind. With the thin sunlight of the autumn morning filtered neutral as a gleam of water through lace curtains, it offered a curious mixture of suggestions. The settee and the screen, the voluptuous cushions and the deep-pink of the camellia petals hinted at exotic or Parisian sensuality. The expanse of parquet floor, the plain dado, the mandolin and the glazed flower-pot evoked the rehearsal room for a dancing-class of little girls. Perhaps it was neither extreme, Swain thought. Or perhaps this was the room in which the extremes met and mingled.

'Mr Swain! I do beg your pardon for keeping you like this.'

Henry Jekyll closed the door of the room behind him and greeted his visitor. He was scarcely the same man in appearance or demeanour. Though nervous, he was brighter. The round face showed anxiety but it was the anxiety of the man who is excited to be up and doing.

'I am pleased to see you better, sir,' said Swain politely.

A quick grimace of self-disparagement came and went in the line of Jekyll's mouth.

'I am in command, Mr Swain. I am well and I do not

believe, as it happens, that I was ever truly ill. A man is sometimes down. That is all.'

'Mr Utterson is not to join us?' Swain inquired. 'You may wish to have a lawyer's advice.'

Jekyll laughed.

'I do not think so, Mr Swain. My conscience is clear in this matter. Besides, a man does not always want a lawyer to know his business.'

He waved the inspector to one end of the settee and took the other himself. It crossed Swain's mind how well-appointed the room must be for the purposes of seduction. Two people were bound to occupy the same couch.

'Very well,' he said courteously. 'Then may we return to the matter of Sir Danvers Carew. It now appears that he was killed with a stick that belonged to you.'

'But not killed by me, Mr Swain.'

'And killed after composing a note in which he threatened you with scandal should you accept a governorship of the Military Incurables Hospital.'

Jekyll was unabashed. He adopted the tone of one gently advising the inspector.

'Mr Swain. I do not know, nor pretend to know, what Sir Danvers Carew may have composed. I received no such note from him. I should have been astonished and mystified had I done so. Therefore, I conclude he did not send it.'

'The stick,' Swain said firmly. 'That first, if you please. I should like an explanation.'

Jekyll gave a weak and wishful smile.

'Then you must seek it from the man who used it, Mr Swain. I do not carry a stick as a rule. I have no need of one. As a dress cane I have a silver-knobbed ebony evening-stick. I rarely use it. For the rest, they have been in the hall or about the house for many years. I do not notice them. Poole fetches the silver-knobbed ebony when I require it. I could not even tell you when I last saw the stick that interests you. Several years ago at least.'

'Even though it was a present to you from Mr Utterson?'

'It was one of many he possessed and had no use for,' Jekyll said dismissively. 'It was not of particular value. I have nothing to say on the matter, Mr Swain. Indeed, there is nothing I can say that would help you. And I mean to help you, if I can.'

'Should it be necessary,' Swain said coolly, 'I must have this house searched for the missing half of the stick that was broken in the attack.'

Jekyll was a little subdued but unmoved.

'Should it be necessary, Mr Swain, I certainly hope that you will do so. Though if I were such a villain as you must then suspect, would I not have disposed of the evidence?'

Swain ignored him. All the same, it was disconcerting to find the sudden self-possession that Jekyll's behaviour now showed.

'Sir Danvers Carew,' he said quietly, 'and Dr Samuel Parr. Tell me about them.'

Jekyll gave an exasperated sigh, his first sign of irritation that morning.

'I was bored with my life here, Mr Swain. I had seen nothing but study and science, experiment and practice. I would happily have taken a commission and gone to the wars. But success disqualifies a man from much of life, Mr Swain. It disqualifies him quite as much as failure. I was a doctor and a man of science. My name was known. I was a Fellow of the Royal Society. The world would not allow me to live in the ordinary way. I wished, for a while, to retire to a lower level. To travel and not be recognised. To see Syria and the Holy Land. To explore Africa a little and learn something of primitive psychology. I chose to disown my past and travel incognito. There was no other way.'

'For an adventure?'

'Yes, Mr Swain. For an adventure, since you put it that way. I adopted the name of Samuel Parr. It would enable me to practise medicine if I wished. There was a Samuel Parr, an obscure country doctor who had just died. I saw a notice of him in the paper, I think. My qualifications were in every way superior to his. My practice was a good deal better. I never once pretended to skills that I did not possess. And so I went.'

103

'I believe you later used that name to write for the medical journals.'

'A *nom de plume*, Mr Swain, for those subjects which the medical world does not yet approve. You would not, I trust, arrest a man for anonymous writing?'

The humour flickered again but not the smile.

'I am not here to arrest you, sir. But I mean to have the truth of Sir Danvers Carew's death. As it stands, he composed a note. In the note he accuses you, while passing as Dr Samuel Parr, of having behaved dishonourably during the engagement with the Zulu tribes at Isandhlwana. The next night, he was beaten to death.'

'But I did not behave so, Mr Swain. There is not the least proof of it. Look where you will, there has never been the least suggestion of it. The camp was overrun, the column forced to withdraw. Some who withdrew were killed and some survived. I was fortunate enough to be among the survivors because I had just ridden out of the position on my return to the brigade. Dr Shepherd was already with the camp and it would have been absurd for me to stay and leave my duties at the brigade unattended. It would have been of no use to return to the camp when the battle began. Sir Danvers Carew might talk of heroics, for he was not there either and never saw the attack. When Lord Chelmsford's column arrived, it was all over.'

'Then,' said Swain gently, 'you have little regard for Sir Danvers Carew and his opinions.'

'I am no alienist, Mr Swain, but human conduct is my study. I tell you that in such danger no man stands and waits his turn to be put to death like a sheep or a calf. And that is hardly cowardice.'

'Indeed, it is not,' Swain said gently. 'However, the suggestion in the note is that you abandoned your duty and that Sir Danvers Carew knew of it. It may be a calumny but no more welcome for that. Many a man would go to some lengths to silence such an accusation against himself.'

'Then let my accusers face me. I did my duty to the uttermost and escaped with my life by pure chance. Neither Carew nor any other man has confronted me to the contrary.'

'And may it continue so,' said Swain quietly.

He had come to the dangerous frontier between those topics on which he was well-informed and those that still lay in darkness.

'There is a man by the name of Hyde who is known to you. Tell me of him.'

'By what right—'

'By no right, Dr Jekyll. But if you choose to reject my questions now, you must answer them more publicly in a little while. Who is Hyde?'

The light in Jekyll's eye betrayed a sudden and deft inspiration.

'I have a patient of that name.'

'And?'

'And, Mr Swain, the affairs of a doctor and patient being matters of confidence, that is all I shall say on the subject of Mr Hyde. Ask them here or elsewhere, there will be no further answer from me.'

Swain nodded, as if he understood and approved.

'Tell me of Trim Street, sir. Are you familiar with it?'

'I cannot say that I am.'

'You do not know a court there called Terminology House?'

'I do not believe so. Perhaps I know it by sight but not by name.'

Swain studied the deep pink leaves of the camellia, suggestive of sweet tropical scents and burning skies.

'Perhaps, though,' he said, 'you can help me. How would it happen that a ruffianly fellow might be pressed for ninety pounds outside a slum court of that kind at three in the morning? How might it happen that he would plead poverty but promise to get a cheque from within? And how could it be that he would enter there and return in a moment with a cheque signed by you for the precise amount and drawn upon your account at Coutts Bank in Piccadilly? If you were familiar with the street and the court, I could understand it. If you are a stranger there, it is a trifle curious to say the least.'

'I could not and do not know of such things!' Henry Jekyll stood up. 'This is done to provoke me! I was ill and now that I

105

am recovered I wished to be of service to you, Mr Swain. But you provoke me, sir! You spy upon my most private financial transactions. And that is all my reward. I know sufficient of the law, sir. I have endured your curiosity long enough. I will have no more of it. You hear me, Mr Swain? My attorney shall answer from now on.'

Swain remained seated.

'This is done to protect you from the worst, Dr Jekyll. Who is this man Hyde? Does he not live at Terminology House? And does he not blackmail you over the matter at Isandhlwana?'

To Swain's astonishment, Jekyll laughed out loud. It was a strangely unbalanced laugh but the relief in it was beyond question.

'I will be damned before I let any man blackmail me for something I did not do! I will face any of you and answer over the matter of Isandhlwana. Let him speak of it who dares!'

'Is not the man at Terminology House the patient you call Hyde?'

'How the devil should I know? He may live in six different houses for all I can tell. And, being my patient, I will speculate no more upon him in your presence.'

Without another word, Jekyll walked from the room. Swain heard him on the stairs. It was by no means clear whether the interview had been broken off or not. Nothing was said to suggest it. Presently the footsteps sounded again and Jekyll returned, flourishing a handkerchief as if he had been to fetch it. His manner had altered. The ebullience of half an hour before was gone. He seemed cowed and apologetic.

'I beg you will excuse me, Mr Swain. I am not so well as I thought. I sleep and wake and sometimes do not quite know which. Last night I slept well and was better this morning. But these questions will not do, Mr Swain. They will not do.'

Swain got up.

'Then we will leave them, sir. For the moment.'

'I did not murder him, Mr Swain. I knew nothing of him or his note. That night I was here and I was not alone. But

106

I will confess to the murder and you may hang me before I will speak the name of my companion.'

'And Poole was here?'

'And Poole was here as well. But he did not see the person and I will not speak that name.'

'The time might come, sir, when the name would speak for itself.'

But Henry Jekyll could endure no more. The self-confident equilibrium he had maintained at Swain's arrival was gone, suddenly and abjectly. It had been no more than a flash of bravado.

'Leave me!' he said quietly. 'Leave me alone, the pack of you! It was not for this that I came back to England.'

Perched on the Egyptian settee, he lowered his face. The inspector waited for a moment and then saw, rather than heard, that his subject had begun to weep. Alfred Swain, disconcerted by the sudden crumpling of assured bonhomie, withdrew quietly from the room and closed the door. It would have been repugnant to him to continue the questioning and, in any case, it could be to no purpose.

'Your master is not as well as he thinks,' he said to Poole as the servant helped him on with his coat.

'He's dying, sir,' said Poole calmly, as if it were the most natural thing in the world, 'that's all it is. Slowly, to be sure. Whether by his own hand or not depends on how you look at it.'

Swain, despite himself, was shocked.

'He's not an old man. He's not diseased, I should have thought.'

The servant gave a wise and quiet smile.

'But he's a man for picking his own time, Mr Swain. That's all.'

'And the fellow Hyde that cashes the doctor's cheques?'

'I don't interfere in such arrangements, sir. It's not part of me nor of my job. I'm treated well. And even when he seems strange in his manner, it's only the chloral speaking.'

Alfred Swain walked down the steps and into the autumn square. There were children playing noisily along the pavement and a nursemaid with a toddler in the gardens. Death of a kind that he did not understand was stamped upon Henry Jekyll. Chloral or morphia might have a part in it. But chloral or morphia would not kill him. Swain thought again of a phrase from the journal of Sir Danvers Carew. Henry Jekyll was the doomed Faust of dark sciences. But if he be Faust, Carew had written, where is his Mephistopheles?

He quickened his pace towards the black shape of the waiting cab.

'Back to Whitehall Place,' he said sharply to the driver, 'and quick as you can.'

12

'I'm not saying it would have made much difference if you'd been here, Mr Swain,' Sergeant Lumley's face was flushed a delicate port-wine shade as after a hearty dinner. 'All I am saying is that you'd have known earlier. And you can have the facts checked. You've been seen off, diddled, fed gammon, by whoever Dr Jekyll may be. That's all.'

'He's a sick man,' said Swain defensively, his eye meditating the blotched chocolate-brown distemper on the lower half of the office wall.

'He's a bleedin' liar,' Lumley said triumphantly. 'He's well enough for that. Samuel Parr wasn't dead when Jekyll went off abroad. He was still in the medical list, come to that. I can't say he went on doctoring, but he was still alive when Jekyll come back from abroad. In fact, he was still alive until four years ago. By then, Jekyll had been going around calling himself Samuel Parr for about ten years. In Africa, in the Levant, and even here from time to time.'

'*Four years ago?*'

'I seen the death certificate in Somerset House,' Lumley said proudly. 'Four years next March. Respiratory failure, whatever that may be when it's at home.'

'It means he stopped breathing,' Swain said boldly.

' 'Course he bloody stopped breathing,' Lumley said indignantly, ' 'e couldn't be dead else, could he? You mark my words, Mr Swain, this whole caper got a real ripe smell about it.'

Swain gave a patient sigh and closed his eyes.

'It means that respiration failed as a result of some other cause.'

'Like a pillow over the poor devil's face or a cord round

his throat,' said Lumley sceptically. 'You never asked me who signed the certificate, however.'

'Who?'

Lumley swelled with the pleasure of it.

'Henry Jekyll, M.D. and a lot of other letters. He had to put his real name, didn't he? I mean he couldn't very well sign it as the cove that was supposed to be dead, could 'e?'

Swain thought about it all. He consulted his watch.

'In half an hour, Mr Lumley, I'm off duty. I shall think over the matter then. Henry Jekyll's not in any state to give us much trouble. As it is, I'm damned if I can see how he murdered Sir Danvers Carew when his description doesn't fit and when his servant and another witness put him somewhere else at the time.'

Lumley stood between the inspector and the door.

'And you never asked me where he died, Mr Swain.'

'Where?'

'The County of Monmouth,' said the sergeant ominously. 'Back of beyond, in other words.'

Swain paused, then pulled his gloves on after all.

'Nothing odd about that, Mr Lumley. Not necessarily odd, I mean. People die in Monmouthshire as easily as anywhere else.'

'My nose says it's odd,' Lumley murmured confidentially. 'A real ripe Gorgonzola smell this one got. You want to get back there, Mr Swain, and give it to old Jekyll hot and strong. He's ill, is he? Yes, and I daresay I could be ill, supposing it suited me!'

Swain's gloves were on now and he was in a hurry.

'Before I do that, Mr Lumley, I shall need to be better briefed. Better informed. Send a wire to the registrar's office in Monmouth, the coroner's office if need be. I want to know just how and where Samuel Parr died. The date isn't enough, you may tell them. Nor the cause. Just see to it, if you please, Mr Lumley.'

A certain warmth gathered in the sergeant's plump face as the tall figure of Alfred Swain – coated, gloved and hatted – swept out of the room.

'Oh, yes,' said Sergeant Lumley with portentous irony. 'I don't know how we should go on round here if there wasn't someone to see to things. Someone that had time to spare from school-books and artistic evenings!'

But before his voice rose to audible indignation at the end, he allowed Inspector Swain to turn the corner of the corridor, out of earshot.

PART 2

The Fairy Feller's Master-Stroke

13

While Lumley saw to the matter of Samuel Parr, a bright November sun lit the last of the pale leaves in the broad walk of Kensington Gardens. Swain had met Romana Utterson that afternoon by appointment, at the gilt and Gothic memorial to the late Prince Consort. They walked together under the arched branches with the sunlight at their feet and the espaliered fruit trees of Kensington Palace close by.

Her walking-costume of short velvet jacket over a dress of cerise velveteen was calculated to match the heat and unpredictability of her temper. For all that, Alfred Swain deplored the fashion. Women in modern dress were freaks compared with the visions of his childhood. There was, he supposed, an explanation in fashion or sexuality for the monstrous bustle that filled out the rear of the skirts. All the same, he could think of it only as an attempt to smuggle a gnome or a small occasional table under the petticoats.

'And what do you do in Pimlico, Alfred Swain?' The eyes quizzed him with a lascivious quality that was of the brain rather than the body.

'Very little, I fear, Miss Utterson. I eat and sleep there. I read a little.'

'And what do you read, Alfred Swain? What do you read just now?'

Whatever it was, she would receive the answer with sardonic acclaim. He might as well tell the truth.

'*The Renaissance*,' he said, 'by Walter Pater.'

Romana Utterson stroked her chestnut hair thoughtfully and gave him a conspiratorial glance, as if they might be sharing a joke at the expense of a third party.

'Not only an aesthete, then, Alfred Swain, but a *savant* into the bargain. We see in you a much-underestimated man.'

'It is the first time I have read it. I daresay it will be the last.'

But she was tired of it now. Above the roof of Kensington Palace the sky had a pure cold blue that suggested early spring rather than autumn. On their trelliswork, the fruit trees appeared about to bud and leaf.

'A man that only reads books once, Mr Swain, has ample time to receive his friends. When am I to inspect the interior of these Pimlico rooms?'

Swain studied his own boots pacing out the length of the broad walk.

'Perhaps you would care to bring Jenny and Dido to tea one afternoon?'

Romana Utterson gave a gasp of laughter at the preposterous suggestion.

'I should care for it very little indeed, Alfred Swain. I do not pay calls with my sisters in tow.'

'Your father may not wish you to do so without them, in this case.'

Her look might have been intended for a slow-witted child.

'I must make you understand, Freddie Swain. My father would not wish you to tell him boldly that I was coming to tea alone with you in your rooms. It would put him in the disagreeable situation of having to protest, or at least having to entertain feelings on the subject. He would prefer not to do so. The mere unremarkable fact that I am in your rooms alone with you having tea would not disturb him. No one obliges him to have feelings on the matter so long as it is not mentioned. Can you still not understand?'

'Oh yes, perfectly,' said Swain coolly. 'But my profession is to understand things and not always to believe them. Let us see if a tea-party cannot be arranged.'

The promise was ambiguous enough to silence her. He sensed that Romana Utterson would now come to the purpose of their meeting. But she did not do so yet. The tall terraces running from Bayswater to Marble Arch were a good deal closer before she brought herself to it.

116

'It was such a silly thing to do,' she said without looking at him. Was it the almost Egyptian slant of the eye, Swain wondered, that gave an impression of danger and unsatisfied desire?

'Silly,' she went on, her tone casual as if the offence did not really matter. 'And spiteful, I think. Yes, spiteful, indeed.'

Swain had thought, and then he had hoped, that the occasion for their meeting like this was to be Romana Utterson's apology for biting his hand.

'I don't know,' she said quietly, 'how a person could do such a thing. Was it to avenge yourself upon him, Alfred Swain, because he loved me when I was a child? Or was it to punish me for treating you as you deserved the other evening – and for daring to mention his name in your presence?'

Swain stopped walking. He should have guessed there was to be no apology. It was his own conduct that was on trial again. Across the grass, where a series of butts had been arranged against the brick wall of the palace garden, a team of Kensington ladies in white blouses and skirts, Robin Hood feathers in their hats, had begun the day's archery practice. The first of the bows was raised to eye-level and an elegant silk-clad arm drew the string. The light spear-tipped wood of the arrow rose straight and true, plopping into the outer ring of the straw-packed target.

'It would have been impossible to exempt Henry Jekyll from questioning,' he said at last, 'supposing you to mean that.'

'But the manner of it!' she said, 'the manner of it in the case of a man who is so sick that he hardly knows what he says!'

'You know perfectly well that it was necessary,' Swain watched the next of the elegant Amazons draw an arrow from her quiver. 'If you do not understand the necessity, your father will explain it to you.'

'My father, Mr Swain, is a man who likes making explanations as little as he cares for receiving them. He prefers a world where all may be known and nothing discussed. Then there can be no scandal, no necessity to be scandalised. He can live his bachelor life, as he calls it, without the

117

disagreeable need for emotions and feelings. He is a companionable man, Mr Swain. But if the rest of the world died tomorrow, he would grieve no more than the gilly-flower on the wall.'

'I shall not believe him to be so hard-hearted, Miss Utterson.'

Another arrow thumped softly into the target. This time the sisterhood of archery gave a collective jump, a clapping of hands and a cry of admiration for the skill of a bull's-eye.

'A heart may be hardened for its own good, Mr Swain, without malice.'

They turned away from the archers and walked on for a moment in silence.

'I will say this,' Swain turned to her but received no more than the scepticism of her profile in exchange. 'Nothing shall be done without need. If there is nothing more to be asked of Henry Jekyll, then I will see to it that he is left alone.'

Romana Utterson was unimpressed by him.

'There is no more to be asked,' she said.

'How can you know that, unless you know the man who murdered Carew?'

'Because you were told, were you not, that another person as well as the servant was with Henry Jekyll when the crime was committed?'

Swain thought for a moment that the circle was complete.

'And you were the person with him?'

'Whether or not I was, Alfred Swain, I would swear it. To stop the persecution of a friend who did not commit murder – and could not to save his own soul.'

'The crime of perjury,' said Swain wistfully, 'you would commit it so lightly?'

Romana Utterson turned and faced him on the leaf-strewn path. Behind her two gardeners were raking the grass. She was not warm with anger but pitilessly clear and elusive as an equation in algebra that he could not reduce to an answer.

'And would you not lie, Alfred Swain, for a dear friend? Does your policeman's conscience forbid untruth to save a wife or a child, a mother or father, a sister or brother? Would you tell the truth and see them destroyed? Or would you tell the noble lie? I would tell it, my dear, to save a cat or a dog that I loved, much more a man or woman. And what would you do?'

'The same,' said Swain with a shrug. 'I should tell the lie without feeling noble. And I should resign from the Metropolitan Police.'

Romana Utterson giggled. She came towards him, hugged his arm, and insinuated her own through it.

'There is more joy over one truth-teller that repenteth,' she said. 'I am so relieved, Alfred Swain, to find you on the side of the dark angels.'

Perhaps there was no more to it, Swain thought. It was his professional interest in Henry Jekyll that had stood between them and nothing more. That interest was dwindling fast, so far as he could see.

'You must understand,' Romana was saying, 'Henry Jekyll and my father are of the same type. There is nothing whatever wrong in my visiting an old friend. But it must never be said that Miss Utterson went alone to visit a gentleman that evening without a chaperone. You see? I believe Henry Jekyll would go to the gallows cheerfully before he would tell the world in whose company he was and where at the time of the Cheyne Walk murder.'

'But his stick was the weapon the murderer used,' Swain insisted, returning a little the pressure of the arm. 'Your friend was bound to be asked about that.'

A sudden access of enthusiasm and energy filled her.

'As to that, Alfred Swain, I have twice lost umbrellas on the railway, which have probably done to death goodness-knows-how-many victims – in other hands.'

'But not in the hands of Mr Hyde?'

'I have not the least idea.'

'And do not know the name?'

'I know very few of Henry Jekyll's friends, outside my own family. There really is no reason why I should. I have never heard the name.'

'I did not say he was Henry Jekyll's friend.'

119

She almost sneered at the glib trick of the professional interrogator.

'You did not, Alfred Swain. But you would not have mentioned him otherwise. Would you?'

They came to the handsome villa in the Bayswater Road with its pillared porch and verandas under wrought-iron canopies.

'You will come in,' Romana Utterson said firmly, 'and I shall make you understand why the matter of Henry Jekyll must go no further.'

Swain gave another shrug and followed. She led him past the usual door and up the stairs to a fine half-landing with a Grecian window arch of blue and green glass. To the left lay a small sitting-room and beyond that, he suspected, a dressing-room. Whatever misgivings he might have had were put aside at once, in the name of curiosity. On the wall in front of him, between two windows that looked across the traffic of hansom cabs and horse-trams, hung an oil painting. It showed a young woman and a girl of seven or eight. Their costume was in the style of an earlier decade. The young woman in a loose gown had her back three quarters turned to the artist and was sitting on an Egyptian settee. She held a guitar as if about to strum it with her fingers. The little girl, watching her own feet, had drawn back the hem of her dress and was practising a dance step.

The oblique profile of the young woman was that repeated in the Tenby photograph. It was hard to see much of the little girl's face. But the room was Henry Jekyll's saloon. The settee with its gilt dolphin-heads and its broad striped silk in green and gold was the one on which Swain had sat. The glazed green pot and its stand were there. Even the camellia. The very walls were still painted in their pale green borders and flowered circles. On the polished blocks of the parquet floor, the light of the tall windows shone as it had done in reality for Swain a little earlier.

'It was painted some years ago,' Romana Utterson said. 'Dido's first lesson in dancing, to the accompaniment of my guitar. Henry Jekyll had it done when he came back from abroad.'

'He kept the house while he was away?'

'Of course,' she said. 'He had nowhere else.'

Swain looked more closely and saw at the bottom of the picture a title, *The First Lesson*, and a signature, 'F. Sydney Muschamp'. It was a charming study of sunlight and gaiety and innocence.

'Henry Jekyll patronised the arts in his youth,' Romana said, 'but the pictures were not always as light-hearted as that.'

She went through into the next room, as if expecting that Swain might follow. When he did not, she returned, carrying a heavy silver bangle.

'This he gave me too,' she said. 'Hold out your hand.'

Swain did as he was told, expecting her to hand it to him. Instead she clipped it carefully and too tightly round his wrist. Swain eased his hand a little.

'Read it,' commanded Romana Utterson.

Only then did he notice that the braided silver contained an incised italic script. There appeared to be four lines of a poem.

What binds the better slave to worse
Swindles soul, body, goods & purse
To unlock the secret cells of dark abyss
The power which never does its victim miss.

Romana Utterson unbuttoned her velvet jacket, took it off, and laid it across the back of an armchair.

'You see?' she said casually. 'Or rather you don't see again. Henry Jekyll's motto. The better slave is always bound to the worse, Freddie Swain, as you are now.'

He twisted the silver round his wrist. There was no obvious device for opening the clasp.

'It's quite safe,' Romana Utterson said. 'It won't come off.'

Swain looked and saw the laughter welling up in her. It was the helpless and wholesome amusement of a child's trick. But the trick had worked. He could see no way, short of extreme force, by which the silver bangle could be removed.

'I do believe,' she said, approaching him with a giggle, 'that the better slave is now truly bound to the worse.'

Swain tried again. As he did so, and failed to open it, he thought of the impossibility of reporting for duty that evening with a woman's bracelet on his wrist. The duty locksmith would get it off for him but Swain shuddered at the stories that would circulate in the Criminal Investigation Department after that. Had he a jacket with sleeves long enough to cover his wrists completely? He thought not and, in any case, it would look absurd. He would have to bandage his wrist on the pretext of a sprain. Or else . . .

'It needs a key,' Romana said gently, 'that's all. Did you think I should keep my better slave in irons?'

'Then,' he said, 'I should be grateful for the key, if you please.'

'It's here,' she said. He watched her walk into the dressing-room and stand there, waiting for him.

'I should prefer—'

'What a goose you are, Fred Swain!' she said. 'Don't you understand? They have given me up. I am universally regarded as incorrigible. I go my own way.'

It crossed his mind again that Romana Utterson, unmarried at twenty-five or twenty-six, was not morally unique in her social class. And if the world were to end that night – even if the little world of his own life were to end – how much he would regret the loss of her that afternoon.

To end the drama one way or another was all that concerned him then. Alfred Swain, so easily taken for a prig, was no more than discreet. Sergeant Lumley and his more earthy companions were probably less sensual in such pleasures but they were a good deal more vociferous. And in any case, Swain noted as a matter of marginal significance, his relationship with Romana Utterson was not strictly speaking professional.

The chestnut hair swirled like a mane across her shoulders as she turned her head to him.

'And is it so irksome a thing, Alfred Swain, for the knight to win his release from captivity?'

When she laughed, all her earlier difficulty and waspishness was only a joke played upon him. They were both in the open now, where matters were upon another footing.

122

'Life is short – we can but try,' she said. 'You may live to regret me, Alfred Swain. But would you not regret self-denial a good deal more? As time goes on, it is opportunity lost for ever that blights one rather than folly committed. Never to have known such mysteries, Freddie Swain. Never even to have known she who was as ordinary as Romana Utterson.'

And that, he thought afterwards when cursing himself as an indescribable fool, was all there was to it. It was one of those moments when he knew, if he had cared to listen to reason, that the indiscretion might have cost him his career. But it was as if he was seized by the madness of daring rather than some sensual compulsion alone. The prudent Inspector Swain for once chose the high-wire or the blindfold duel and found a dimension of excitement beyond the cool and naked limbs of Romana Utterson.

When their faces were close in the exercise of passion, the mysterious quality of the eyes was lost at such range. The contact of her pale skin was less exciting than its contemplation behind the scrapbook screen. Only in the blood and in the loins was the power of Eros triumphant.

Swain, caressing the light dew of exertion on the anonymous Venus, as Romana Utterson had become, felt the first misgivings that overcame the exhilaration of desire. It was the danger of this quizzical, exotic, devious woman that had enticed him. Precisely those same qualities might be the means of his destruction at any moment of her choice. *What binds the better slave to worse* . . . As he watched her turn the little key and draw the silver band from his wrist, the meaning of the italic script acquired a deeper significance.

Swain's finger traced the line of her nape and shoulder as his pencil had once done.

'What was the poem?'

Romana Utterson smiled and rubbed her head against his hand like a cat. She turned the silver bangle and showed him the inside. It was there in the same italic script.

The Fairy Feller's Master-Stroke.

'Who wrote it?' he asked.

She shook her head.

'A poor mad painter called Richard Dadd, whose pictures Henry Jekyll collected and whose case he studied. A man that had murdered his father. Or perhaps it was truly Henry Jekyll himself who wrote them. See the other side.'

'They represent vagary wild,' Swain read out, 'and mental aberration styled. Now unto Nature clinging close. Now wildly out away they toss.'

'They,' she said, 'are dreams. Henry Jekyll's last paper was on the nature of dreams and their control. Whether it might be possible for a person of sufficient will and insight to control the dreams of another. But in all this he was diagnosing his own sickness. The mind that fails increasingly to distinguish dream from reality. That is the man with whom you must share me, Alfred Swain.'

He looked at her and saw not the least irony in her eyes or mouth.

'No,' he said quietly, 'I claim no share in such a situation.'

The eyes shone then with mockery and anger.

'Poor Alfred Swain who must have all or nothing! And so he has none – like the littlest pig in the rhyme!'

'Or perhaps he knows that loyalty cannot be divided,' Swain suggested.

After that she would say no more on the subject. Swain took his leave with no promise between them to meet again, though both knew that there would be such a meeting. It might be in the perfumed dressing-room or in the drab setting of Pimlico. Whether they would ever again meet in the drawing-room below – with its Pre-Raphaelite sketches on the wall and Mendelssohn's reassuring arpeggios drifting through the lamplight – was something Swain doubted. He went down the stairs with her and she let him out into the rumble and clatter of iron-rimmed wheels along the Bayswater Road. The gaslight was coming out down the row of street-lamps. Beyond the dark skeletons of the park trees the last of the day appeared in the sky over Kensington with a glow of frosty fire. Autumn was turning at last to winter.

In the hours that followed, Swain was troubled by feelings that he could not precisely define and ideas that hovered like

124

ghosts, seen only from the corner of the eye. There was something beneath all that he had learnt. It was compounded of madness and paintings, lust and dishonour. But most of all it had to do with shame and fear. Its subject eluded him. Its method was surely blackmail.

To say that the spirit of Romana Utterson haunted him was to Swain an absurdity. Yet she was present in his mind as he walked from Bayswater to Westminster and later that night from Westminster to Pimlico. He held conversations with her in his mind and explained to her the nature of his feelings. He criticised and warned her. Then he caught himself in this folly and made a conscious effort to avoid it.

That night he thought she had appeared to him in a dream. But though the face was like hers, he knew it was Dido the youngest sister.

They were standing in an open space and Dido took him by the hand.

'I want you to meet my mother,' she said.

Alfred Swain knew he was dreaming then. In sleep the logic of his mind still insisted that Amelia Utterson had been dead fifteen years or more. It was not a graveyard upon which the tall iron gates opened. More like a temple, he thought. It was not a nightmare vision. Swain knew before the bronze doors opened what he would find within. There was a great throne raised above a flight of steps and an infinite sky of warm blue behind it. He saw it through a romanesque arch of twisted columns. Everywhere there were tall fans of peacock feathers, jewels and wreaths of gaudy flowers. With a sense of annoyance at having been duped, Swain in his dream saw that it was Romana Utterson who sat on the throne. She was naked but for her jewels. A child sat, or rather sprawled upon her knee. It was the double of the Dido Utterson beside him and he was irritated again by such evidence of a gimcrack deception. As he woke, he recalled that the scene was a painting by Gustave Moreau, a coloured print of which he had been shown on one of his visits to the Uttersons. He had thought it florid and overdone, the subject being Salomé or something of the sort.

Fully awake, he struck a match. It was just after three in the morning. But Alfred Swain got out of bed and found a pencil. The notion of Romana as the mother of Dido, perhaps by Henry Jekyll, was absurd. But absurdities existed to be disproved.

On his slip of paper, he made Romana twenty-six and Dido sixteen, the greatest gap between them. It might be less. Romana then would have given birth to Dido at the age of ten and conceived her at the age of nine. It was both absurd and vexing to be woken by such nonsense. Cursing the waywardness of dreams, Alfred Swain blew the candle out and tried without success to sleep again. Something intangible was wrong. But neither his waking nor his sleeping mind had yet come near the answer.

14

Superintendent Toplady seemed almost to caper on the points of his toes as he moved excitedly behind his desk. The long green curtains were closed across the windows, shutting out the raw twilight and the gathering river mist. He grinned at Swain in furious triumph.

'I'll say this, mister. Folly brews a long time before it boils. Yours has come to the bubble at last!' He rattled in his hand a sheet of paper with the inspector's handwriting on it. 'London to be searched for any man called Hyde that might correspond to the maid's description in Cheyne Walk, eh? A warrant to search the premises in Trim Street that they call Terminology House? That it, mister?'

'It might have been a week ago, sir. The place seems to have been deserted now. As for the man Hyde, he has some questions to answer, whoever he may be.'

'And so have you, mister!' Toplady whispered the words softly, as if to the love of his life. 'Do you know that trespass is actionable? And false arrest and wrongful imprisonment? Know that? Eh, mister? Know it?'

'There are grounds for action, sir.'

Toplady chuckled in his anger.

'There are grounds for investigating a scoundrel like Jekyll more like! Ah, but he mewls and pukes and he talks of his pretty books that are spoilt and his pictures that are torn. And so he must be molly-coddled. No more, mister! He shall be no more.'

'The maid's description of the attacker is nothing like Dr Jekyll, sir,' Swain began, but Toplady talked him down.

'The maid? Call her a maid, mister? Well, you may for her profession. She was no maid otherwise. Eh? Read the inquest this morning, did you? She was gravid, sir. With child. Fecund. By Carew or another. Balance of mind disturbed by being left to face the consequences. Coroner found it so. And you would put the case on such trumpery evidence as hers, when you have Jekyll's stick that did it and Carew's threat that made him do it?'

'If the man Hyde, answering her description of him, can be found—'

But Toplady would have none of it.

'Evidence of a lunatic girl that's dead and can't be questioned? And the man Hyde that no one's ever seen and don't exist but for Jekyll's account of him? Ask me to go to court with that, eh? Indict a phantom, while the true villain sits and smirks among his nastiness in Caleb Square? That the idea, mister?'

'What else can there be, sir, but a search for Hyde of Terminology House?'

Even as he spoke, Swain knew the weakness of his words. Toplady snapped at them like a hungry terrier.

'What else! A member of parliament murdered! A crime that cries out for solving! And y'have closed down the entire investigation by such mishandling!'

'Sir?' said Swain. Watching Toplady, he did not doubt that a thunderbolt was being aimed. From what quarter, he could not say. The superintendent studied a second sheet of paper.

'Lawyer Utterson informs the commissioner that the health of Dr Henry Jekyll cannot sustain further questioning or visits by the Metropolitan Police. See, mister? Lawyer Utterson requires assurance from the commissioner that he will be informed if Dr Jekyll's assistance is required again. In the event of a further visit, Mr Utterson will require to be present. See it? Eh?'

'Yes, sir.' Swain tried to sound humble and reasonable simultaneously.

'A pretty bog!' Toplady's manic zeal shone in his narrowed eyes. 'A pretty bog y'have led us into. Jekyll goes scot-free! And why was nothing said to me, mister, of your personal attachment to Lawyer Utterson?'

'I knew Mr Utterson before the attack upon Sir Danvers Carew, sir. Since then I have seen him once, I believe. It was the occasion when he informed me that the lower half of the stick found near the body resembled one that had belonged to Dr Jekyll.'

The starched collar-edges dry-razored the superintendent's cheeks.

'And did y'never think fit to tell me of those evenings spent with Lawyer Utterson's daughters? I hear of 'em now, mister! Schoolmiss poems and governess sketching-parties.'

Swain felt only a limitless relief that Toplady did not connect his name specifically with Romana's. He chose to risk a lie.

'Since the death of Sir Danvers Carew, sir, I have seen nothing of the family except upon that one occasion when Mr Utterson wished to tell me of the broken stick.'

Toplady grunted, his triumph tossed aside.

'May see as much of 'em as you wish now, mister. Shall make no odds.'

Swain's first thought was that he had been dismissed from the Metropolitan Police. But that was impossible. There had been no disciplinary hearing.

'Sir?' he said patiently.

'You shall be compromised no longer, mister. It shall not matter. You have yielded place in the investigation.'

And still Swain could not understand what had happened.

'I'll speak plain, mister. Y'have had your run. And what results? Sir Danvers Carew killed with a stick belonging to Henry Jekyll but by a man described as looking unlike him. Described by a kitchen maid who hanged herself for blighted passion! Henry Jekyll sworn to be at home when it happened. But you must put the miserable devil on his guard by your questions. He never killed Carew – oh, he never did! He is the sickly fellow blackmailed by a villain who did the murder – so you say. But a man can't be blackmailed unless he complains of it, mister. And he don't complain. Eh?'

'No, sir.'

'And so you ask about one of his patients. A fellow Hyde that no one knows and can't be identified as having anything to do with Carew. Eh?'

'Under investigation, sir, as the brute that had Terminology House.'

'Under investigation!' Toplady rolled the contempt round his mouth like a choice claret. 'Y'may find yourself under investigation before this is done, mister. The division is not a hair's breadth nearer finding the murderer of Sir Danvers Carew than it was the day he died. Henry Jekyll's stick was used. And he was threatened by Carew. The silly maid that hanged herself saw a ruffian she said wasn't Jekyll. She might be Jekyll's woman, you poor fool!'

'A good deal of the investigation is of a delicate nature, sir,' said Swain firmly. 'We shall have to find our way through private information.'

'Delicate nature! Private information!' It was as near a scream as Toplady had ever come in Swain's presence. 'Is this a police force or a pope's confessional, mister? The law of England knows nothing of private information, sir! Evidence, mister! There must be evidence! Unless you would transform us to a convent school where milky girls shall have their little nastinesses mumbled over by a fat fellow in a cassock! By God, old Lady Carew is right!'

'Sir?'

'She wanted you put under orders long ago, mister. I stood up for you then. No longer. As from this moment the investigation passes to Chief Inspector Newcomen. Her ladyship employed him once, in the days of hiring, to trace some silver that the country servants had purloined while she was in town at Cheyne Walk. Thanks to your conduct of the case, mister, her ladyship reposes less confidence than she did in the Criminal Investigation Department. Let us see if Newcomen can restore her.'

'Mr Newcomen?' Even in his present situation, Swain found it hard to conceal his dismay. 'With respect, sir, Mr Newcomen was always a hiring man while the system lasted. The best man in the world for missing silver. But a murder in the street—'

130

'If a murder in the street is beyond him, mister, you may be sure it has proved beyond you likewise. You have not the sense to see it, I believe. This is no ordinary murder. A man that is a power in the land is killed. And you deceive yourself that you can treat him as if he had been an ordinary clerk or Haymarket dollymop. This was a member of the House of Commons and a man of title. He has family and party to represent him.'

'And is equal in death with the clerk and the dollymop, sir,' said Swain, permitting himself a moment's indignation.

Toplady grinned, delighted that his victim promised him some sport by a show of spirit. But the grin was checked almost at once.

'Let that be an end, mister. The man that boxes clever with me shall have a bloody nose! If there is leave due to you, I shall be obliged for you taking it at the first chance. Till then you shall give place in this matter and work under orders from Chief Inspector Newcomen. You have no tact with your superiors in society and are a damned sight too familiar with the riff-raff. And now, mister, my compliments to Mr Newcomen in the corridor outside and I will see him at once.'

Toplady turned his back and waved the inspector away.

It was far the worst encounter of Swain's career. That Toplady treated others in the same manner was little consolation. It was of no use to be certain that the murder of Sir Danvers Carew depended on delicate investigation and private knowledge, that Newcomen would never solve the crime. The ancient delight of the superintendent in martyring his subordinates had found its fulfilment with Alfred Swain. It had been a pleasure long denied to Toplady and was the sweeter for that.

Lumley was waiting for him downstairs with a blue telegraph-form.

'That business about Samuel Parr dying because he stopped breathing,' said the sergeant cheerfully. 'Seems he died of drink in the public asylum at Monmouth after having been nursed for years by a private keeper. Wire from the clerk of the visiting magistrates.'

'Give it to Chief Inspector Newcomen,' said Swain ungratefully, leaving Sergeant Lumley without further explanation.

131

Swain spoke to no one else that evening. He went out into the thin cold rain and walked through streets where the wet reflected lamplight shimmered and twinkled and melted together on the dark puddled surfaces. From the riverside near St George's Square the clattering keys of a barrel-organ ground through the melody of 'My Flo from Pim-li-co'. He came at last to the newer streets of coloured brick and patched stone, the little shops selling tobacco and boiled sweets. Above one of these shops were his rooms. He let himself in by the side door and picked up an envelope from the mat, where the afternoon post had left it. Walking upstairs, he set a match to the mantle. The harsh white radiance lit the varnished wood and dusty cushions of his sitting-room. There was a shelf upon which were collected Lyell's *Geology* and Mr Swinburne's *Atalanta in Calydon*, Tait's *Recent Advances in Physical Science* and the Laureate's *Idylls of the King*. To these had lately been added Professor Ruskin's *Stones of Venice* and Mr Pater's *Renaissance*.

Alfred Swain, who liked to regard himself in a small way as a thinking man of the modern world, slit open the envelope he had just picked up. It contained a single sheet of notepaper, vellum-laid and of the best quality. With a little frown of concentration he read the message, written in an unfamiliar hand.

Goldhurst Terrace,
South Hampstead.
Tuesday 28th November.

Mr F. Sydney Muschamp is in receipt of Mr Swain's inquiry, respecting the painting of *The First Lesson*. Mr Muschamp has consulted his diaries and is unable to find any commission corresponding to this at the date to which Mr Swain refers. He is, however, able to trace it to an entry ten years previously when the *The First Lesson* was executed as a portrait of a lady and her daughter. The commission was, indeed, from Dr Henry Jekyll. The further circumstances are no-longer precisely clear in Mr Muschamp's mind. But of the facts which he has communicated here he is quite certain.

132

Mr Muschamp ventures to hope that this communication will be of assistance to Mr Swain in his researches.

F. Sydney Muschamp, A.R.A.

Alfred Swain went across to the window that looked into the narrow Pimlico street where, despite the raw darkness, boys in shabby trousers and girls in thin frocks were skipping and jumping about the chalked squares of their pavement games. He closed the velvet curtains and turned back to the gas–lit room. Then he stood at the arm of the scuffed leather chair and read through the artist's letter again. Romana Utterson's lie to him was not important in itself. Why should it matter that the dead mother, Amelia Utterson, was the figure on the settee and Romana herself the infant dancer? That she should have bothered to tell a lie was surely of some significance. Was it adult vanity of some kind that made Romana substitute Dido, in her own account, as the model for the child dancer? Or was there some more sinister reason for altering the date of the painting of Henry Jekyll's saloon by ten years?

Perhaps it was no more than Romana's vanity, her desire to steal Amelia Utterson's own adult beauty and parade it as her own. And perhaps it was a clumsy defence for a secret that was instinctively to be protected.

Inspector Swain sat down at the little table that served him as a desk. Fitting a new nib into his pen, he dipped it in the ink-bottle and began to compose a letter of thanks to Sydney Muschamp.

15

In the week that followed, the relationship between Newcomen and Alfred Swain did not prosper. A hairy man who sprouted improbable tufts from ears and moles, Newcomen began with a great display of deference. He tipped an invisible hat to Swain's greater knowledge of the case and infinitely greater experience in the matter of common crime. But his past employment, in the days before 1879 when officers might be hired for private service, stamped him for what he was. At the mention of a professional or titled name, Newcomen grew deferential. Confronted by disrespect in the streets, he became loud and hectoring. He was feared in one or two places by petty thieves and respected nowhere.

It was a few hours after being placed in charge of the Carew murder investigation that the chief inspector first mentioned to Swain others who had been his 'second-in-command' on previous cases. Good fellows, all of them, when led by Charles Newcomen. Thereafter the term 'second-in-command' was aired once or twice a day as a matter of form. Swain ground his teeth privately and maintained outwardly his mild horse-faced intelligence. At the end of the first week, an interesting bottle and a large ham wrapped in muslin were seen in Chief Inspector Newcomen's possession. They had been delivered by carriage as the first visible sign of Lady Carew's confidence.

Alfred Swain's mind underwent a curious and uncharacteristic alteration. The case had been taken from him. Endeavour and success alike lost their savour. After a day or two, he began to take a morose pleasure in the failure of the investigation. Henry Jekyll was innocent of the murder, though possibly guilty of masquerading in the past under the name of Samuel Parr. Even there the law was uncertain. He had never pretended to qualifications or abilities which he did not possess in his own name. As for the murder, Carew was killed by a ruffianly fellow. Jekyll was or was not blackmailed by a man called Hyde. Hyde and the ruffian might or might not be identical. Romana Utterson was a liar in one instance and might not, after all, provide an alibi for Henry Jekyll. This last item was one that Swain kept to himself. Jekyll's innocence was vouched for by the servant Poole and the maid Mary Smith. The inspector had no intention of offering his stock of 'private information' to Newcomen. At every utterance of 'second-in-command' Alfred Swain held such intelligence more tightly to him.

On Newcomen's part, there was no search for the ruffian – Hyde or not – and Terminology House remained undisturbed. Newcomen paid several visits to Lady Carew and, on her authority, bullied the servants in the Cheyne Walk houses. It was received doctrine on the upper floor of the Criminal Investigation Department that the villain who had clubbed Sir Danvers was Henry Jekyll in some form. It was only necessary to shout long and loud at the servants to produce a favourable witness and confound the obstructive Lawyer Utterson. The fact that a vanished ruffian once lived in Terminology House was no proof that the mysterious Hyde had ever existed.

But the shouting produced nothing and, at last, Newcomen seemed to lose confidence. He spent a good deal of time behind the closed door of his office. So long as Lady Carew believed in him, he was content and secure.

Superintendent Toplady was occupied by higher things. A penny-a-line journalist, abetted by the Salvation Army, was preparing a denunciation of the white-slave trade. Young women from England were being escorted abroad in sinister circumstances. It was not enough that Mr Stead proposed to call his salacious *exposé* 'The Maiden Tribute of Modern Babylon'. He had aimed his remarks at some of the most famous names in the Brigade of Guards. The evidence which he possessed about certain proclivities of the King of the Belgians threatened a diplomatic incident. The law must punish such indecent scribble. By contrast, the murder of Sir Danvers Carew dwindled from a headline drama to a four-line comment on the inner page of an evening paper.

'I always think,' said Newcomen one day with tooth-sucking reflection, 'that it was a bad bargain when the reward system was abolished. A policeman often works better and certainly no worse when something of that sort is in prospect. I was glad of it as a young constable in the business of Lady Carew's silver. Even now her ladyship has consented to put up a pocketful of chinkers to have her son's murderer brought to justice. So our Governor tells me. But a policeman cannot be eligible for a reward. Nowadays the public conscience would not stand for it.'

That was the other thing, Swain thought, Newcomen's habit of referring to Toplady deferentially and almost ecclesiastically as 'our Governor'. There, for the time being, the relationship stood.

In the days that followed, Swain saw nothing of Romana Utterson. He wrote two notes and presented himself once to the door of the villa in the Bayswater Road. Miss Utterson was not at home.

She, not her sister Dido, had been the child practising a dance-step in the painting of Henry Jekyll's saloon. The untruth might be important or not. Swain, deprived of the right to ask by Superintendent Toplady's tantrum, wished to know. The identity of the young Utterson female on the sofa was impossible to guess from the slight profile shown in the painting. But Sydney Muschamp rather than Romana was to be believed.

Frustrated in other methods of inquiry, Swain wrote a final note, dating the picture and making his objection plain. To his surprise, an answer came by return. He received it in the first post after Christmas. It was frank and unapologetic, in the style of what she had called 'the noble lie'.

You are right, to be sure. It was Mama who sat upon the sofa (with the guitar) and I who danced so prettily. I do not, however, care to present myself to my admirers as a child. All the same, that you should have failed to recognise me, even so obliquely and at such a distance in time, is less than flattering. I hope that you will feel moved to make amends for the error. R.U.

That was to be all, so far as he could see. The same archness appeared in the note, the same hint that there was much to be taken if he would avail himself of it. But no invitation. No suggestion now that she would like to see his rented rooms in Pimlico. Nothing that gave him the least sense of attachment between them.

The beginning of the New Year found Alfred Swain surprisingly contented. Chief Inspector Newcomen's case would get nowhere. He was sure of that. It was possible, after all, to live without Romana Utterson. He would regret the lost evenings of modelling and sketching but he feared the relationship upon which they had begun that November afternoon in Bayswater. There were depths and complexities from which, in his cautious and cerebral way, he drew back.

The second Sunday of the year was bright and cold. When lunch was over, Swain promised himself a modest treat. Laying aside a shabby book-barrow copy of Mackay's *Extraordinary Popular Delusions and the Madness of Crowds*, he decided that he would walk through the bright January afternoon as far as the Soho house of William Blake. There would be little to see but it would make a point to aim at.

As it happened, he was not more than ten minutes beyond Trafalgar Square, in a quiet street of prosperous and freshly-painted little shops, when he saw Utterson walking in conversation with a younger man. The second man was a stranger to Alfred Swain. Yet he had the fine profile and leonine head of one whose portrait might be in the prints of booksellers' windows.

Swain paused. He would have preferred to avoid Utterson. Yet they were on the same pavement and he would never get past merely by crossing the road. He must turn at once and walk back the way he had come. But that sudden turning in his tracks was bound to draw attention. He was caught like a duck in a shooting gallery.

'Mr Swain!' Utterson's voice was that of a man sincerely pleased at the coincidence. 'What a fortunate encounter. Do you know Mr Richard Enfield, my young cousin? He moves much in society, which I abhor. And he is the most handsome devil that ever preached at Exeter Hall. And Mr Swain, Enfield, is a Scotland Yard man. No less.'

'Indeed?' Enfield contrived to sound a note of personal and surprised delight. 'Of the Criminal Investigation Department, no doubt? But not on duty just now, I hope.'

'Not the least,' said Swain mildly. 'I was walking to see the house of William Blake in Marshall Street.'

He had hoped to detach himself by this pretext but they were ready for him.

'Then we shall show you the way,' Utterson said. 'It will suit us very well to take a cut through here. Unlikely fellows though we are, Enfield and I enjoy a weekly stroll together. The freedom of bachelors. I think, Mr Swain, you have chosen to be a bachelor for the present?'

The question, gentle though it was, cut the ground from under the inspector's self-assurance. He had no notion what Romana might have said to her father. Was that father chiding him for neglect of his eldest girl or congratulating him on an escape? How much did Gabriel Utterson know? Under the bright insistent enquiry of the lawyer's eyes, Alfred Swain faltered. His confusion was confounded by a heat of guilty self-awareness – that he had deceived and abused the trust of this decent and generous man by his conduct with the daughter of the house.

Uncharacteristically, Alfred Swain hesitated.

'I think— I think, sir, I have no choice in the matter. The ladies seem to have given me up.'

The other two men laughed, not at his wit but to reassure him. To his relief, Mr Utterson made no direct reference to Romana or her sisters.

Pointing with his stick, the lawyer led the way across the road to a blank wall patched by damp. A low communal door stood at one end, matched by a house door but no windows at the other. The wood of the communal door, swollen by rain, stuck for a moment. Then Utterson gave it an imperious shove and it opened with a groan of dry hinges. Swain, following the other two through and then closing the door again, found himself in a narrow mews. The stables and cottages were of lichened stone. Enclosed on either side, the air of the cobbled lane seemed suddenly damp and cold to breathe.

'This,' said Utterson for Swain's benefit, 'is where Enfield had his little adventure one night. Terminology House, as they call it. A brute of a fellow making his way there trampled over a little girl when she fell on the pavement outside. There was a public row got up in the street. Enfield pacified the child's family by making the coward pay for the injury. He went into the private door just down the street and came out two minutes later with a cheque for exactly ninety pounds made out to cash. Drawn by Henry Jekyll on his account at Coutts.'

'I should be more careful how I handed round cheques drawn for cash,' Enfield said, 'but it was taken to the bank in Piccadilly next morning and paid without a murmur.'

'And the name of the ruffian?' Swain inquired blandly.

Enfield laughed at the inspector's simplicity.

'It might have been anything under the sun. A callous devil like that has more names than there are sins to commit. He was not Henry Jekyll. Of that you may be quite certain.'

'Yet one may cut through to the square and Jekyll's house by this way,' Utterson said.

Enfield seemed a little put out, as if his story had been doubted.

'You might cut through in twenty minutes, Utterson, not in two. The fellow dived in and out again with the cheque so fast that he had scarcely more than time for it to be written and signed.'

Swain listened to them a moment longer. With some reluctance, he put aside William Blake.

'I should be obliged, Mr Enfield, if you would show me the way by which this connects with Dr Jekyll's house.'

Enfield shrugged.

'If you wish. But the fastest horse in the world would not get you there and back in two minutes with a cheque made out for precisely the odd sum required.'

'Henry Jekyll was already in Terminology House and signed the cheque there,' Swain suggested.

Utterson maintained a prudent detachment from their conversation. Enfield frowned.

'If he was at home, why did the brute who trampled the girl have to unlock and unbar to let himself in? No, I do not think anyone else was there.'

'Then,' said Swain patiently, 'the cheque must have been written before. If it had been made out by your ruffian, it would have been challenged as a forgery.'

Utterson, who had been studying the frosty fire of the sunset over the rooftops, turned at last to the other two.

'Unless it were a matter of blackmail. Unless a challenge was more than Henry Jekyll dared. And were that the case, the sin you speak of may go by the name of Hyde.'

Prudence had been set aside for ever by these words. The Law Society might do its worst. When he realised the extent of Utterson's indiscretion, Swain knew that Henry Jekyll was in mortal danger. And yet the man was beyond help, unless he would ask for it. The three of them walked on in silence for several minutes.

'By turning here,' Utterson said at length, 'one enters the mews behind Caleb Square. There is, I think, a way to the old surgical theatre that Dr Denman built in the garden many years ago. There were stairs at that time to the coachman's attic above the stables.'

'Lucky the fellow whose coachman would consent to live in an attic now!' Enfield remarked cheerfully.

They turned the corner and came into Caleb Square. In the winter sunset the first gaslamps were lit and the uncurtained windows of the Georgian houses revealed well-warmed and log-scented rooms. The evening air of the pavements was

140

faintly gritted with the taste and smell of domestic soot from the chimneys.

'Two sides of the square,' said Enfield briskly, 'and we shall be back on our route again. I fear you will see very little of William Blake's house by the time we get there, Mr Swain!'

Swain pulled a mouth of wry resignation, like the victim of a practical joke.

It was Utterson who interrupted before he could reply.

'By God!' said the lawyer, with a short laugh of relief. 'There he is! See! In the public view at last.'

Following the line of the lawyer's raised arm, Swain saw that the sash window of Henry Jekyll's saloon on the first floor was raised as high as it would go. Jekyll himself was sitting immediately within, as if taking the air while he could. It was impossible to see much more of him than his head, shoulders and torso, even when he stood up in some surprise at the sight of Utterson. No meeting had been intended just then but the lawyer was clearly pleased and greatly relieved to have found his friend in this way. Swain stood back a little in the shadows with his hat on, preferring not to be seen.

'I would as soon not be introduced just now,' he said softly.

The other two men stopped by the area railings and Utterson called up.

'Jekyll! How are you? You look much better than you were. I trust you are recovered.'

'I think I am, somewhat. But I am still very low, Utterson. Very low. I thank God that it will not last much longer.'

To Swain the voice was faint and uncertain. Jekyll spoke like a man who could give his attention to no one but himself and to nothing else but his own malady.

'Then take heart, man!' Utterson began to laugh his friend out of such gloom. 'You are too much indoors, my dear fellow. You should be out, whipping up the circulation like Mr Enfield and me. This is my cousin, by the way. Mr Enfield – Dr Jekyll. Come, now! Get your hat and take a quick turn round the square with us.'

Swain watched from the shadows. The hints of longing, apprehension and despair followed one another in Henry Jekyll's face like clouds chased by the wind across a summer sky.

'You are very good,' he said at last, as if he might begin to cry. 'My dearest friend. I should like to very much—'

'In that case,' Utterson began. But Jekyll's voice, crying as if with a terror suddenly perceived, cut across the lawyer's words.

'No! No! No! It is quite impossible.' The voice dropped to a quiet misery. 'But, indeed Utterson, I am very glad to see you. This is really a great pleasure. I would ask you and Mr Enfield up but the place is not fit.'

'The fitness matters nothing, my dear old friend—'

'No!' shouted the prisoner at the window. 'No! You cannot come up! I regret it but you cannot. You must not . . . shall not . . .'

To Swain, it was like the slow denouement of some moralistic melodrama, with the window-frame serving as the arch of a stage. What else that room contained, he could scarcely imagine.

'Very well,' Utterson was saying good-naturedly. 'Then the best thing will be for us to stay down here and speak with you from where we are.'

'That is just what I would propose.' The relief in Jekyll's voice was plain.

At that moment Swain took a step to one side, hoping to see into the room at a new angle. Jekyll's eyes moved in his direction with a look of alarm. That instant the window was slammed down in a thump of sudden ferocity. Utterson and Enfield were too close to see much. Swain, standing further back, was able to determine from the angle of the movement that the hand which slammed the window down could not possibly have been Henry Jekyll's. The curtains were violently drawn across and presently the light in the saloon was turned down.

The inspector joined the other two.

'God forgive us! God forgive us!' said Utterson quietly. 'This is surely the worst ever.'

'I think it was my fault,' Swain said meekly. 'I moved aside and perhaps he saw me. Or at least he saw a dark figure in the shadows. Alarming to him in his present state.'

Utterson shook his head as they walked on.

'I think not, Mr Swain. What was so terrible in that room that he could not receive us? What terror or what vileness? And why must he propose to talk with us from the window – and the next second slam it shut with such a fearful look?'

'He is not well, sir,' Swain said pacifically.

'If that were all!' Utterson dropped behind a little so that he and the inspector might be out of Enfield's hearing. 'I thought it madness at first, Mr Swain. I feared more powerfully when I read the will that it might be dishonour. For that reason, though as a lawyer I had custody of the document, I would take no part in drawing it up.'

'You could scarcely be blamed for that, sir.'

'But, Mr Swain, I will go further now. This is no time for etiquette. Henry Jekyll may be destroyed at any moment. Let me tell you openly what you must already have guessed. You were correct in identifying the name represented by the letter 'H'. There was something else in the provisions of the will on that topic. The man who answered to that name was described as being the tenant of Terminology House. And that name, in turn, was mentioned to me by Mr Toplady in connection with the murder of Sir Danvers Carew.'

'And yet, sir,' said Swain carefully, 'the murder of that gentleman can have nothing to do with Dr Jekyll.'

Utterson looked past him, as if by avoiding his eyes he might seem not to be betraying a confidence.

'Think of this, Mr Swain. Suppose Henry Jekyll was somehow in the grip of an extortioner. Suppose furthermore that Sir Danvers Carew held him guilty of a second dishonourable act and threatened to tell the world. If that were to happen, the extortioner would be greatly the loser. Would he not? His victim would be done for. His source of revenue would run dry. Might not a blackmailer, Mr Swain, conclude the necessity for silencing Sir Danvers Carew in the quiet of the grave?'

Swain shook his head.

143

'If that were all, sir, the extortioner's crime would then place him in Henry Jekyll's hands. He might reveal a scandal about the doctor. But the doctor, if he guessed the truth, might see his persecutor hanged for murder.'

The first chill of the night wind scuffed a few leaves in the gutter of the lamplit street.

'What then?' asked Utterson helplessly. 'What could there be worse than murder and the gallows?'

'Henry Jekyll's true crime.' Swain thoughtfully put aside a vision of Romana Utterson kneeling naked before the settee in Jekyll's saloon. 'Not scandal and not dishonour. An act so infamous in the scale of his own life that he would suffer extortion and condone murder rather than that the ghost of it should walk.'

Utterson shook his head and they paced slowly up to the corner where Enfield stood waiting. It was evident that they must part at the junction of the two roads.

'I will see what more I can discover about our poor friend,' the lawyer said to the inspector. 'To be sure he was distressed a week or so back over the death of Dr Hastie-Lanyon, who had been a friend to us both. But he was not more overcome than might be expected. You have not reached our age, Mr Swain. Nor has my cousin Enfield. The death of friends in middle life rings the curtain down for us all. One does not make such friendships again as those which had lasted from our youth.'

'All this,' said Swain, 'does little to resolve the mystery of the murder in Cheyne Walk. Unless the man Hyde can be identified from so many of his kind. The name means little. Any man may take a name.'

Utterson appeared reluctant to commit himself further. It was Enfield who intervened.

'My dear Mr Swain. It is wrong that you should take upon you more responsibility than your duty permits. I have a little influence and I am listened to by those who have a good deal more. Old Lady Carew attends the meetings at Exeter Hall when she is in town. I would not call her a member of the congregation but I am sure she wishes us well. I shall tell her

144

of the incident, when the child was trampled underfoot by the monster in Trim Street that night. I shall add that he is known to be a man of a bad reputation – a cruel reputation – with poor men and women alike. He is the very person whom Sir Danvers Carew would abominate. From my own observation, I shall add that his description – the stamping and the growling as well – match the account given by the poor maid, Mary Smith. And I shall say what I believe to be the truth. That since the murder was discovered and the hue and cry raised, the devil of whom I speak has gone to ground in his lair and been seen nowhere.'

Swain could not bring himself to mention the name of Newcomen.

'I daresay, Mr Enfield, that any pressure brought to bear on the feelings of Lady Carew might do good for us. As it stands, a warrant for Terminology House would not be easily granted. But this might bring us forward a good few strides.'

'Perhaps,' added Utterson soberly, 'perhaps with sufficient speed to save our poor friend Henry Jekyll.'

Swain shook hands with his two companions and turned away. He walked back through the square and the little streets, seeing Jekyll's house now entirely in darkness. He had lately begun to read Maudsley *On the Pathology of the Mind* and had copied laboriously from the encyclopedia an entire article on 'Insanity' by Dr J. Batty Tuke. But though he sympathised with the victims of the disease, his own direct and vigorous mentality made it impossible for him to imagine the symptoms described. A hundred years before, he would have advocated beating the patients out of their silliness. The thought of this made him a little ashamed. But in the end he had given up trying to grasp the fundamentals of the science, returning instead to amateur geology and physics.

Perhaps Mr Enfield would do good after all. At the least, this secret foreknowledge of an approach by Lady Carew revived Swain's enthusiasm for the case. It was as good as watching a fuse lit under Chief Inspector Newcomen.

16

If Alfred Swain had a palely intellectual appearance and was self-improving by nature, these qualities were emphasised in the presence of Chief Inspector Newcomen. Amply moustached and assertive, the chief inspector was proud to have been a commercial policeman. Newcomen sighed monotonously for the good old days of the hiring-room, of service and reward. To be consulted man-to-man by a duke and lodged in the humblest quarters of a great house was more to him than to take Toplady's place at Scotland Yard.

There was in Newcomen a peculiar combination of deference and aggression. Swain felt uneasy. The chief inspector's fallibility in dealing with street people and colleagues alike was betrayed by every word and gesture. All the same, Mr Enfield had spoken to Lady Carew and her ladyship had communicated with her husband's former comrade-in-arms, now Chief Commissioner of the Metropolitan Police. Within a few days, Newcomen came red-faced from Toplady's sneering. He confided his orders to Swain, as if they were all his own doing.

'It seems, Mr Swain, that at last we have contrived a warrant for the search of the premises in Trim Street. If it can be found that an Edward Hyde lives there, we have a warrant for his arrest on charges of assault upon a child. If he does not live there, the warrant lapses. We cannot arrest every Edward Hyde in the kingdom and therefore we shall arrest none. But we may get the truth of Terminology House. We have the assistance of Lady Carew and the good offices of our Governor to thank for this opportunity.'

'Indeed?' said Swain politely, but Newcomen was not to be drawn.

If the search of Terminology House was intended to come

146

as a surprise to the neighbourhood, it was a failure from the start. By the time that the Black Maria carrying Swain, Newcomen and two uniformed constables arrived, Trim Street was lined as if for a ceremonial procession. The crowd stood silent along either pavement, showing neither enthusiasm nor resentment. The people pressed towards the carriage, faces dumb and curious as fish in an aquarium. Swain, who had spoken to no one of the search, cursed Newcomen silently. There had been some ill-considered boast, some *braggadocio* by the chief inspector, that had led to this.

At the shabby end of Trim Street, where the blank wall rose above the little door, the police van stopped. The inspector waited, allowing Newcomen and the uniformed constables to hammer for entrance. He heard Newcomen's voice, harsh and hectoring in his dealings with the lower orders.

'The person Edward Hyde! And if you understand what's best for you, my good woman, there will be no prevarication in the matter!'

The response to this was a stream of soprano obscenity that had the entire street in an uproar. The inhabitants of the Soho backwater cared nothing for the ruffian in Terminology House and nothing for Newcomen either. With the impartiality of the disaffected, they cheered on the winner. Swain guessed that Newcomen was not winning.

'See here, ma'am! I hold a warrant from the justices in respect of these premises—'

But all round the chief inspector there were faces contorted in an ecstasy of derision and delight. Infant voices shrieked, 'See here, ma'am! I've got a warrant, I have! Oh, yus, not half I ain't!' Newcomen laid about with the flat of his hand, scattering the urchins but failing to contact a single head among them.

With equal feelings of gloom and rancour, Alfred Swain got down from the van. He pushed his way past the two uniformed men and stood shoulder to shoulder with Newcomen. Pent in by the crowd, they faced the termagent who filled the low doorway. She had been woken suddenly from an unnatural sleep, to judge from the puffed pallor of her face, the bruise-coloured darkness under her eyes, and the manner in which

147

the henna'd hair rose in an appearance of fright. Swain hoped that the shawl held about her was more securely gripped than Romana Utterson's.

'Aggie York?' he said amiably.

'Oo says I am?' The eyes narrowed as if against strong light.

'Dear me,' said Swain gently. 'Name wrong on the charge sheet last time round? Was it? Razoring a cove that was too concerned for his wife's peace of mind to press charges? Something of that, anyway.'

A craquelure of wrinkles appeared in the powder as Aggie's mouth split in a smile like a wound.

'Mr Swain!' she said with an archness that made him flinch. 'You was never announced. I saw this face, 'ere. His! Never knew him from Adam. If I'd known it was you, Mr Swain—'

'That's all right, Miss Agnes. This is Mr Newcomen, a friend of mine. He has a warrant to search the premises, if that's convenient just now.'

'I was asked to mind, Mr Swain. On behalf of Mr Josiah Butter that owns the ground lease. Rummy cove that rented the rooms moved out suddenly. He might come back, or Mr Jos might be bilked. I'm here to mind. That's all. Been here since last night.'

'Then I should say it's convenient after all,' said Swain for Newcomen's benefit. 'Mad Billy keeping you company, is he?'

Aggie York attempted a girlish giggle and Swain flinched again.

'He's a lovely caution. Ain't he? But no. At present 'is lordship is out of town, you might say.'

'Then you won't mind, Aggie, if we look about.'

'Liberty 'all, Mr Swain. Do as you please. In course, you won't be needin' me.'

'I daresay we shan't, Aggie. But you'd oblige the two uniformed gentlemen by keeping them company until we finish.'

'I'd oblige you rather, Mr Swain.'

'And a lucky fellow I should be, Miss Agnes.' Alfred

Swain wore his smile like a carnival mask over the distaste that gathered in his eyes.

Aggie York stepped back and the four men went in through the low doorway.

Swain followed Newcomen up a windowless flight of stairs covered by a dusty carpet. The gaslight showed a large framed print of *The Odalisque and the Servant* by Ingres, the Sultan's favourite twisting in languorous contentment on her rich cushions at the sound of the servant's lute. On the plain wall opposite hung the peep-show voyeurism of Maurin's study, *The Lustful Sheikhs*. Elsewhere, the same pictures would have attracted little notice. Here they seemed to be flaunted as a foretaste of pleasures to come.

Swain had noticed that under Terminology House there was a stable opening into the mews court at the back. Mr Enfield had been right. This flight of stairs was the only entrance or exit for the house itself. At the head of the stairs a green baize door, securely locked, closed off the living quarters.

'I never seen,' whined Aggie York behind them. 'Take my Bible oath I don't know more of what's in there than the child new-born.'

The clichés of pretended innocence came to her easily after so many years of practice.

'Course you don't, Aggie,' said Swain reassuringly. 'You're a good girl, you are.'

'Yes I am!' The voice was vibrant yet fearful in its emphasis.

Chief Inspector Newcomen took from his cloak a steel pick polished to regulation brightness. He slid the edge as far into the crack between door and frame as it would go. Then with a sudden expert shove, he wrenched the wood clear of the lock-fastenings. The mutilated door swung inwards upon its hinges.

'I'll be skinned for this!' whimpered Aggie York. 'There'll be the devil to pay!'

Swain and Newcomen ignored her. Leaving the bawd on the stairs with the two uniformed men, they entered the dim rooms of Terminology House. It was Newcomen who set a match to the mantle and lit the gas. In the first place, Swain

149

noticed, the windows were curiously covered. The glass was veiled with stretched art muslin, then by dark curtains, and finally by curtains of Nottingham lace gathered on the inside. Daylight had never entered here. On tables and sideboard, Egyptian lamps of beaten brass and red inlay had been fitted with shades of royal blue, or crimson, or sea green. It was possible to bathe the rich velvet sofa and silk cushions of Regency stripe with whatever hue the visitor favoured. Midnight blue or infernal red, apricot sunlight or subaqueous green.

There was an odour of burnt spice in the musty air, a suggestion of stale incense. A woman's stockings lay folded on a cushion. The walls were covered by deep cherry damask that looked darkened by smoke. A brass bowl and a jade pipe on the mantel-shelf might have been the tools of the opium dreamer. There were several more framed prints on the wall, matching the theme of those above the stairs. *The Happy Slave, Arabian Women, Beauty Behind Bars*. The names of the artists meant nothing to Swain. A cheval glass and a plain mirror had been arranged to reflect the sofa and the chairs.

'Looks like our man's lodgings to you, Mr Swain? Does it? Or Henry Jekyll's private rooms where he could do what might be indiscreet at home?'

The chief inspector spoke with an air of firmly controlled distaste.

'I wouldn't think these were Jekyll's rooms, Mr Newcomen,' Swain said coolly. 'Not much here but cheap-jack rubbish. Not his style at all. If you believe Aggie York, the lease belongs to Josh Butter, a young gentleman that spent his fortune and then smashed. He's her keeper, or was until Mad Billy bought her. This is the sort of place you might hire for a month, a week, or ten minutes, if you chose. People use houses like this. They don't live in 'em. But a man of strong enough tastes might have a permanent use for this one.'

Newcomen grunted. He put his hat on a walnut-grain sofa table and began to open the drawers of a corner cupboard. Swain walked through to the other rooms. There was a small and plainly furnished parlour, a bathroom with florid Portuguese tiling in blue and white, and the bedroom.

In contrast to the drawing-room, the last of these contained only the bed itself, and a half-size marble reproduction of Bell's *Andromeda* from the Great Exhibition catalogue. Once again, there was nothing sinister in the statue itself. But the naked girl with her head bowed and hand behind her, the flesh folding softly across the abdomen, and the chain of the slave about her thigh took on an obsessive quality in its present surroundings.

By the time that he returned to the drawing-room, Newcomen was emptying the drawers in the brass-railed curve of a Carlton House table.

'There's nothing here that seems to belong to anyone,' he said sourly. 'Nothing with a name. Nothing that attaches to a particular person in any way at all.'

Swain made a sound of sympathy and watched Newcomen draw a volume of *Mademoiselle de Maupin* from a box covered in white silk. With its illustrations in pastel colours, it had an air of luxury and impropriety, perfumed languor and secret passion. Newcomen closed it with a snap and put it back.

'French nastiness,' he said with a sniff.

Swain himself began on the drawers of the sideboard, using a bunch of variable keys that seldom failed to unlock domestic furniture of this kind. There was silverware and linen in the first layer, none of it marked with a name or initials. Putting this away, he pulled open the lower drawer. At the first glance, he knew he was going to be luckier than Newcomen. For the moment he refrained from saying so. The drawer of the desk was wide and shallow. On top of the pile was a sheet of cerulean blue letter-paper. It was covered in rusting ink by a column of names. Or, rather, it was the same name written repeatedly in careful italic. *Henry Jekyll . . . Henry Jekyll . . . Henry Jekyll . . .*

Swain put it to one side and examined with growing apprehension what lay underneath. There was a sepia photograph. It might have been a second exposure but he thought it was more probably a second print of the group that Romana Utterson had shown him – Henry Jekyll and his

151

friends in the hazy sunshine of Tenby so many summers
ago.

It had been clipped to what felt like a sheet of ply-
wood, about twelve inches square and scarcely thicker than
cardboard. This was folded in tissue paper. He unwrapped it
with great care. To his surprise he found an original painting
in oils. Or, at least, a study for such a painting. It was
an odd and disturbing composition, identified on the back
as *Circe*. An androgynous head, which was none the less
female, appeared through blades of grass and a thin screen
of leaves. It was flanked by two half-faces of satyrs, staring
and sneering, as if with the pleasure of having the woman
in thrall.

But it was her eyes that held Swain's attention. On the
painted wood, the unknown artist had captured, as Swain had
failed to, the tight-lidded ellipse, the sensuality and unbalance,
of Romana Utterson.

But it was not Romana Utterson. Surely it had been painted
too long ago. In the bottom right-hand corner of the picture
was an inscription, written in a rather square and regular
hand: 'R. Dadd, refecit 1869'. And across the picture, as if
to cancel it, a thin brush-script had written in a hand recog-
nisably like that of Jekyll's in defacing his books: 'Est suum
cuique dunc dictum. . . . Transupra et ecce sinistrum. . . .
Simile similibus addendum. . . . Daemoni date debendum
m–m–m–m. . . .'

Swain was not sure whether he had discovered some secret
horde of Henry Jekyll's or the tools of a blackmailer who
had stolen the painting and the sepia photograph from Caleb
Square. He thought they were probably stolen.

'And what's all that nonsense about, then?' asked Newcomen
scornfully over his shoulder.

For the second time in his recent career as a policeman,
Swain blessed the schoolmaster father who had drilled him in
Latin at six years old. The writing scrawled on the painting of
Circe was clear enough.

'It means,' said Swain pedantically, ' "Each person is allotted
an unlucky fate, here and in the Beyond. Like must be added

to like. Our debts must be discharged to the demon appointed over us." And then it tails off, scrawling the last letter "m" over and over.'

'And the paper?' Newcomen scowled at the column of writing.

'Henry Jekyll's signature, as it might be practised over and over by someone who wanted to imitate it.'

'The same that spoiled the picture,' Newcomen said.

'Perhaps,' said Swain. 'I think the hand that spoiled his books and ripped his father's portrait was not, after all, his own. Poor fellow.'

'Demons and unlucky fates,' said Newcomen scornfully. 'You think yourself a man of sense, Swain. A man that reads. You can tell this for the nonsense that it is. We'll leave that lot in the drawer for now, seal the door, and make a note of what's here.'

Then, with an unaccustomed sense of the theatrical, Newcomen brought out from behind the desk the upper half of a polished and silver-bound stick. The wood was hardened and dark red. It had been shattered by a blow that made Swain shudder to imagine it. But even Newcomen could not fail to prove it the weapon with which Sir Danvers Carew had been beaten to death.

'Hyde,' said Newcomen, his voice rich with self-satisfaction, 'or more likely Jekyll in the disguise he called Hyde. Whichever of 'em we get, this whole business can be laid to rest.'

Swain got to his feet, offering congratulations to his senior officer. As he did so, he slid into his pocket the sepia photograph which he had carefully and improperly kept out of Chief Inspector Newcomen's sight. The door of Terminology House was sealed and two uniformed constables remained on duty at the top of the stairs.

'If I was asked,' said Newcomen, folding away the shattered stick with jealous care, 'I'd say that was very nearly that. Whether Edward Hyde exists or if this comes home to Henry Jekyll, we can all sleep easy. I'd say my bit of stick should do us all a lot of good. And when I make the announcement

153

to Lady Carew and the newspapers, I shan't forget your part, Swain. Fair's fair, after all.'

Alfred Swain kept his peace. His fingers touched the square card of the photographic print in his pocket. For reasons that Newcomen would never know, he profoundly hoped 'that was very nearly that'. But not for one moment did he believe that it could be.

17

'The fool! The prime fool!' Sergeant Lumley's face split in a grin of frenzied congratulation. He was delighted on Swain's behalf. 'I'd hate to be wearing old Newcomen's backside when Toplady finishes with him. It's the end of his case, this is! Oh, yes, it really is! Worth waiting for, I call it!'

'It was a natural mistake,' Swain said modestly. Three days after the search in Trim Street, he was still overawed by the speed and simplicity of Chief Inspector Newcomen's downfall. 'Anyone would have thought the same. One half of a silver-bound stick in dark red wood, found by Sir Danvers Carew's body. Another half found on suspect premises. Obvious conclusion.'

Lumley sniggered.

'Still, Mr Swain! Not everyone'd put a trumpet to the seat of the trousers and tell the newspaper writers outside the dictionary house that they'd found the top end of the stick – and then discover next day it don't match the lower half. Why didn't he try the two halves first? Or why not just say it could be a match but he wasn't sure?'

'Anyone might have drawn the same conclusion, Mr Lumley.' Swain felt he could afford a certain generosity and nobility in the completeness of his vindication.

'I call it beautiful!' Sergeant Lumley crooned. 'Cards, trumps and a beating, as you might say.'

Swain put it as gently as he could.

'Not exactly that, Mr Lumley. Someone's got to explain what the broken top half of a walking-stick was doing in Terminology House. Put there as if we were expected to find it. True, it's

155

not a match. And that's what's odd. But it points a finger at whoever lived there or visited.'

'It's knowing which one's being pointed at,' said Lumley with a significant nod.

'No, Mr Lumley. I'd much rather know whose finger is doing the pointing.'

'Depends if the ruffian that Mr Enfield saw lived there.'

'Or if Henry Jekyll used it as a house of assignation.'

'High class pork-shop,' said Lumley knowledgeably. 'All them pictures and coloured lights and the curtains always drawn.'

Swain sat down again on the edge of his desk.

'Sitting like that is how you broke a piece off the beading last time,' Lumley said reproachfully. The inspector ignored him.

'All it amounts to, Mr Lumley, is that we've beaten through the undergrowth of this case. If there's villainy in it, those that are guilty of it may be startled enough to fly up into sight. And then we shall have them.'

'And if they don't,' said Lumley sceptically, 'we conclude that Sir Danvers Carew made away with hisself by beating hisself to death with his own stick.'

Swain walked round to his chair.

'On your way out, Mr Lumley, you might—'

'Another thing,' Lumley said, standing his ground, 'that you was so anxious to know.'

'Yes, Mr Lumley?'

'That painter chap whose name you come across in Terminology House. Richard Dadd. I turned him up here. Criminal records, of all places. Stabbed his father to death in 1844. Unfit to plead. Mad as a March hare. Confined in Bedlam and transferred to Broadmoor when they opened it in 1862. Never left there. Harmless ever afterwards. Quite bright in himself. Painting pictures. But seventy years old and completely off his head. Horrors and visions of devils, mostly.'

'Yes,' Swain said, 'I gathered that. Still in Broadmoor?'

'In a manner of speaking.'

'I've never tried to question a criminal lunatic, Mr Lumley. Let alone one with a dark genius for painting.'

'No,' Lumley said, 'I suppose not. And you won't be questioning this one either. You was too slow, Mr Swain. And a bit unlucky as well. The part of Broadmoor he's in now is the cemetery. Mr Dadd went to his last long home a week or two back. On 8 January, to be precise.'

Alfred Swain checked himself, knowing better than to profane the presence of a man's death by expletives.

'I'll be engaged the rest of the day, Mr Lumley. Here but engaged.'

'Oh,' said Lumley, 'seeing witnesses I suppose? Putting old Jekyll through the mangle? Depositions? Affidavits? Tidying it all away?'

'No, Mr Lumley,' said Alfred Swain with his sternest rebuke. 'Thinking things out. There's a lot less thinking goes on round here than there ought to be. And as for tidying away murder—'

Lumley withdrew to the sergeants' room and indulged himself in the luxury of a long grumble.

Swain took a chess-board and several counters from the drawer of his desk. He had never had leisure nor inclination to play the games for which they were designed. But now he marked a letter on each counter, so that one stood for Sir Danvers Carew and another for Henry Jekyll. There was Samuel Parr and the man – or men – known as Hyde. Poole the manservant was there and Mary Smith. There was Utterson and Enfield. After some hesitation, he took another counter and marked it Romana Utterson. Having done that, there were three more counters called Jenny, Dido and Amelia. At one corner of the board there was a counter that never moved. He called it Richard Dadd.

The darkness of winter afternoon gathered in the river sky. White gaslights measured the handsome length of Northumberland Avenue and the embankment. A last icy sun fired the sky above Brompton and Knightsbridge. Swain, hunched and scowling, trained his formidable intelligence upon the board and the pieces. The supple mind performed loops

157

and arabesques of logic. It balanced circumstance against probability and evil against opportunity.

But in the end, he sat back and swore every oath that came to mind.

After a supper break, his duty continued until midnight. There were reports yet to be written on Terminology House and Mary Smith. There was the proposed interrogation of Henry Jekyll to be noted. Quite enough to occupy the evening. Perhaps, after all, Lumley was right. Carew and Mary Smith were dead. Samuel Parr and Richard Dadd were dead. Edward Hyde, if he had any independent existence, was lost to sight. Henry Jekyll was a harmless derelict and Romana Utterson a frustrated spinster no longer in her first bloom. The whole damned thing just needed tidying away.

He was just pondering whether the phrase 'met her death' would best describe the present view of Mary Smith in his report, when he heard a disturbance in the corridor outside. There was a woman's voice, shrill and insistent. There were cautious and helpful growlings from one of the duty sergeants. Swain pulled out his watch and saw that it was just after nine. Here was an end of whether Mary Smith 'met her death' or not. He was the inspector on duty. Even before the fist thumped on his door, he knew he was wanted.

The girl who stood in her brown holland cloak between two sergeants was familiar to him, though he could not quite place her. Her face seemed full and flushed, as if at any second she might burst into tears. Sergeant Skinner, at her side, kept a sympathetic but controlling grip on her arm.

'Miss Lottie Bow, sir,' said Skinner apologetically. 'A matter of some urgency, Miss Bow insists. For your attention, sir.'

To Swain, her name meant nothing at all. The girl, calmer now, shook off the sergeant's hand.

'Lottie Bow, sir! From Dr Jekyll's!'

Swain understood and recalled the face, seen under a maid's cap. She had been somewhere in the shadows as Poole helped him on with his coat.

'Of course.' Swain led her gently into the room while the two sergeants watched. 'And how may I be of service, Miss Bow?'

'It's the master – Dr Jekyll!' Her tone suggested that she would whimper now, if she could move him in no other way. 'He's locked himself in.'

'In where?'

'His study – laboratory – whatever you call it. We can still hear him in there. But he won't come out.'

Swain sat her gently in the chair kept for visitors.

'And how long has Dr Jekyll been locked in like this?'

'A week,' she said hesitantly. 'Best part of the week anyhow.'

'A week?' Swain looked at her in astonishment. 'In one room?'

'Yes, sir!' Now the tears began to flow and he saw how terrified she must have been. 'And we can still hear him in there. And I was so frightened tonight. Suppose he died and it was said we had a hand! And Mr Poole told me the best thing was for him to fetch Mr Utterson. And for him to put me in a cab and send me here to fetch you, sir. Oh, Mr Swain! You will come, won't you?'

'Yes,' Swain said, 'I shall come at once. Of course I shall.'

He turned to Sergeant Skinner.

'Where's Mr Newcomen?'

'He wouldn't be here now, sir. Past his time.'

'Yes,' Swain looked about him and picked up his coat, 'I suppose it is. If you can find Mr Lumley or get a message to him, ask him to meet me at 2 Caleb Square as soon as he can. All right?'

'Sir!'

'And see that Mr Toplady gets the news of this the minute he comes in.'

'Won't be till tomorrow now, sir.'

'Send him a message, then.'

'Would he be at home or at his club, sir?'

'How the deuce should I know?' said Swain ungratefully. 'Send to both.'

He put an escorting arm round Lottie, drawing her along the corridor and down the stairs. They emerged into the frosted wind of the city night and stepped into the cab. Chess was forgotten. The real game had begun again.

18

There was no sign of any other cab by the area railings of the house in Caleb Square. Either Utterson had arrived with Poole on foot or else Swain supposed that he himself was the first to arrive. Telling Lottie Bow to remain in the hansom, he stepped out into the lamplit square. It was a wild night of the late winter. A flying tracery of dark cloud raced across a moon that seemed tilted on its back by the storm. The pavements were deserted in such weather. The Georgian square was full of wind and dust, the thin trees in the central garden lashing themselves along the railing.

Swain went up the steps, banged on the door with his fist and listened. At first he thought the house must be empty and that the servants had fled. Then he heard a metallic rattle and someone opened the door a little on its steel chain.

'Is that you, Mr Poole?' With the light in his eyes, he could see only the shape of a head. 'Is Mr Utterson here yet?'

The door closed and then opened freely. Poole looked past Swain, searching for someone else.

'Where is the maid, Lottie Bow?'

'In the cab,' Swain said. 'She is better there. What of Mr Utterson?'

Poole led the way into the hall where several of the servants, whom Swain had not seen on his previous visits, were standing about in attitudes of curiosity or apprehension. Poole summoned the boy who was kept to clean the knives.

'Take the candle, lad, and light us the way through the back.'

Like a ritual procession, they set off across the courtyard that had once been a back-garden of the house. The knife-boy led the way, sheltering the flame with his hand, followed by Poole, with Swain bringing up the rear. When they approached the entrance to the anatomy theatre, as it had been in Dr Denman's time, the candle blew out. But beyond the doorway Swain could see a lantern. Utterson and two of the servants were standing among the crates and bottles that now littered the ground-level.

'Thank God,' Utterson said, recognising the inspector. 'Are you alone?'

'At present I am. I left word for Sergeant Lumley to join me here, if he could be reached.'

'Is he discreet?'

'I believe so.'

'I hope so,' the lawyer said. 'But, my dear Swain, here is a pretty kettle of fish. Or rather, to speak frankly, I cannot make out what it is.'

'Or who it is, sir,' said Poole close behind them. 'I have seen him once this past week when I came suddenly into the anatomy theatre from the garden. The door to the study was open and he was down here, searching among the crates and bottles. When I came in, he gave an exclamation and whipped back up the stairs again. I saw him only for a minute but the shock might have made my hair stand on end. He wore a grotesque mask, which my master would never have done. He cried out like a rat and ran from me, which Dr Jekyll had never done. And he seemed more than anything a dwarf.'

'Whereas you have seen Henry Jekyll,' said Utterson turning to Swain. 'He is as tall as you.'

'Then it was not Henry Jekyll who cried out and wore a mask,' Swain said simply. 'A man may appear taller than he is. He can hardly make himself look shorter.'

Poole looked up the stairs at the study door.

'It was not Dr Jekyll as I know him, Mr Swain,' he said softly.

'And there have been messages scrawled and thrown out for the servants to pick up,' Utterson added to Poole's explanation, 'sending for drugs to Maw's the chemist. And then complaining that what was sent for was never pure.'

'I still have that note, sir,' Poole said. 'The gentleman at Maw's was so angry that he threw it back at me. It is in Dr Jekyll's hand.'

Swain looked at the others.

'Whatever the explanation, we must have him out of there. He may do no damage to others, perhaps, but he may destroy himself.'

'Try him, Poole,' the lawyer said, 'try him again.'

The butler took the candle from the knife-boy and lit it once more. He walked slowly up the stairs to the red baize door of the study and knocked.

'Mr Utterson, sir, asking to see you.'

Poole turned and gestured to them to listen.

'Tell him I cannot see anyone.'

Swain heard the words faintly through the thickness of the door. The butler came back down the stairs and confronted Utterson.

'Sir, was that my master's voice?'

'It may be changed,' the lawyer said.

'Changed?' Poole shook his head. 'Well, I think so indeed. Have I been in his service so many years to be deceived about his voice?'

Alfred Swain took the candle from the butler's hand. Poole had begun to enjoy being the centre of attention rather too much for the inspector's taste.

'It would be hard to tell, Mr Poole. The door is so thick and lined with baize. I have met Dr Jekyll twice. The voice just now might be his, but no one could swear to it.'

Holding the candle, he went softly up to the door and listened. Someone – or something – was moving inside. There was a busy stamping tread. Swain listened a moment more and then came back.

'He is walking up and down, I believe.'

'True, Mr Swain,' Poole said, 'and with a footstep harder and flatter than Dr Jekyll's ever used to be. We have heard it every day – and every night. And once I heard weeping – like a woman's.'

Swain looked at him carefully but there was no evasion or subterfuge in the man. He was in fear for his master and his own place.

'A woman?'

'Or a lost soul.'

162

'A man may weep or a woman may weep, Mr Poole. But there is a difference between them if they are loud enough to be heard through that door.'

He had hoped that Lumley would arrive before the crisis of Jekyll's self-incarceration had to be resolved. But Utterson had had enough.

'Let the footman get an axe,' Utterson said, 'and let the coachman guard the other stairs. You will make no objection, Mr Swain?'

'Speak to him once more, sir,' Swain said. 'Let him hear your voice and see if he will open the door.'

With every sign of reluctance, Utterson led the others to the baize door. Swain took the axe from the returning footman. The lawyer laid his cheek to the red baize and cried out.

'Jekyll! This is Gabriel Utterson! I demand to see you!'

At first there was no response. Utterson tried again.

'Jekyll! I give you fair warning. Our suspicions are roused. I must and shall see you.'

There was stillness for a second and then, against the wind and wildness of the trees outside, there came a scream that turned Swain's heart to ice. The sound, like almost every sound that he had heard from that imprisoned voice, was beyond human identity.

The scream broke at last in a groaning, shuddering prayer.

'For God's sake have mercy!'

Utterson shouted for the axe but the inspector had already swung it back and then brought it down with a blow that seemed to shake the building. The baize door jumped against the fastenings of lock and hinges. A screech of pain and terror came from within. Swain knew that anything was now justified to force an entry. He had not the least doubt that murder or self-destruction was being carried out on the other side of the door. The axe crashed again upon the lock and the wood bounded against its frame.

'Again!' shouted Utterson. 'Quick and hard as you can.'

Twice more Swain felt his own arms almost jolted from their shoulder sockets by the force of the blows. And then he knew it was done. With a powerful blow of his boot, the door flew inwards. He stared at the scene before him, uncomprehending.

The cabinet, as Jekyll called his study, was bathed in quiet lamplight. The fire danced and sputtered in the grate. One or two drawers were open and there was a great disorder of papers on the table. The glazed presses with their rows of chemicals in bottles seemed undisturbed and, indeed, unopened. How long the smaller table had been laid for tea or the kettle had been singing on the hob it was impossible to say. But there was no sign in the room of Henry Jekyll. On the carpet before the fire lay the body of a dwarfish man, younger than Jekyll but his face prematurely lined. He was dressed in clothes that seemed too big for him.

Swain went first into the room as a matter of habit, motioning the others to keep back. He thought that a spasm briefly contracted the muscles in the dead man's face and he saw in the right hand a glass phial that had been crushed in a last spasm of agony. Kneeling down, he smelt an odour of almonds.

'That's 'im!' said a confident voice in the doorway. 'That's the cove that caused the rumpus outside Terminology House that night. When Waistcoat Charlie was nabbed. And, in that case, he must be number one for being Edward Hyde.'

Swain glanced up, relieved to hear that Sergeant Lumley had arrived at last.

'We'll need a doctor as soon as possible,' he said quietly. 'I want no one to move and nothing to be disturbed in here.'

'Mr Swain,' said Poole quietly. 'That poor devil is the patient who came to my master in the name of Edward Hyde. I have opened the door to him a score of times. How many visits he made privately to this room by way of the mews entrance, I cannot tell. I think it must be he who wore a mask the other day.'

Swain nodded and waved him away. Presently he could hear Poole and the others banging about in the corridor below, shouting for Henry Jekyll.

'Mr Swain!' Utterson was at his side. 'I defer to your authority in this situation. Indeed I do. But there are sealed papers on the business table. Two or three of them are addressed to me. If we are to find my poor friend, they must be opened and read without delay.'

Swain nodded and the two of them went over to the table.

'There is a note,' Utterson said, 'bearing today's date and signed. Listen. It is addressed to me. "When this shall fall into your hands, I shall have disappeared, under what circumstances I have not the penetration to foresee. My instincts and all the circumstances of my nameless situation tell me that the end is sure and must be early." It is a curious note, Mr Swain and uncharacteristic of Jekyll in its way. He wrote a straightforward style. I cannot imagine him saying "under what circumstances I have not the penetration to foresee". There is a scrawl upon the bottom of the paper. He says, "Read first the narrative that Lanyon warned me he was to place in your hands." I cannot tell what that means, Mr Swain. Of Lanyon's narrative I know nothing. I have received no such paper, nor was there anything among his effects.'

'Dr Hastie-Lanyon of Cavendish Square, who died in January?'

'It must be,' said the lawyer with a frown. 'Charles Hastie-Lanyon. He and I and Jekyll have been friends since our schooldays. You know as much from what I told you and Enfield the other day. But if he wrote a narrative for my eyes, why have I not received it before and what would it be doing in the hands of Henry Jekyll? How did he come by it or know about it?'

Swain picked up a bulky envelope from the table. It had been carefully sealed.

'These papers must be held as evidence, Mr Utterson. You know that better than any man.'

'And yet Jekyll's safety depends on their being read now, Mr Swain.'

Swain looked about him to make sure that there was no one to hear.

'I intend you to read them, Mr Utterson. We shall go into Dr Jekyll's saloon. You may read them there. If you are asked for, it shall be said that you have gone home on urgent business to do with Henry Jekyll's disappearance. When you have read the documents, you may call Mr Lumley and give him your statement. Then I shall take the papers with me to Scotland Yard.'

Utterson nodded and the two men went back across the courtyard to the main house. The gaslit saloon with its Egyptian settee and medallioned walls was huge and cold in the night air. The lawyer sat down to read, handing the pages one by one to Swain who then read them also.

At last he looked up at the inspector.

'Mr Swain! Either this is the wildest lunacy and criminality – or else it is worse witchcraft than the Dark Ages ever knew. That poor Jekyll is deranged, I will concede. But Hastie-Lanyon was as rational a man as ever walked this earth.'

Swain finished the final page.

'Lunacy and criminality I believe in, Mr Utterson. I owe them my livelihood. But until witchcraft becomes amenable to forensic investigation, I'll trust the physical sciences.'

'But Lanyon was a doctor, Mr Swain. A man of science. And so was Jekyll. Indeed, he is still, if his poor mind was well. Lanyon was rigorous in investigation and analysis. Yet see what he puts here and what Jekyll adds to it!'

Swain walked across to the uncurtained windows and looked down into the square. A black police van had drawn up outside and two uniformed constables had been posted at the main door of the house. The police surgeon had finished his first examination and the body of the man believed to be Edward Hyde was being carried out in a municipal coffin. Inspector Swain shivered in the chill of the unheated saloon. There had been no fire in the grate for a week or more, he was sure of that. Through the bitter wind he heard a church clock beginning to chime from the direction of St Giles. Torn drifts of cloud still raced across the sickle-blade moon. Impervious to the cold and blustery midnight, a crowd of idlers pressed against the area railings and waited expectantly.

19

'Read it,' said Swain sternly.

Sergeant Lumley fingered the handwritten pages as if they might be the bearers of contagion.

'All of it?'

'Of course all of it. It's evidence, Mr Lumley. Prime evidence in the cases of two dead men. Sir Danvers Carew and Edward Hyde. And possibly Henry Jekyll. That paper is Dr Lanyon's last testament, written two days before he died of peritonitis. Read it and tell me what you think.'

The great building was silent in the last hours of night.

'Tomorrow would do.'

'Read it now, if you please, Mr Lumley!' Alfred Swain's eyes glittered with exasperation. Sergeant Lumley was sitting unhappily in the chair before the inspector's desk. If this was the only way to get clear and home to bed, he would have to read the dead man's statement. With a frown of concentration, the sergeant gave his attention to the firm and upright script of the late Charles Hastie-Lanyon.

On the ninth day of January, now four days ago, I received by the evening delivery a registered envelope, addressed in the hand of my colleague and old school companion, Henry Jekyll. I was a good deal surprised by this, for we were by no means in the habit of correspondence. I had seen the man, dined with him indeed the night before. I could imagine nothing in our intercourse that should justify the formality of registration. The contents increased my wonder, for this is how the letter ran.

'10th December 1884

'Dear Lanyon, – You are one of my oldest friends, and although we may have differed at times on scientific questions, I cannot remember, at least on my side, any break in our affection. There was never a day when, if you had said to me, "Jekyll, my life, my honour, my reason depend upon you," I would not have sacrificed my fortune or my left hand to help you. Lanyon, my life, my honour, my reason, are all at your mercy. If you fail me tonight, I am lost. You might suppose, after this preface, that I am going to ask you for something dishonourable. Judge for yourself.

'I want you to postpone all other engagements for tonight – even if you were summoned to the bedside of an emperor. Take a cab, unless your carriage should be actually at your door, and with this letter in your hand for consultation, drive straight to my house. Poole, my butler, has his orders. You will find him waiting your arrival with a locksmith.

'The door of my cabinet is then to be forced and you are to go in alone. Open the glazed press (letter E) on the left hand, breaking the lock if it be shut. Draw out, with all its contents as they stand, the fourth drawer from the top or (which is the same thing) the third from the bottom. In my extreme distress of mind I have a morbid fear of misdirecting you. But even if I am in error, you may know the right drawer by its contents: some powders, a phial, and a paper book. This drawer I beg you to carry home with you to Cavendish Square exactly as it stands.

'That is the first part of the service. Now for the second. You should be back, if you set out at once on receipt of this, long before midnight. But I will leave you that amount of margin, not only in fear of one of those obstacles that can neither be prevented nor foreseen, but because an hour when your servants are in bed is to be preferred for what will then remain to do.

'At midnight, then, I have to ask you to be alone in your consulting-room to admit with your own hand into the house a man who will present himself in my name. Place in his hands the drawer that you will have brought with you from my cabinet. Then you will have played your part and earned my gratitude completely. Five minutes afterwards, if you insist upon an explanation, you will have understood that these arrangements are of capital importance. By the neglect of one of them, fantastic as they must appear, you might have charged your conscience with my death or the shipwreck of my reason.

'Confident as I am that you will not trifle with this appeal, my heart sinks and my hand trembles at the bare thought of such a possibility. Think of me at this hour, in a strange place, labouring under a blackness of distress that no fancy can exaggerate, and yet well aware that if you will but punctually serve me, my troubles will roll away like a story that is told. Serve me, my dear Lanyon, and save

Your friend,
H.J.

'P.S. – I had already sealed this up when a fresh terror struck upon my soul. It is possible that the post office may fail me, and this letter not come into your hands until to-morrow morning. In that case, dear Lanyon, do my errand when it shall be most convenient to you in the course of the day. Once more expect my messenger at midnight. It may then already be too late. If that night passes without event, you will know that you have seen the last of Henry Jekyll.'

Upon the reading of this letter I was sure my colleague was insane. But till that was proved beyond the possibility of doubt, I felt bound to do as he requested. The less I understood of this farrago, the less I was in a position to judge of its importance. An appeal so worded could not be set aside without a grave responsibility. I rose accordingly from table, got into a hansom, and drove straight to Jekyll's house.

The butler was awaiting my arrival. He had received by the same post as mine a registered letter of instruction, and had sent at once for a locksmith and a carpenter. The tradesmen came while we were yet speaking. We moved in a body to old Dr Denman's surgical theatre, from which (as you are doubtless aware) Jekyll's private cabinet is most conveniently entered.

The door was very strong, the lock excellent. The carpenter vowed he would have great trouble and have to do much damage if force were to be used. The locksmith was near despair. But this last was a handy fellow and after two hours' work the door stood open. The press marked E was unlocked. I took out the drawer, had it filled up with straw and tied in a sheet, and returned with it to Cavendish Square.

Here I proceeded to examine its contents. The powders were neatly enough made up, but not with the nicety of the dispensing chemist; so that it was plain they were of Jekyll's private manufacture. When I opened one of the wrappers, I found what seemed to me a simple crystalline salt of a white colour. The phial, to which I next turned my attention, might have been half-full of a blood-red liquor, which was highly pungent to the sense of smell and seemed to me to contain phosphorus and some volatile ether. At the other ingredients I could make no guess.

The book was an ordinary version-book, and contained little but a series of dates. These covered a period of many years. But I observed that the entries ceased nearly a year ago, and quite abruptly. Here and there a brief remark was appended to a date, usually no more than a single word: 'double' occurring perhaps six times in a total of several hundred entries; and once very early in the list, and followed by several marks of exclamation, 'total failure!!!' All this, though it whetted my curiosity, told me little that was definite.

Here was a phial of some tincture, a paper of some salt, and a record of a series of experiments that had led (like too many of Jekyll's investigations) to no end of practical usefulness. How could the presence of these articles in my house affect either the honour, the sanity, or the life of my flighty colleague? If his messenger could go to one place, why could he not go to another? And even granting some impediment, why was this gentleman to be received by me in secret? The more I reflected, the more convinced I grew that I was dealing with a case of cerebral disease. And though I dismissed my servants to bed, I loaded an old revolver that I might be found in some posture of self-defence.

Twelve o'clock had scarce rung out over London, ere the knocker sounded very gently on the door. I went myself at the summons, and found a small man crouching against the pillars of the portico.

'Are you come from Dr Jekyll?' I asked.

He told me 'yes' by a constrained gesture. When I had bidden him enter, he did not obey me without a searching backward glance in the darkness of the square. There was a policeman not far off, advancing with his bull's-eye open; and at the sight I thought my visitor started and made greater haste.

The particulars struck me, I confess, disagreeably. As I followed him into the bright light of the consulting-room, I kept my hand ready on my weapon.

Here, at last, I had a chance of clearly seeing him. I had never set eyes on him before, so much was certain. He was small, as I have said. I was struck besides with the shocking expression of his face, with his remarkable combination of great muscular activity and great apparent debility of con-stitution, and – last but not least – with the odd subjective disturbance caused by his neighbourhood. This bore some resemblance to incipient rigor, and was accompanied by a marked sinking of the pulse.

At the time, I set it down to some idiosyncratic personal distaste, and merely wondered at the acuteness of the symp-toms. But I have since had reason to believe the cause to lie much deeper in the nature of man, and to turn on some nobler hinge than the principle of hatred.

This person (who had thus, from the first moment of his entrance, struck in me what I can only describe as a disgustful curiosity) was dressed in a fashion that would have made an ordinary person laughable. His clothes, that is to say, although they were of rich and sober fabric, were enormously too large for him in every measurement – the trousers hanging on his legs and rolled up to keep them from the ground, the waist of the coat below his haunches, and the collar sprawling wide upon his shoulders.

Strange to relate, this ludicrous accoutrement was far from moving me to laughter. Rather, as there was something abnormal and misbegotten in the very essence of the creature that now faced me – something seizing, surprising, and revolting – this fresh disparity seemed but to fit in with and to reinforce it. So that to my interest in the man's nature and character there was added a curiosity as to his origin, his life, his fortune and status in the world.

These observations, though they have taken so great a space to be set down in, were yet the work of a few seconds. My visitor was, indeed, on fire with sombre excitement.

'Have you got it?' he cried. 'Have you?' So lively was his impatience that he even laid his hand along my arm and sought to shake me.

I put him back, conscious at his touch of a certain icy pang along my blood.

'Come, sir,' I said, 'you forget that I have not yet had the pleasure of your acquaintance. Be seated, if you please.'

'I beg your pardon, Dr Lanyon,' he replied, civilly enough. 'What you say is very well founded. I come here at the instance of your colleague Dr Henry Jekyll, and I understood—' He paused and put a hand to his throat. I could see, in spite of his collected manner, that he was wrestling against the approaches of hysteria – 'I understood a drawer—'

But here I took pity on my visitor's suspense, and some perhaps on my own growing curiosity.

'There it is, sir,' I said, pointing to the drawer, where it lay on the floor behind a table, and still covered with the sheet.

He sprang to it, and then paused and laid his hand upon his heart. I could hear his teeth grate with the convulsive

172

action of his jaws. His face was so ghastly to see that I grew alarmed both for his life and reason.

'Compose yourself,' I said.

He turned a dreadful smile to me and, as if with the decision of despair, plucked away the sheet. At the sight of the contents he uttered one loud sob of such immense relief that I sat petrified. And the next moment, in a voice that was already fairly well under control, he asked,

'Have you a measuring glass?'

I rose from my place with something of an effort and gave him what he asked.

He thanked me with a smiling nod, measured out a few minims of the red tincture and added one of the powders. The mixture which was at first of a reddish hue began, as the crystals melted, to brighten in colour, to effervesce audibly, and to throw off small fumes of vapour. Suddenly the ebullition ceased. The compound changed to a dark purple, which faded again more slowly to a watery green. My visitor, who had watched these metamorphoses with a keen eye, smiled, set down his glass upon the table, and then turned and looked upon me with an air of scrutiny.

'And now,' he said, 'will you be wise? Will you be guided? Will you let me take the glass and go from your house? Or has the greed of curiosity too much command of you? Think before you answer. If you shall so choose, a new province of knowledge and new avenues to fame and power shall be laid open to you in this room, upon the instant. Your sight shall be blasted by a prodigy to stagger the unbelief of Satan.'

'Sir,' I said, affecting a coolness I was far from truly possessing, 'you speak enigmas. But I have gone too far in the way of inexplicable services to pause before I see the end.'

'It is well,' replied my visitor. 'Lanyon, you remember your vows. What follows is under the seal of our profession. Now, you who have so long been bound to the most narrow and material views, you who have been denied the virtue

173

of transcendental medicine – you who have derided your superiors – behold!'

He put the glass to his lips, and drank at one gulp. A cry followed. He reeled, staggered, clutched at the table and held on, staring with bloodshot eyes, gasping with open mouth. As I looked, I thought there came a change. He seemed to swell. His face became suddenly black and the features seemed to melt and alter. The next moment I had sprung to my feet and leaped back against the wall, my arm raised to shield me from that prodigy, my mind submerged in terror.

'O God!' I screamed, and 'O God!' again and again. For there before my eyes – pale and shaken, and half fainting, and groping before him with his hands, like a man restored from death – there stood Henry Jekyll!

What he told me in the next hour I cannot bring my mind to set on paper. When that sight has faded from my eyes, I ask myself if I believe it – and I cannot answer. My life is shaken to its roots. Sleep has left me. The deadliest terror sits by me at all hours of the day and night. I feel that my days are numbered.

As for the moral turpitude that man unveiled to me, even with tears of penitence, I cannot even in memory dwell on it without a start of horror. I will say but one thing, Utterson, and that (if you can bring your mind to credit it) will be more than enough. The creature who crept into my house that night was, on Jekyll's own confession, known by the name of Hyde, and hunted for in every corner of the land as the murderer of Carew.

Charles Hastie-Lanyon

Sergeant Lumley looked up at Swain without speaking for a moment. Then he gave vent to an expressive sniff.

'You was thinking of going to Superintendent Toplady with this, was you, Mr Swain?'

'Perhaps. Why?'

'Because,' said Lumley confidently, 'it's the biggest load of old cod I've read in a statement – ever. Whatever happened anywhere, it never happened like that. One man swallows a funny drink and turns into another? You take that to old Toplady and he'll have the skin off of you in nice thin strips.'

'It's not the magic that's wrong,' Swain said thoughtfully, 'it's other things that bother me.'

Lumley snorted at the preposterousness of it all.

'Well, 'f that don't worry you, Mr Swain, you ain't got much to concern you at all. Just go into court, tell the judge and jury that old Jekyll took a fizzy drink, turned into Hyde, and coopered Sir Danvers Carew for a lark. You'd be lucky to be kept on as constabulary dog-catcher after that.'

'Listen,' said Swain, 'just listen for a minute. It's not the magic. That letter from Jekyll to Lanyon was written as stated. There's the original of it in its envelope with the papers. It went through the post, registered. And it was the real letter. The post office wax soaked through the envelope and marked the writing-paper. Poole took it from Jekyll's own hand to post it.'

Lumley shrugged.

'I don't see it, then.'

'Look at the dates,' Swain insisted. 'Lanyon says that he had this visit from Hyde on 9 January. But the letter from Jekyll, supposed to be so urgent, is dated 10 December. And he talks about 'tonight'. Now registered post may be slow at times, Mr Lumley, but it wouldn't take more than two days from one part of London to another. A month! That's absurd. And if it took that long, how would Jekyll know which day it was going to arrive?'

Lumley shifted in his chair.

'Mistake?' he said hopefully.

'And another thing, Mr Lumley. The handwriting.'

The sergeant studied the paper.

'Good firm upright hand,' he said defensively.

'Just so, Mr Lumley. That's what's wrong with it. It looks like Lanyon's hand. But not as he wrote on 13 January. The letter says he was dying of shock. He died of a burst appendix and peritonitis, according to the evidence. And by 13 January he was about done for. Two days from death. Anything he wrote would be in a hand that looked like a spider-trail. This is much too good. And that's not all.'

'Why not?'

'Mr Poole, the butler. Jekyll told him to have a locksmith ready, if necessary, to open the drawer of the medical cabinet on the night of 11 December. Mr Poole did as he was told. Lanyon came for the powders, the drawer was opened and off he went. It only took a key to do it. Poole might be a liar and all this might have happened on 9 January – but it didn't. It couldn't have. And that's not all either, Mr Lumley.'

'Ain't it?' said Lumley, swallowing a yawn.

'No, it isn't. If Lanyon wrote this to warn Utterson that Jekyll was Hyde and a murderer, what was it doing tonight in Jekyll's house rather than Utterson's? How did it get there? Jekyll never saw Lanyon again after 13 January so he could hardly have been given it. Utterson was the lawyer who went through his effects, but he never found the paper among them. And Jekyll or Hyde wouldn't burgle Lanyon's house to get it after he died, because they wouldn't know he'd written it. Why write a letter warning Utterson against Jekyll, and then send it to Jekyll? It never was sent, Mr Lumley. It was made up by Hyde in Caleb Square. This week. That's what makes it a fake.'

'Fake?' said Lumley suddenly, as if waking from a doze.

'Of course, Mr Lumley. Good God, man! You surely don't believe this fairy-story of men changing shapes?'

'But what sort of fake?'

Swain relaxed, as if after considerable effort.'

'The last forgery of Edward Hyde, the last of many,' he said contentedly, 'Written this past week where he'd gone to ground, in his victim's room in Caleb Square. The brute must have been there a long time, a month or more, holding Jekyll to ransom. He must have known the hunt was on for him after we searched Terminology House. No wonder Jekyll wouldn't open the door to me and Utterson and Enfield that Sunday afternoon! But the past few days, Edward Hyde's been there alone. Either he killed Jekyll or Jekyll killed him.'

176

'We could start on that tomorrow,' Lumley said hopefully. 'Start with old Lanyon's confession.'

Swain glared and took back Hastie-Lanyon's statement.

'Can't you see it, Mr Lumley? This is Hyde's work, not Lanyon's. Based on a letter that he knew Jekyll had written, to procure the drug that was Hyde's addiction. The rest was fake and forgery – Hyde's profession – done in a perfect copy of Lanyon's hand. Much more ambitious than putting Jekyll's name to cheques. Believe his letter, Mr Lumley, and you believe that the murderer of Sir Danvers Carew was Henry Jekyll disguised.'

'Don't see why he went to that much trouble,' Lumley said gloomily.

'So that Henry Jekyll should be tailor-made for the murder of Danvers Carew. Edward Hyde knew about the Zulu war and what Carew was threatening. Perhaps he purloined Carew's note – more likely Jekyll showed it him. If Carew exposed Jekyll, there was an end of Hyde's extortion. So Carew must die. But if ever the hunt for Carew's murderer got close, there must be evidence that it was Henry Jekyll who killed him. So the villain took a gamble to send Jekyll to the gallows or the madhouse as the man who masqueraded in the name and appearance of Edward Hyde. In its way, it's ingenious. The inspiration of a man floating in an opium dream. But just too good to be true.'

'There's witnesses,' Lumley said.

Swain was unimpressed.

'Mary Smith who told a story to protect her father. Poole the butler who says Jekyll was in the house at the time but never saw him. And Miss Utterson who would tell any lie to save him. Let Sir Charles Russell or Sir Edward Clarke cross-examine her for five minutes and the rope would be round Henry Jekyll's neck. The motive for murdering Carew belonged to him and so did the weapon. And if you don't believe that the Lanyon letter is a forgery, Mr Lumley, you have to believe that Henry Jekyll clubbed Sir Danvers Carew to death.'

Lumley yawned again.

'Henry Jekyll and Miss Utterson ain't the murdering type,' he said helpfully.

A twitch of annoyance pulled at Swain's features.

'One or both of them, Mr Lumley, is the murderer of Edward Hyde. Never mind Carew and blackmail. The roots of this go deeper than the Zulu war. I want to know where it all began.'

20

'Inform me, mister,' said Superintendent Toplady cautiously. 'Illuminate this claptrap, if you please.'

He glittered behind his desk, waiting like a crab to pounce upon a dozing shrimp. But in the background the inspector sensed the malign presence of Lady Carew as a new burden for his commander to bear.

'Before Terminology House was searched, Edward Hyde must have fled to Caleb Square. There, under threat, he demanded shelter from Henry Jekyll. During that week, Jekyll himself found refuge somewhere else, leaving Hyde master of the place. The Lanyon letter to Mr Utterson, I take to be a forgery by the man Hyde, done in a mad and drugged inspiration. Perhaps not long before he took poison. If he were believed, then Henry Jekyll might be tried and hanged for the murder of Sir Danvers Carew.'

'And how d'he die, mister? This scoundrel Hyde? Eh?' The cruel collar edge rasped a little on the shaven gill.

'Accident, sir, or suicide, or possibly murder.'

Toplady gave him a grin devoid of mirth.

'I'll say this, mister. Y'place your bets wide.'

'Blackmail is certain, sir. Nothing to do with the scandal of Henry Jekyll posing as Samuel Parr or going to the Zulu wars. Hyde had got him for the act that made him leave England in the first place. Whatever that was. Sir Danvers Carew recognised Jekyll in London last year as the man who he thought had played the coward in Africa. He threatened him with scandal. Hyde, seeing his source of good things in danger, murdered Sir Danvers Carew. Jekyll knew this but dared not tell and so became the murderer's accessory after the fact. Hyde would forge cheques on his bank account and

179

his victim dared not complain. Even without such persecution, Henry Jekyll was half way to the kingdom of the mad.'

'And what of the papers, mister?'

'The letter of 10 December from Jekyll to Lanyon, asking Lanyon to fetch certain powders and take them to Cavendish Square that night for an unnamed visitor appears genuine, sir. But what purports to be Lanyon's account of a satanic transformation is a forgery. Not an exceptional forgery but good enough as a copy of Lanyon's normal script. But his script was far from normal by 13 January. He was in agony by then, half-drugged for it, and in his last hours.'

'Forged by Hyde, d'ye say, mister?'

'The man was a forger, sir. It was his profession. The cheques he signed with Jekyll's name prove that.'

Toplady grumbled to himself a little.

'And what of the visitor that Jekyll truly sent to Lanyon on the night of 10 December?'

'I believe, sir, that it was one of the few traps that Jekyll or his friends ever laid for his blackmailer. Hyde was a drug-taker, had been for years. I believe that on 10 December Dr Jekyll told him that he had no morphia in his cabinet. Hyde must go to his friend Dr Lanyon at midnight. You may be sure he did so. Now this was the one time when Jekyll could be sure that Hyde would not be at Terminology House. That house was entered by Jekyll or someone on his behalf. The top half of a broken stick, a twin for the one that killed Sir Danvers Carew, was concealed there. Lodged behind a sideboard where Hyde might not notice it but a police search would turn it up. A clumsy attempt to hang Hyde for the murder. But it might have done, sir.'

Toplady danced up and down a little.

'And how might Jekyll or such a person enter Terminology House at the precise hour to do this?'

'Perhaps, sir, by being let in. Someone who had a key and loved the intruder well enough to do it.'

'And this fellow Hyde, mister?'

'Got his powder from Lanyon and took it in the normal way. Asked for Jekyll's letter back. Conceived a notion by which he might disappear and Jekyll be hunted as the murderer of Carew. Made it seem that Hyde existed only as Jekyll's disguise. In such disguise he killed Carew. When Lanyon died and could not contradict him, Hyde forged Lanyon's account of the satanic transformation.'

'Say so, mister? Eh?'

'Sir,' said Swain insistently, 'if Hyde were not dead and his body found, we would now hunt Henry Jekyll as if Hyde were merely his disguise. How the disguise was effected we might not know. But Henry Jekyll would be sought for the murder in Cheyne Walk.'

'And Hyde himself?'

'Died of poison, sir. Dr Collins will tell us what. As I knelt down to look at him, I smelt an odour of kernels.'

'Kernels, mister? Peach, cherry, almond?'

'Something that would yield prussic acid, sir, in crystalline form. There were notes sent to Maw's the chemist, signed by Jekyll, complaining that the powders were not so pure as they used to be. Hyde was in possession of the cabinet for the last week. Drugs were procured for his craving. I believe that one prescription was deliberately written for cyanide in its purest form, mingled in a tincture of morphia. A physician's authority would do for that. Minute quantities could be used in treatment. Jekyll wrapped it as a single dose of morphia alone. He knew his blackmailer would take it, sooner or later, believing it to be an opiate. The death would appear as pure misadventure. And so the victim destroyed his tormentor.'

'Did he, by Jove!' Toplady repeated the humourless grin. 'I like the devil Jekyll for that immensely!'

'Or perhaps Hyde planned his dupe should take it in mistake for morphia,' Swain said and saw the superintendent frown, 'but at the last minute, Hyde knew he was caught – that the police were at the door. So he took the poison himself, as his last escape.'

Toplady turned and stared into the chill azure of the morning sky. Presently he confronted Swain again.

'So, mister. Y'have the fellow Hyde blackmailing Jekyll over something we don't know. Y'have Hyde murdering Carew who

181

threatens to destroy his milch-cow over something unmanly in the Zulu war. But Hyde's name is mentioned in connection with Carew's murder. And so y'have Hyde putting the murder off on Jekyll by forging some nonsense from Lanyon after Lanyon's death.'

'I believe so, sir.'

'And meantime, mister, y'have Jekyll or someone striking back at the scoundrel. Half a broken stick is hidden in Hyde's room for us to find. Hyde takes flight when wanted for questioning, holds Jekyll almost hostage in his own house. Jekyll, more than half-mad, runs away but leaves a powder among the morphine that shall destroy Hyde once for all?'

'Something like that, sir.'

'And Jekyll could never be brought to account for a powder a man might have stolen, taken by accident, or taken to do away with himself deliberately.'

'Yes, sir.'

Toplady did not like this part of it at all.

'Then all y'have, mister, is the destruction of the scoundrel Hyde by misadventure or his own hand. Coroner's jury never would bring in murder on such evidence. Never would. And y'have the case of Sir Danvers Carew that can never come to court. Eh? Murder by person or persons unknown, the coroner will say. Can't say else. A damned unsatisfactory conclusion that will prove. What we shall tell Lady Carew, I cannot think.'

For the first time in their acquaintanceship, Swain saw a mist of self-pity clouding the superintendent's eyes.

'There's one other paper, sir,' Swain said tactfully. 'A confession left by Dr Jekyll for Mr Utterson. I take this to be in his own hand. I believe it explains all. He tells us that he also began to take a certain tincture. This I think was after his return from Africa. Under its influence he began to imagine things that could not be and to feel desires he could not appease. He believed himself to be Edward Hyde. But he writes of Hyde, sir, as a man who already existed and not as a name he invented. In other words, sir, under the influence of cocaine or whatever it might be, he imagined himself as the

182

man who was his own blackmailer. He writes of himself as having two separate bodies at the same time, inhabiting one while the other slept elsewhere.'

Toplady growled again, as if warning the inspector not to go too far.

'It is what he said to me, sir,' Swain insisted, 'that he could not tell dreaming from waking in the end. When he slept, he believed that he had already woken up and was forever imprisoned in the mind of Edward Hyde. He talks of sensual indulgences but with no evidence that they took place. He accuses himself of the murder of Carew while under the influence of the drug, but he offers not a shred of evidence to support this. Indeed, he denied it to me. There is not a man in London who might not make out as good a case for his own guilt.'

The superintendent rummaged on his desk for a moment and then held up a sheet of paper.

'I have read his confession, mister. It is tosh and little more. But I think old Jekyll is more cunning than you would have us believe. Mad he may be. Yet the man is devious, mister. See what he writes.'

Toplady handed Swain the paper, stabbing a finger at the final paragraph.

Will Hyde die upon the scaffold? Or will he find the courage to release himself at the last moment? God knows. I do not care. This is the hour of my true death, and what is to concern another than myself. Here, then, as I lay down my pen, and proceed to seal up my confession, I bring the life of that unhappy Henry Jekyll to an end.

The inspector looked up from his reading.

'Well, mister? What d'ye say to that? Eh?'

Swain looked past the superintendent's shoulder at the Westminster flags by the river, straining in the cold March breeze.

'That we are supposed to believe Hyde took his own life, sir. Whereas Henry Jekyll, deranged though he may be, probably seized the chance to destroy his persecutor by inserting a deadly poison among the tinctures of morphia.'

183

'Beyond proof, mister. Have the goodness to look at me when y'speak. I abominate an evasive man. What else?'

'That the future is to be determined by a third person, sir,' said Swain carefully, 'a person who is neither Jekyll nor his blackmailer.'

'Then there is no question left, sir, for the Criminal Investigation Department,' Toplady formed a sour quirk of the mouth. 'It seems we have Carew's murderer in the body of Hyde. Jekyll may have been a fool and a dupe. He was, I believe, a madman. Whether they were the same or different makes no odds now. The person of Jekyll committed many follies but no crime, except perhaps when he called himself Samuel Parr.'

'There is one matter unresolved, sir,' said Swain firmly.

'Then you may ask it now.'

Swain turned his eyes upon Toplady at last.

'Where, sir, is Henry Jekyll? He cannot vanish into thin air. His body, alive or dead, is somewhere. Where is he?'

A contemptuous reassurance animated Toplady's gnome-like features.

'As to that, mister, y'can have no answer. Nor need you inquire further. There is still leave due to you?'

'A week, sir,' Swain said, not understanding the connection, 'to be taken before the year's end.'

'Take it now, mister!' Toplady snapped with ill-concealed triumph. 'Keep out of my sight and set your mind to rights. There has been enough of this case. I shall have work for you when you come back. The South-Western Railway Company requires a man. Young ladies travelling first-class between Aldershot and Waterloo have been subject to enforced familiarities from military gentlemen. I shall look to you to put a stop to it, mister.'

Swain was horrified. The sentence pronounced upon him was worse than any he had feared.

'But surely, sir, the railway company's police—'

Toplady grinned and the spikes of his grey hair seemed to stand stiffer than ever.

'Y'shall thrive upon it, mister. It is the work just fitted for

184

you. And if it is not, y'may choose a career outside the Metropolitan Police. Schoolmiss work, poetry books and sketching! Y'have only to indicate the wish!'

Toplady's grin assumed a more vicious energy and his mouth worked about with an epileptic compulsion. The case of the mad Henry Jekyll was over and done with. Montague Toplady was his old self again. He danced on his toes and the points of the collars menaced his eyeballs once more with the agitation of his head. Like a game-cock he moved from foot to foot in the dismissal of Alfred Swain from his presence.

'See to it, mister!' he said happily, revelling in Swain's misery. 'See to it as soon as y'may!'

PART 3

The Real Alfred Swain

21

'It's not that bad,' Sergeant Lumley said consolingly, 'and it's not for ever. Not half as bad as what old Newcomen got.'

Swain, who had just imparted the news about the South-Western Railway Company to his sergeant, looked up from his desk with a flicker of interest.

'Newcomen?'

Lumley gave an emphatic nod.

'Dog-stealers,' he said with ill-concealed satisfaction. 'Someone down Southwark or Lambeth steals dogs off the nobs in Portman Square or Audley Street. Sends 'em a ransom note. Twenty guineas or the animal goes in the Thames with a brick round its neck. Always pay up they do. You or I could starve in the street for all they care. But they can't bear the thought of harm coming to some mongrel or even a mog. There's Whistling Jack and a hundred more down Southwark make a living by it. They've put Newcomen in command of the dog-stealing. Walking a beat round the slums to look for any signs of animals that shouldn't be there. Watching for when they have to be took out to squat on the pavement and all that.'

Swain sat in awe of the majesty of Toplady's vengeance.

'You're right, Mr Lumley,' he said at length. 'I could have come off worse! A sight worse!'

'And you got a week,' Lumley insisted. 'Lot can happen in a week.'

'A lot's got to happen, Mr Lumley. One more tiff with Mr Toplady and it could be worse than dog-catching.'

'Yes,' Lumley said with a significant look. 'There's the urinal patrol and the midnight-till-eight beat down Rotherhithe arresting drunkards for being sick in public. I'd say either of those

189

was worse than subalterns touching up young persons in railway carriages. At least you've got first-class conveyances.'

Swain got up.

'Right, Mr Lumley. I'll see you next week.'

Lumley relaxed.

'Going to Margate or somewhere, Mr Swain?'

'No,' said Swain thoughtfully, 'too cold for that. I'm taking a trip down to Broadmoor.'

'Oh yes, Mr Swain?' The name appeared to mean no more to the sergeant just then than Brighton or York.

'A painter whose work interests me. The late Richard Dadd.'

Lumley's face filled with alarm at the realisation.

'For God's sake, Mr Swain! Leave well alone! There's enough bother in the department without you wading any deeper into the regimental cess-pool. You could catch it as bad as Newcomen after all!'

'Just a day's outing, Mr Lumley. Nothing more than that.'

It was on the following morning that Swain got up before dawn and walked from Pimlico to Hyde Park Corner, across the crisp and frozen turf to the Edgware Road, and so to the terminus of the Great Western Railway at Paddington. Under the broad curve of the glass roof, the chill of the sooty air resounded with the respiration of steam, gasping and inhaling by turns. It was the beginning of his journey to the criminal lunatic asylum, lately transferred from Bethlehem Hospital in Southwark to Broadmoor in the Berkshire countryside.

That the new asylum was a change for the better could not be doubted. As Swain approached the last mile on foot, he was astonished by the grandeur and openness of the place. The hospital ran along the crest of a hill, its buildings resembling a series of country mansions or perhaps the skyline of a Tuscan city. There were square Italianate towers and lofty colonnades, handsome galleries and elegant windows. It did not look in the least the sort of place to immure murderers and the perpetrators of appalling injury.

Perhaps the most striking feature, Swain thought, was the apparent absence of a high wall or any other means of separating the prisoners from the world. As he came closer, he saw that this was a skilful and humane illusion. The walls were high and secure as those of any prison. But the builders had taken advantage of the slope of the hill. From the upper terraces, the prisoners could look out across the tops of the walls far below, their view of the Berkshire countryside free and uninterrupted. Swain came to the gate.

'Inspector Swain of Scotland Yard to see the Superintendent, Dr Orange. A matter of some urgency.'

He was escorted up a driveway between bushes of laurel and rhododendron which gave the feeling of a rich man's park to the outer gardens. Beyond the inner gate there was silence and a sense of order that Swain found intimidating. As he came to the steps, a man appeared at the top of them. He was in his middle years, black-haired and trimly bearded with a broad forehead and keen dark eyes. He stretched out his hand to the inspector, without smiling.

'I am Dr Orange, Mr Swain. What can it be that is so urgent?'

'The safety of Dr Henry Jekyll, sir.'

Dr Orange frowned, as if this only made matters worse.

'He is not here, Mr Swain. I assure you of that.'

'He may no longer be alive, sir,' said Swain carefully, 'but I believe he was known here.'

The superintendent relaxed a little.

'He was, Mr Swain. I knew him a little myself, from the occasional visits his researches required.'

The two men entered the building and walked down a long vaulted corridor. To one side was a well-proportioned but simply-furnished day-room. Men who were for the most part elderly talked together in pairs, or sat at plain tables and read books, or lounged on the side-seats with their hands thrust into their jacket-pockets, staring into space. It might have been the reading-room of a mechanics' institute or a philosophical society. Swain found it hard to imagine that these old men who sat so quietly and intently together had committed some of the most pitiless and blood-chilling crimes of their day.

On the other side of the corridor the windows overlooked the terrace with its pavilion roofs and country views. Dr Orange opened a door and ushered Swain into a sitting-room.

'And now, Mr Swain,' he said with the air of a busy man interrupted, 'what is it that I can do for you?'

'Henry Jekyll,' said Swain patiently, 'was the patron of a painter, Richard Dadd, who died here a month or two ago.'

'Many people were, Mr Swain,' the superintendent worked his fingers together with enthusiasm. 'There were numerous commissions for pictures and the decorations of sets of chairs. We have a theatre here, where the patients act little plays. Richard Dadd decorated the panels of that also. There was tragedy in his life, Mr Swain, but his life was not all tragedy. You take my meaning?'

Swain nodded.

'And how did Henry Jekyll's interest in this place begin? Was it with Mr Dadd?'

Dr Orange smiled and shook his head.

'It was before my time. I think it was an interest in certain forms of mental aberration. Perhaps it was the crime of Richard Dadd that began it.'

The inspector assumed the expression of a man in a great and delicate difficulty.

'Dr Orange, I beg you to believe me that Henry Jekyll's safety – even his life – must be at risk if he is not found soon. I know there is some story connecting him with this place and with Richard Dadd. Yet I cannot hit upon it. Will you help me?'

The superintendent hesitated, but Swain was not to be put off.

'Tell me, Dr Orange, of the paintings that were done by this poor fellow. Was there not one called *Circe*?'

Dr Orange shook his head.

'It was first called that but the title was not thought suitable. It was painted in 1862 and changed soon afterwards to *Bacchanalian Scene*.'

'I speak, Dr Orange, of the second version. The one that is still called *Circe* and bears upon it the words "*refecit*, 1869". It belonged, did it not, to Henry Jekyll?'

'You know more of this, Mr Swain, than I had supposed.'

'But not enough, sir, to show why a poor mad painter should have done such a lascivious likeness of a lady of the Utterson family.'

Dr Orange sighed in token of defeat.

'Mrs Utterson was brought here—'

'Mrs Utterson? Mrs Amelia Utterson? The wife of Gabriel Utterson, the lawyer?'

'To be sure, Mr Swain. It was she whom Dr Jekyll brought here. Dr Jekyll was a good friend to the Utterson family. And to the Carew family for that matter. Mrs Amelia Utterson was daughter to Lady Carew and the elder sister of Sir Danvers. But if you know so much, Mr Swain, I am sure you know that.'

Swain ignored the invitation to comment and clung to his main purpose.

'Mrs Utterson was surely not brought here as a criminal?'

'No, sir. Dr Jekyll came in search of a keeper that would care for her. They were here as visitors – doctor and patient – for no more than a couple of days. Richard Dadd saw her several times from the window. He was seized by a quality of her beauty, a distracted and perverse ghost of former loveliness, I daresay. From this, he painted his bacchanalian scene again and made her the wild creature at its centre. Dr Jekyll bought the picture when it was done, in order that it should fall into no other hands.'

'And her madness was incurable?'

'It was before my time, Mr Swain. What do you know of puerperal insanity?'

'Little enough, sir, except that it affects women sometimes after a child is born.'

Dr Orange relaxed a little.

'True, Mr Swain. It takes variant forms. It may be no worse than low spirits. It may be psychotic and incurable, leading to self-destruction or infanticide. In this case it was, I believe, a tendency to self-destruction.'

'Of Amelia Utterson, sir?'

'Her child was born, Mr Swain, and the onset of the disease was within the fortnight, as it commonly is. It was a very bad

193

case, as I am told. The poor soul was raving in her distress for a good deal of the time. Dr Jekyll arranged for her to be privately superintended and kept away from her family. It was impossible that she should be left in a normal domestic household, where there were other children. She had a private keeper and the best that could be done by her physician. In her case, it was in vain. She died, I believe, after about six months. Dr Jekyll brought her here soon after the onset of her illness, seeking a humane and experienced keeper that might look after her in confidence. Without gossip and scandal, Mr Swain. Such men are not always easy to find.'

'The keeper, sir?' Swain asked. 'Who was he?'

Dr Orange shook his head.

'It was before my time.'

'He was a keeper here? Is that so?'

'I believe he was. It often happens that a man will turn to caring for a private patient. He is well equipped for it after his time with us.'

'The name of the keeper, sir. Might it have been Parr? Or Hyde?'

'I cannot promise, Mr Swain, it was long before my time. I knew Henry Jekyll only in later years as the collector of poor Richard Dadd's visions of lunacy and damnation.'

'Were there other pictures in which his vision of Mrs Utterson appeared?'

'I believe there were, Mr Swain. Of a kind one would not wish to display. I think Henry Jekyll bought them to save them from other hands and eyes.'

'Or perhaps, sir, because the poor mad painter saw a truth that the rest of the world was blind to.'

'Speculation, Mr Swain. Dangerous speculation.'

'The house,' Swain coaxed him again. 'The house where she was cared for. Where might that have been?'

Dr Orange frowned but this time with an effort of recollection.

'It was a romantic spot somewhere, as I heard. I can scarcely tell you where. Somewhere out of the way. In cases of puerperal insanity a change of scene, they say, is the best remedy.'

194

'And you cannot tell me where the house was, whether it was a private asylum or a private house with a keeper?'

'Indeed I cannot, Mr Swain. I heard it as no more than a story which happened before my time – just as you hear it now. Henry Jekyll played the part of a friend to the family rather than a doctor.'

It was hard for Swain to conceal his disappointment.

'Then you can help me no more.' It was a statement rather than a question.

'You have already overpersuaded me, Mr Swain. It is, I suppose, your profession.'

A few minutes later they walked together back down the drive where the thin and icy sunlight had done no more than melt a few sparkles on the frozen grass of the terrace. Swain sensed that Dr Orange was trying to formulate a confession. As they were about to shake hands, the asylum superintendent looked at his visitor.

'Mr Swain, I would not mislead you in such a matter as this. I speak tentatively, you understand. It was before I came here. But I believe that the keeper employed was indeed a young man called Hyde. More than that I cannot say. I would not say as much, were it not for the danger in which you tell me Henry Jekyll is placed.'

By the time that he reached the rooms above the little shop in Pimlico, Swain could think of nothing but that Henry Jekyll must be found, alive or dead. He unlocked the street door to let himself in and remembered that just this afternoon, in a bare panelled room in Westminster, a coroner's jury would be sitting in inquest upon the mortal remains of Edward Hyde.

Stooping down, he picked up several letters from the doormat. One of them caught his attention immediately. He opened the pale pink envelope.

The matter is serious. I have gone to Henry Jekyll. You will understand why. R.U.

Gone to him? Where? And when? Swain remembered the words of Poole, the butler. The voice like a woman weeping in the room where Hyde's body was later found. And when

195

had she written the present note? Before or after the night of Edward Hyde's death? He turned it over again, but there was no date upon it. The postmark was two days earlier, 'London SW'. She might still have been in London then or it might have been posted for her. Perhaps, since she had written it, Henry Jekyll was dead as well.

That was what Alfred Swain proposed to find out as he folded her note back into the envelope and slid it into his pocket.

Like an unquiet spirit laid to rest, the case could not be closed until Henry Jekyll or his body had been found. And that, Swain thought, was the same thing as finding Romana Utterson. The prospect was one that quickened his pulse with an ill-defined excitement and alarm.

22

'Mr Swain? Mr Alfred Swain from Scotland Yard?'

Mr Learman in his parliamentary livery stood on a diagonal pattern of summer-bright Pugin tiles. He peered at his visitor through the Plantagenet arch. In the long mural, Cardinal Wolsey still confronted Sir Thomas More with an expression of astonished rebuke.

'Swain,' said Swain, stepping from the shadows and acknowledging the fact.

'Another matter to do with the late Sir Danvers Carew, perhaps?'

'Indeed,' said Swain, disguising the prompt deception with a suggestion of deep significance. 'Mr Learman, I have to ask for your help in a small matter.'

'Not the room again I hope, Mr Swain? The room has been emptied and tidied.' Learman gave a slight snuffling laugh at his own propriety. 'It is occupied now by Mr Adshead, the member for Hull.'

'Not the room,' said Swain reassuringly. 'A matter of papers, Mr Learman. State papers. Not kept at Scotland Yard, you understand. The Annual Report volumes of the Commissioners in Lunacy.'

'Yes, Mr Swain?'

'For the years 1870 to the present.'

'Yes?'

'I should like to consult them,' Swain said sharply. Learman drew in his breath, as if he had just hurt himself in some way.

'The library is not, Mr Swain—'

'Anywhere. A cubby-hole. A boot-cupboard. Porter's lodge. I don't mind where I see them.'

'Parliamentary privilege, Mr Swain—'

'Will not protect another honourable gentleman from being beaten to death on the public pavement, Mr Learman. Unless something is done to prevent it.'

'In that case, Mr Swain—'

'Thank you, Mr Learman. I shall wait here.'

Learman executed one of his running, backward bows, as if thanking Swain for the pleasure of a dance, and disappeared into a corridor at one side.

Swain walked up and down under the medieval fantasies of the industrial age. He paced a brief and frustrated sentry-go. Henry Jekyll and Romana Utterson had vanished from London and, indeed, from the face of the earth. Alfred Swain, at his wits' end, concluded at last that both had found refuge in the strange legal kingdom of lunacy and confinement. Mr Utterson was at home to no one and even the servants had left the house in Caleb Square.

Swain stared morosely at Cardinal Wolsey and waited for Mr Learman. Somewhere in the depths of the building he thought he heard a buzz of voices, here and there a door slammed, the echoes carrying and multiplying through high vaulting and along infinite corridors. At last Mr Learman returned, walking with short and strained steps under the weight of a pile of ledgers. Each one seemed the size of a York stone paving slab.

'Perhaps in here, Mr Swain?' he suggested plaintively.

The door, panelled as if for a Tudor banqueting hall, opened upon a small room that smelt of wax and polished leather. A large table with a reading-stand occupied most of the space. It was illuminated by a pale wintry sun, the river-light filtered through the leaded panes of parliamentary windows. Swain thanked Learman and opened the first of the heavy leather-bound volumes.

For the best part of an hour, he scanned the tables of figures and categories for the years when Amelia Utterson might have been cared for in a private asylum. There was nothing for the whole of Monmouthshire. The names of Jekyll and Parr, Hyde and Utterson were nowhere to be found on any of the pages. All along, Swain had feared this might be so. It seemed there was nothing more to be done. He turned to Learman in despair.

'Is this all, Mr Learman?'

'Every last one, Mr Swain. Enough in all conscience, I should say.'

'What I'm looking for isn't in here, Mr Learman.'

'Then perhaps it don't exist, Mr Swain. Think of it that way.'

'Any private house licensed to receive lunatics in the year of each report must be in these lists?'

Learman looked a little pained, as if Swain should have known better.

'The law required it, Mr Swain. Even in those days. Except where only one poor soul was under confinement. That was not cause for a licence. After all, a family might care for one of its members at home.'

'And where that was done, Mr Learman, there would be no entry here?'

'None, Mr Swain.'

Swain looked at him in dismay.

'I am searching for a man who is probably detained in such a house as that. You tell me, then, I might be looking for any house in the country!'

'You might, sir,' said Learman gently, 'you might indeed.'

It was the worst, Swain thought. He closed the volumes and stood up. As he was about to turn and take his leave of Mr Learman, the light from the river outside seemed to pierce his thoughts like a shaft of sun.

'If there was a death, Mr Learman! If a patient died, even in a house where that was the only patient! What then?'

Learman shook his head.

'You would not find it there, sir. A matter for the visiting magistrates of the district. Before you could go further, you would need to know the house in question, which is what eludes you at present.'

It was hopeless, Swain thought. The supervision of madness was itself madness. Then the sunlight broke through again.

Money! No public body ever performed a duty without charging somebody else for the service.

'Mr Learman! Suppose there was such a case. Suppose a patient died. Who would bear the cost of investigation in the beginning?'

'The visiting magistrates and the parish board.'

'And who would bear it in the end?'

'Why, Mr Swain, the Commissioners in Lunacy, to be sure.'

'Then, Mr Learman, for the years in question there must be records of the accounting between the visiting magistrates and the commissioners.'

A dismal apprehension appeared on Learman's face.

'The Treasurer's Account books, Mr Swain? There are thousands of entries under a host of headings!'

'I should be deeply grateful, Mr Learman.'

There was a longer pause this time. On their arrival, the volumes of the Treasurer's Accounts were of such size and weight that the table and reading stand were almost too puny for them. While Learman looked on, downcast, Alfred Swain turned the thick and crackling pages of the printed ledgers. Still it was useless. There was nothing in the accounting of the Monmouth magistrates with the Commissioners in Lunacy that matched the death of Amelia Utterson.

When it was all over, Swain knew that he had had his share of misfortunes in the case. But there was one exception. He continued to scan the Monmouthshire entries. As he did so, his eye caught an entry in an adjoining column headed 'Brecknock'. It was for a payment made four years earlier.

For counsel's opinion in the matter of an ex-parte injunction, seeking discharge, brought on behalf of Henry Smith-Billington, an infant, against the assigns of Samuel Parr, Observatory House, Gospel Pass, Brecknock, by Maybury, Utterson, & Parke of Gaunt Street, EC4. Twenty-one guineas.

In Swain's mind there was a memory of Mad Billy in the receiving-room, talking about the tenant of Terminology

200

House. 'An old master of mine.' That was what Billy had called Edward Hyde.

'Mr Learman!' The warmth of the inspector's gratitude to the little man was undisguised. 'I believe I have got the place at last!'

Learman looked over his shoulder.

'Indeed, sir? I should prefer to be in Westminster myself, at such a time of year as this.'

'And so should I, Mr Learman. But a life is running to its end and may take another with it. I must go at once to see what can be done.'

'Dear me!' said the little man, impressed and respectful. 'As bad as that, is it?'

'If anything,' Swain said with a sense of occasion, 'it may be worse.'

He left Mr Learman, went back to the plain little rooms in Pimlico and packed everything that he might need into a travelling bag. He paused only to check that an ex-parte injunction was an unopposed application. That all men and women are infants in law until the age of twenty-one was already familiar to him. How the paths of Mad Billy and Henry Jekyll had crossed was something he did not yet understand. At the cost of abandoning his brushes, he found room for a lantern and a small geographer's guide to West Britain. Carrying his bag, he set out on foot again for the Great Western Railway terminus at Paddington. He left no messages and no indication as to where he had gone. In his mind he nourished an ill-formed argument that he was on leave and, therefore, whatever he did was his own private business. Death, not murder, was that business now.

Alfred Swain travelled the rest of the day, and the night, and much of the following day. His route lay through country that was as foreign to him as the plains of Bengal. There were ranges of hills that seemed to increase in height with every mile that passed. Once he saw a broad river estuary of brown water and frozen mud. There were streams from banks overhead that hung in long and fantastic icicle-shapes. From time to time a clear cold rain fell against the flanks and windows of the train.

The journey gave him time to consider his situation. He was hunting a man who was deranged and disgraced, who might be alive or dead. That mattered very little to him. The true justification of his journey was that he sought the truth of a riddle, the ancient wrong of which Henry Jekyll had been guilty. But Alfred Swain knew perfectly well that he would not have made the journey for that alone. There was also a matter of the eyes he could never capture in his sketching, the enigmatic and lascivious slant of them. There was the shawl that had fallen and the voice that had mocked his prudery. The strange enactment of submissive kneeling and the savage amusement of the teeth fastening in the flesh of his hand filled him with a quickening anticipation. He thought it probable that she was the murderer of Edward Hyde and that, if his own death were necessary to protect Henry Jekyll, she would not hesitate. Yet Alfred Swain, the rational thinking man of his time and the representative of law and justice, longed more than anything else to be King Cophetua with such a beggar maid.

In his head he carried the details of a map and a list of names. At last he stood on the station-platform of a small market town that might have been almost anywhere in the British Isles. Rows of well-kept cottages and the houses of professional men breathed out their thin chimney-smoke against the coming dusk. Swain was cold the moment he stood outside the train, despite his coat, his gloves, and his hat. The early sunset had a frosty fire that had characterised the great part of a bitter winter. A new chill in the breeze cut his face like a knife. He could feel the skin drying and cracking on his lips and on the knuckles of his hands.

There was a broad main street with a pavement built up very high on one side. Even had there been a carriage for hire, it would have been too great a risk. A man of influence in such a place would surely have the cabmen in his pay. For the sake of a few miles and the safety of two lives, it was not worth it. So Alfred Swain walked the length of the street and beyond it, into the darkness of the country road. The last of the daylight showed him a signpost, pointing one way to Brecon and the other to Hay-on-Wye.

Putting the bag down, he opened it and took out a dark-lantern, carefully packed and prepared. He set a match to the wick and half-closed the shutter. Just at that moment a white squall came down from the black shape of the mountain to his left and he felt the freezing sting of hail in the sharp burst of rain.

Swain balanced the two certainties in his mind. First, he was ill-advised to attempt the journey by night. Second, he would be more ill-advised to approach the house by daylight, if its secret corresponded at all to what he expected. In any case, by the next day he might be too late.

The yellow glimmer of the oil-lamp caught the first sparkle of frost where the crystals were forming on the hard mud of the roadway. But Swain's lamp showed him a fork in the highway, the left-hand side leading up the steep and winding track towards the black mountain. Two houses stood at the junction, one in darkness, the other with a light in the parlour window. He supposed that they were the last he would see. In his calculations, he had allowed five miles as the distance to be walked. But in these conditions and with the ascent of the mountain ahead of him, it might as well have been fifty.

Bracing himself for the long climb, Swain turned into the little road that was no more than a lane. Picking his way along rutted mud by the glimmer of the oil-lamp, he began the ascent to Gospel Pass.

From time to time the squalls blew down, carrying ice in the wind with a savagery that made him gasp. Here and there, he caught a glimpse of lamplight showing through a curtain, offering warmth and company. But it was always, he suspected, deceptively far off.

The last of the dusk had gone and there was complete darkness except for a slight luminescence from the few cold and shimmering stars. In a moment he saw or thought he saw the way ahead, a steep incline that was tall as it was long. Ice scorched his lungs each time that he drew in air and he heard his breath sawing in his throat with the exertion. Alfred

Swain had lived too long in cities, it seemed to him now. His confidence that he could find the house he wanted by day or night began to weigh on his thoughts as a fatal stupidity.

Oddest of all, to his own perception, there seemed to be no living creature of any kind. He had expected that owls would hoot or foxes bark. Badgers might stumble across his path or rats scuttle in the hedges. But there was nothing, only the terrible silence of the cold mountain broken occasionally by a clout of icy rain.

So long as he could keep going, so long as he could walk and keep his circulation in order, he would be all right. But at this rate, he might have to walk until daybreak and that, he thought, would be beyond him. After what seemed like two or three hours, the hedges to one side fell away. He was suddenly conscious of standing on a bare and rocky slope, lit only by a curious and delusive phosphorescence from some of the stones. The track was narrower and more stony than it had been, flanked on either side by frozen turf. It took him a moment to realise how high he had climbed. To his right, the ground dropped sharply. In the faint light, he could just make out a vast and uneven landscape far below. It seemed to be an opening deep into the ranges of the Cambrian mountains, a sublime and menacing night scene that ran as far as Cader Idris and Plynlimon.

Swain shook himself and knew that it could not be. But as the oil-lamp flickered ominously, he sensed that the track had levelled out. He was climbing no longer. With less peril than he had feared, he must be approaching Gospel Pass.

Now every gate and turning would have to be inspected, though the one he wanted would be on his left. It was possible that he might make out the shape of the building against the slight and frosty pallor of the starlight in the momentary parting of clouds.

He saw nothing. There was a gate closed across the track to prevent the mountain sheep straying but no sign of an opening. In about twenty minutes, he felt sure that the narrow lane had begun again. There were hedges to either side. The name of Observatory House was a polite fiction. Madness behind bars, rather than astronomy, was the subject of its observation. But it would be where the land was highest. His foot slipped on a smooth and ice-rimed stone, so that he fell sideways into the hedge and swore out loud. As he pulled himself up, a shape lumbered across the pool of oil-light and he saw that it was a sheep disturbed by his fall.

Swain picked his way more carefully, aware of the stunted trees at the verge of the lamplight on either side and the faint chuckle of a stream that had not yet frozen over entirely. There was a hump-backed bridge, just wide enough for a horse and rider. And then nothing.

But he had read his map with care. It had shown him a bridge over water. Only one in the whole of the journey. And it had been shortly before the track that turned off to Observatory House. To his irritation, the flame in the oil-lamp quivered and then went out. But it was irritation, after all, and not despair. Twenty yards in front of him he had glimpsed a gap in the hedge and a path of some kind leading to the left. It might have been no more than the opening to a field. Alfred Swain knew that it must be the approach to Samuel Parr's private asylum.

Without the lamp it was almost necessary to feel his way in front of him. But in any case he would have had to extinguish it by now. Putting one foot carefully before the other, he turned from the lane and felt a rough but definable path. After seventy or eighty yards of this, he knew he was right. Ahead of him there was the dark shape of a building against a dim flush of starlight. No lantern-light showed anywhere but, at the very least, there would be shelter of some sort.

Half way between the track of Gospel Pass and the building, there was a small copse of wind-blown trees. He felt rather than saw the kerbs of a small group of gravestones. From time to time the families of the patients in a private asylum preferred that their dead should be buried quietly far away from home. He struck a match and was lucky at the first attempt. The plain curved headstone was darkened by lichen and time but the lettering had been cut deep.

In Memory of Amelia Jane Utterson,
who died 20 March 1871, aged 31 years.

'A happy lover who has come
To look on her that loves him well,
Who 'lights and rings the gateway bell,
And learns her gone and far from home.'

In the last sputtering of the flame he made out the line of a stone kerb and a space that had every appearance of a grave rather than a mere commemorative stone. He frowned in the darkness. The lines of verse he recognised as coming from the Poet Laureate's *In Memoriam*. But that was the least puzzling aspect of the matter. It was the grave at Gospel Pass that stirred a cold thought in him. Amelia Utterson had spent her last and tranquil week at home in Bayswater. As the register made clear, she had died there and was buried in the cemetery at Kensal Green. Whose was the grave before him now?

Still there was no sign of light or movement from the house. He came carefully towards it, as quietly as he could. There was little to distinguish Observatory House from any prosperous home in the land of the Welsh border squirarchy. It was four-square and plain, in the substantial country style that marked the building of a hundred years before. There were yards and outbuildings of a later and less elegant kind. But there was nothing to suggest that it had ever been used as an astronomical observatory nor that it was occupied now.

The windows were shuttered, or perhaps boarded over on the inside. They might have remained so since the death of Samuel Parr. Making his inspection with care, Swain turned his attention to the stone-built sheds and other buildings of the yard. There was nothing remarkable about them at first. But as he came to the last of the low-roofed structures he saw and felt by stretching out his arms that the windows were securely barred on the outside. The iron burnt him with the intensity of its cold. But there was no longer any doubt. A man or woman might be kept here as securely as in Her Majesty's prisons.

There was still no movement, so far as he could see. In the shelter of the outbuilding and hidden by it from the main house, he struck a light and held the flame to the window. Through the dusty glass he had a brief and flickering view of a whitewashed space with a pile of straw in one corner. If ever it had been used to confine a lunatic, that usage had ceased a long time ago.

He dropped the match and trod it out as the flame scorched his fingers. Then he struck another and tried to see into the next room. But the window had been boarded over on the inside. Even so, it was impossible that a human being could be kept there in such conditions without dying in a little while. If there was a room that imprisoned the strange duality of Dr Jekyll's mind it must lie in the house itself. Oblivious for the moment of the tightening grip of cold upon him, Alfred Swain moved to the corner of the building.

Surely the windows were shuttered and boarded. The house was empty and dark. There was just one window that made him uncertain. A tiny sliver that was not quite light and not quite dark. Perhaps a knife-edge of light between two shutters or perhaps a faint reflection of the stars' glimmer. And perhaps nothing at all.

He took a step towards it. As he did so, a shadow moved behind him in the stillness. A dull reverberating pain seemed to originate in the centre of his brain and blossom outwards. He registered the event with a detachment that astonished him, while he still stood upright. By the time that he fell to his knees the darkness was unbroken by starlight and the world of the mountains closed upon him in unrelieved black.

'Sorry I had to do that,' said someone amiably. 'Didn't want to hurt you, old fellow. Feeling all right, are you? Steady the Buffs! Best let me give you a hand.'

23

'You fool! You fool, Alfred Swain! Why could you not leave it be?'

The voice, like the last memory of the explosion in his head, came from somewhere deep inside him. He was aware that the sentiments were his own. But he disowned the sound of the voice. In the confusion of recollection, he thought that this was how it must have been when Jekyll heard another man talking in his own most private thoughts. It was happening again. And when he knew this, Swain felt that it was all right. He had explained it all to himself and it did not matter.

But why in that case could he not open his eyes? It was not for want of trying. He could feel the lids straining upwards into the sockets and he could see nothing. There was not even the pricking sense of vision in darkness. Something was wrong with him. Something was profoundly and inexplicably wrong.

'You fool!' Now he was pitying himself, by the sound of the voice. 'Why did you have to do it?'

Do what? He wondered about it. Leave London? Speak to Dr Orange? Search the records at Westminster? Wander about on the mountains at night? Something had hit him. Swain tried to grope his way back through the memory of events. Keep to the sequence. Someone had hit him. That was what had happened. He understood now why he was here – wherever that might be. That was why he was blind. And because he understood, in a curious way that seemed to make it all right. There was nothing to worry about.

'If only you had understood!' the voice said.

Alfred Swain mobilised his tongue to reply, to assure himself or the voice that he understood perfectly and that it was all right. But his tongue declined to obey him. It lay in his mouth speechless and motionless as a pork chop on a dinner plate.

'No one wanted you to die,' the voice said plaintively.

If his tongue could have managed it, Swain would have said that he had no wish to die either. There seemed to be general agreement on this and so it really did not matter. But his tongue lay like meat against his teeth and, in any case, the voice had stopped talking. He rather thought it had gone away. Moreover, he felt far from well. He needed sleep. And so Alfred Swain slept.

He woke, a long time later, as if at the drumming of a gong or the ringing of a firebell. With complete clarity, he knew that he was lying under a heavy blanket. The room was in darkness, sealed so that it excluded every atom of light. He supposed that someone might have intended to kill him. When he tried to say so, there was not a sound in his throat. He felt dry and rather sick.

From somewhere in the outer and invisible world of light, he heard a chuckle but saw no one and no light.

'You'd do a lot of harm to people if you had the chance, old fellow. I'd say you're a sight better off where you are.'

It was a voice that he had heard before but he could not put a face to it. In London. In Scotland Yard.

'You're a policeman,' Swain said in a hoarse exclamation.

There was a shout of laughter.

'I wish I was, old fellow. I like a bit of fun that way! But you're the policeman, my dear chap, and that's all about that. Still, I can't say I envy you just this minute.'

'Who are you?'

'Oh, no!' The voice grew waggish and reprimanding. 'I don't give my name like that, old boy. Not without I know what this is all about.'

It came to Swain then and he knew that he was recovering his wits. There was a taste in his mouth as if he had been drugged. Perhaps it was only bile. His head ached but he could think clearly.

'I know you,' he said quietly. 'You're Mad Billy.'

'I say!' Now the voice was impressed, despite a certain disappointment. 'I call that smart as new paint. How did you do that, then?'

'Henry Smith-Billington,' Swain said reassuringly, 'you'll be all right, Billy. The others will be here presently.'

'Others?'

'Sergeant Lumley and the others.'

'Oh, I say!' said Billy thoughtfully. 'I hope they won't. I don't know that that would do at all.'

Swain wondered if he had said the wrong thing. Billy lapsed into silence for a moment. Then he said brightly,

'I hope I didn't hurt you last night. I didn't want to. It wasn't too bad, was it?'

'No,' Swain said, 'not too bad at all.'

'Oh,' said Billy, 'jolly good. I'm glad about that.'

There was silence again between them. Swain heard Billy moving about and knew that he was in the room. Bare boards. Hard uncovered walls.Either in one of the cells at the end of the outbuildings or else in the house itself. A door opened and there was a glimmer of yellow oil-light. He thought at first that Mad Billy had left him. But it was someone else who had come in. This time he knew the voice from its first word.

'Why couldn't you leave us alone?' Romana Utterson said softly. 'Why couldn't you?'

'A man is missing in suspicious circumstances,' Swain said, seeing her silhouette against a faint illumination of bare walls and boards. 'A man who was – perhaps is – your lover. A man who may now be dead. Henry Jekyll.'

She stood before him, the lantern moving to show her posed and self-conscious as if he had been sketching her. Resolve and revenge. That was what the enigmatic slant of the eyes meant to him now.

'Henry Jekyll is safe.' Her voice was little more than a whisper. 'He is here. Safe at last from all of you.'

Swain nodded.

'You could never love any man as you loved him. Your own words. At the time I thought they were just a manner of speech.'

She began to laugh and then broke off.

'The world of Alfred Swain!' she said at last. 'The world where love has one meaning.'

'Not quite.' He snatched at a second chance. 'You lied about the painting of Henry Jekyll's saloon. You lied to keep your mother out of it. That was when I first supposed that Henry Jekyll might be your natural father.'

'Father?' Romana Utterson shook her chestnut hair into place, 'or lover? Which is it to be? Or is it to be both?'

'I had thought of that too,' he said quietly.

Then she laughed again, with scorn rather than amusement.

'He is not my father. I wish he were. He is not my lover. Yet he is the only man I have loved. The words I used were not a manner of speaking.'

Swain cleared the huskiness that had gathered in his throat again.

'Then he was the lover of Amelia Utterson. But which Amelia Utterson? She who lies in Kensal Green cemetery – or she whose grave is a few yards from this room?'

Mad Billy, who had been looking from one of them to the other at every exchange of speech, stepped forward with a friendly grin to Swain.

'Oh, that's only old Dr Parr out there. Keeper Hyde had him put there when the old boy died. Nice old fellow. Hyde was a devil. When he had me here, it took the lawyers to get me out again. Never such a devil for squeezing gold from his patients.'

It was almost the last piece of the puzzle to take its place in Swain's mind.

'Go and tell Dr Jekyll that I am ready, Billy,' Romana Utterson said.

The expression on the young man's face was that of a boy chosen for an errand by an adored schoolmistress. Alone with Swain, she took a step towards him.

'All this time, Alfred Swain,' she said, 'you have been like a man looking for the truth in a fog. Walking within inches of it, never quite finding it. Henry Jekyll was neither my father nor my lover. He was – is – the father of Dido Utterson.'

The fog parted and Swain saw the whole truth, as he thought.

'Henry Jekyll was your mother's lover. Edward Hyde knew of it and blackmailed them.'

Again she shook her head.

'He was her lover for a day,' she said, 'when I was ten years old. That summer at Tenby, after my father had been called back to London. I saw them. The two-backed beast. I went into her bedroom one afternoon in the house that overlooked the sea. There were long net curtains blowing a little in the draught and a view across to the castle. Waves glittering like broken glass and the room full of reflected sun. I saw them. Mama and Henry Jekyll. And I was happy. They were the two people I adored most in the world – not Gabriel Utterson. Not he. I had a dream that we should never go back to him in London but stay as we were, by the sea, always in summer. Dido was born next year. But when I opened the door into their room that afternoon, I destroyed the very thing that made me so happy. They were frightened, I suppose, and guilty. And so they put an end to it.'

'Your father,' Swain said, 'did he know?'

She frowned a little.

'I think he did not even guess. But you remember that he is a man who can endure anything provided that he is not obliged to acknowledge it. Provided that he is not told or that it is not thrust upon him as undeniable truth. When the time came, he went back to his bachelor life. He never spoke of himself as a widower. It was as if she had never existed. But I do not think he knew – or knows – that his greatest friend was the lover of his wife. So long as you did not confront him with it, perhaps he would not care. And that is the secret of his strength. Mr Utterson the lawyer cares for nothing. He gives no hostages to fortune.'

Romana Utterson turned from him, as if there were no more to tell. When she spoke again, her voice rehearsed the facts with no more feeling than if they had been a railway timetable.

212

'The rest you know. She was ill after Dido's birth. My father, in his precise manner, knew that it would be better for a mad wife to be away from the children. Henry Jekyll was distraught but he bought this house from Dr Parr and hired an experienced keeper – Edward Hyde – so that she could be looked after privately with every care. It was far enough away. My father could not endure such disturbance to his gin and water in Bayswater. In the following year she died. Before that, in her misery and fever, she told the entire story of Henry Jekyll and her love. Told it to Keeper Hyde. Here. In this house.'

'And so the blackmail came about?'

'No blackmailer could torture him more than Henry Jekyll tormented himself. He accused himself as her seducer, as the man who had destroyed her reason and her life. After her death, Edward Hyde took into his keeping the old medical man who had once owned the house. An irreclaimable drunkard whose reason had gone – Samuel Parr. The poor creature would never leave his madhouse cell alive. Hyde's trade was forgery and he pillaged the old man's allowances. By that time, Henry Jekyll had thrown away his own career and fame. He thought himself the murderer of Amelia Utterson and the betrayer of friendship. He took the name of a man who was dead to the rest of the world and went abroad as Dr Samuel Parr.'

'It was the story of Amelia Utterson with which Sir Danvers Carew threatened Henry Jekyll?'

She nodded and sat on the side of the bed.

'Mama was a Carew before her marriage, the eldest of the children. Somewhen, in the months she carried Dido, she must have said something to Danvers about her lover. Uncle Danvers had no feeling for my father at all. But when mama died, Danvers swore that Henry Jekyll had first unhinged his sister's mind by his seduction and then brought about her death. Henry Jekyll never denied it. He bore guilt upon him. He accepted the cruelties of Edward Hyde as if they were a deserved judgement. As for his other cowardice, when he rode away from the Zulu battle, it was to avoid meeting Sir Danvers Carew, not to escape the enemy. After that, he came back to

England with his mind in disorder and Edward Hyde's claws were sharpened for him.'

'Henry Jekyll did not resist him or ask for help?'

'He could not endure to think my father should be told of the ancient crime. So his bank account was open to Edward Hyde's forgeries and his cabinets supplied the man's craving for opium. But Sir Danvers Carew recognised Henry Jekyll at once in the bogus Samuel Parr and threatened him with destruction. It came to a head with the nomination to a governorship of the Military Incurables Hospital. Danvers Carew's note to Henry Jekyll was received. Hyde read it. He took care to protect his interest by murder – and to involve our friend closely in suspicion. When you read the copy of that note, it was natural you should think that there was some question of military cowardice.'

Swain moved too suddenly and felt a sick throbbing at the back of his skull.

'There is one question I must answer for myself. I conclude that after the search of Terminology House, Hyde took refuge in Caleb Square. Henry Jekyll turned to murder in his despair and destroyed Edward Hyde by poison.'

She looked at him with pity at last.

'You will never understand humanity, Freddie Swain. Henry Jekyll is no murderer. Grief and shame drove him half mad when my mother died. Edward Hyde's brutality completed the work. But Henry Jekyll never murdered anyone. It is quite beyond him.'

That was it then, Swain thought. The fog cleared at last.

'You,' he said. 'Then it was you who filled the opiate with crystals of prussic acid.'

He strained to see the expression on Romana Utterson's face as she turned into the oil-lamp's shadow. By her tone, she shrugged off the accusation.

'In the end, a man trapped as Hyde was would drink anything with a touch of opium, blind to the danger. I regret that the creature was not destroyed long, long before. But opportunity is sometimes delayed. There could be no hope, no peace but through the death of Edward Hyde. Henry Jekyll would not harm a fly. But I have waited more than a year for my chance. Tell me, Alfred Swain, will it be a feather in your constabulary hat to arrest Romana Utterson for the murder of Edward Hyde?'

Of all the enigmas suggested to Swain by the beauty of Romana Utterson – sensuality, perversity, deceit and even madness – he had for too long missed the most obvious. A resolute and cunning intent to murder the tormentor of the man she cared for. While he sketched and admired her, envied and loved her, she was waiting her chance to free Henry Jekyll by the death of his blackmailer. The nature of their love was plain to him at last.

'If Samuel Parr lies buried out there by the memorial stone to Amelia Utterson, who was the derelict that died in Monmouth asylum?'

She shrugged again.

'Edward Hyde could have told you. Samuel Parr was a man of some wealth with no relatives to take an interest in him. When he died, Keeper Hyde buried him and found a pauper madman whom he kept as Parr and continued to milk the estate. When the money was gone and Hyde had Henry Jekyll in his claws, he sent the poor devil to the public asylum to end his days, under the name of Samuel Parr.'

'And Mad Billy?'

'A patient whom Hyde held in confinement for a grasping family. Another lucrative prisoner in this house until the courts released the poor boy. He is Silly Billy, but there is no harm in him. Henry Jekyll privately persuaded Dr Lanyon to act on Billy's behalf. The boy adores him. It was Billy and Aggie York who opened the door of Terminology House for me that night. Do you not see, Fred Swain? It was I who left the broken stick there. It was a poor effort, but I cannot regret it.'

He had no need for questions now. There was nothing that he could not have guessed. But Alfred Swain had made one fundamental misjudgement. He had thought Romana Utterson might be the mistress or daughter of Henry Jekyll. It had

215

not seemed possible that she might be neither and yet would commit murder for him.

'And me?' he said quietly. 'What do you want of me?'

Romana Utterson frowned, as if she would have preferred him to avoid the topic.

'That you should bother us no more.'

'If a crime has been committed—'

As his eyes grew more accustomed to the oil-light, he saw that Romana was wearing a green velveteen coat and bonnet.

'You will never understand, Alfred Swain,' she said gently, 'the crime of Henry Jekyll! It was no worse than the crime that you committed with me, one afternoon in Bayswater. That was all. Unless you count it a crime to care for her afterwards. But from that one crime of yours, nothing came. From his, there came exile, delusion, blackmail and death.'

'I don't deny it. But what will you do with him now?'

His own voice came weakly to his ears.

'I mean to put him beyond harm.'

'You mean to kill him!'

'No,' said Romana softly, 'I do not mean that. But for you, Fred Swain, death is the worst thing, is it not? For others, it is not always so. I mean to put him beyond harm in life or death. I would kill him to save him. But that will not be necessary. He will choose his own time.'

She might live with Jekyll, of course. Somewhere abroad, at Bruges or Montpellier, where they would lead a kind of life together. Not as lovers, not as father and daughter. As something stranger and inexplicable. A human curiosity in a genteel city.

'I came here to find you,' Swain said, 'that was all. I'm not even a policeman just now. A traveller on holiday. And even if I were a policeman, I should want nothing but to see that you and he are safe. Perhaps you killed Hyde. But only you could prove it. Let it end there.'

'And Mad Billy?'

He smiled in the dark.

'I saw nothing. Only Billy could say whether he laid me out.'

Her hand touched him for the first time.

'As you came in friendship, Alfred Swain, leave us as a friend tomorrow. There is nothing for you here.'

Swain made no reply. He watched her turn without a word and go out through the door. His eyes met the reassuring smile of Mad Billy.

'You'll be all right now, old fellow,' said the amiable giant. 'Any friend of Dr Jekyll's is a friend of mine. He found the sawbones that got me discharged from Keeper Hyde's asylum. I'd do anything for him and Miss Utterson. You'll be all right with me, Fred Swain.'

It was a large and comfortable bunk. The frame was softly padded and soothing to the nerves. It had, Swain supposed, been constructed to comfort the mad. While he was thinking about this, aware of Billy still somewhere in the darkened room, he drifted into sleep.

When he came to himself again, the room was still dark, except that daylight was visible indirectly through the door. Billy was no longer to be seen. Swain recalled the conversation with Romana Utterson during the night. It might have been one of his recurring dreams. But he knew it was not. She had made a confession of the most important kind. If only in order to quieten his own tidy mind, Swain knew that there were questions still to be asked.

He got to his feet and his head throbbed dangerously again. But he persevered and walked slowly to the door. Mad Billy was singing softly to himself and there was an encouraging sound of crockery rattling. Swain found the young man in a quarry-tiled kitchen. Mad Billy turned to him with a grin of welcome. He gave a simultaneous sideways nod and a click of his tongue.

'Feeling brighter, old fellow?'

'Yes,' said Swain. 'And where's Miss Utterson? And Henry Jekyll?'

'No Miss Utterson here, old boy. No Henry Jekyll either. There's just the two of us. You and me.'

'They were here last night.'

Billy chuckled at his own cleverness.

217

'So they were. But they ain't here now, old bean. They've gone.'

'Where?'

Billy spread jam across two slices of bread at once to save labour.

'Nowhere. Just gone. Good few hours ago.'

'That's absurd. It can't have been hours ago.'

'Oh yes it can, old chap.' The mouth was packed comfortingly full of soft bread and sticky fruit. 'You had a thick night last night and that often puts a fellow out.'

'What time is it?'

'Can't you tell, old boy? Not exactly crack of dawn. I'm eating bread and jam, aren't I? That means tea. Half-past three, in other words.'

Swain gave it up. He thought of Romana Utterson with a pang. To kill Edward Hyde for the man she loved raised her inestimably in his view. And yet it was his duty to bring her to justice. The thought that she might have killed for him as well was profoundly exciting to Swain. But he knew that to take her side was a betrayal of his constabulary oath.

He wanted her back, but that was impossible. With her protective passion, there was no separating her from Henry Jekyll now. They would disappear. It was to be Bruges or Montpellier after all, a curious English couple who would live under an assumed name. Their hosts would regard the ambivalent relationship with tolerance and keep well clear. At last they would lie in some far off Protestant or English cemetery in a quiet corner of France or Holland. The suffering of Henry Jekyll would be forgotten. The savage crimes of Edward Hyde might be remembered.

A cold sunlight lay across the bare tiled kitchen. There was already a hint of evening in the sky beyond the window. Swain sat down opposite Mad Billy on a wooden chair. He reached for the bread and jam just before Billy could snatch it again.

'Tell me,' he said conversationally, 'just what was it that made a police uniform so attractive, old fellow?'

24

In the weeks and months that followed, Alfred Swain's conscience grew reconciled to the lack of a dramatic arrest in Gospel Pass. He even felt a secret pride in his failure to present Romana Utterson before the bar of justice on a charge of murdering Edward Hyde. In the end, she had been right about Inspector Swain. He would lie to save a woman he loved, even a cat or a dog. He supposed that even a policeman must learn to live with his weaknesses. Lesser men would take a drink from a publican or a favour from a Haymarket draggle-tail. Swain indulged the grander vices of sentiment. He had pitied Henry Jekyll and, now that it was too late, he loved Romana Utterson. Or, at least, he knew that he had done so once. And he had ignored his duty accordingly. What Toplady called the schoolmiss poetry-books and the sketching parties had corroded his resolve.

The case itself had faded from the press with the violent death of Edward Hyde. Swain, seconded to the constabulary duties of the South-Western Railway, had had no more to do with it. Only in midsummer did he see, on his return to Scotland Yard, a trolley laden with Mepo files, destined for the basement archives of the Home Office. As it passed him in the corridor, he read the label on the spine of the uppermost cover.

'Jekyll,' it said, 'alias Hyde.'

In the labyrinth of the official mind the two names were now linked for eternity. Had they got them the right way round? He supposed so. If they believed that Hyde was merely a masquerade of Jekyll's, then the death of Hyde was the death of both. And if not . . . Alfred Swain had sighed and called up the file of Colonel Valentine Baker, commanding the 10th

Prince of Wales' Hussars, charged with kissing a young lady on the Aldershot express and sent to prison for a year.

By the time that he had served his own sentence with the railway police, the Carew murder case had been forgotten in favour of that summer's white-slave scandal. Mr Stead of the *Pall Mall Gazette* and Bramwell Booth of the Salvation Army had revealed the horrors of English maidenhood, bound and gagged in coffins for shipment across the channel. The law, with a proper sense of decorum, had ignored the trade and prosecuted Booth and Stead. But the resulting protests and particularly the incompetence of Chief Inspector Newcomen in the case secured Swain's recall from Waterloo Station.

Being on early turn and having just come off duty, he was walking home through a sunlit afternoon in late August. Someone had that morning sent him a small clipping from *The Times* of the previous day. It had arrived anonymously through the post in a plain envelope.

> The marriage, previously postponed, between Captain Henry Smith-Billington, only son of Sir William Smith-Billington and the late Lady Smith-Billington of Thorpe House, Hereford, and Miss Agnes Louisa York of Clock Gardens, Chelsea, took place yesterday at Chelsea Old Church. The ceremony was privately held, at the wish of both parties. The honeymoon is to be passed at Biarritz.

Swain read the clipping again as he walked. Then he shook his head, crumpled the slip of paper, and threw it down. The Pimlico barrel-organ in St George's Square was grinding away at the children's delight, a song to have every urchin in the neighbourhood shouting the chorus.

'Ho, whenever I go out. . . . Yer can 'ear the people shout . . . "Git yer 'air cut! Git yer 'air cut! . . ." But I'll meet 'em when the sun goes down. . . .'

Having lunched at a coffee stall, Alfred Swain rather thought he might spend the afternoon with Walter Pater. There had been no further invitations to Bayswater. Mr Utterson had been unable to bring himself to discuss the matter of Henry Jekyll with his former friend. But Swain had spent his summer leisure in museums and galleries with a hunger for their beauty. He had got everything he could from Pater's *Renaissance*. To his surprise, he found that his idol had also written a recent novel. *Marius the Epicurean*. In the normal way, Alfred Swain avoided novels and did not much approve of them. But for Mr Pater, he would make an exception. The two volumes, wrapped by Hatchards of Piccadilly, had been delivered the day before.

He slipped the key into the lock, the heat of the sun fierce on Pimlico brick, and went enthusiastically upstairs. His lips were half-pursed to whistle as he opened the door. Then the figure by the window turned upon him and he felt a shock that was almost fright.

'Well, Alfred Swain,' she said, 'I think a person might expect something more than that. Under the circumstances.'

'I'm sorry. I had no idea. Not even that you were in England.'

'Your Mrs Platt let me in to wait. I hope that was in order.'

'Of course it was. It was a surprise. That's all.'

'Pleasant or unpleasant, as the case may be.'

Romana Utterson drew the pins from her hat, shook loose her chestnut hair, and set the hat itself upon a table.

'Pleasant, of course,' he said foolishly, drawing out a chair for her. 'But how are you? And how is our friend?'

'Henry Jekyll?' She spoke as if with an effort of recollection. 'Henry Jekyll died two weeks ago in Pisa. Peacefully, of a broken constitution. He was buried in the English cemetery at Florence.'

'I'm sorry. Of course, I had no idea.'

From her chair, she looked up at him.

'Don't be sorry, Freddie Swain. He had suffered a great deal but he was as happy as he had ever been for six months. And then he died as easily as closing a door for the night.'

'And you?'

Romana smiled at last, perhaps at the incongruity of her situation.

'I am his heir. Half the world will believe that I was his mistress and the other half will think him my natural father. And both will be in error. I shall settle somewhere. Perhaps in Pisa again or Basle. And I shall grow old as a strange English lady, living alone with her doubtful past. Don't protest, Fred Swain. I shall be perfectly content.'

'And your father?'

She swept a stray tendril of hair into place with the back of her hand.

'I should like to see Dido again, for Henry Jekyll's sake. And Jenny perhaps. But I cannot say that my mind is drawn much to Gabriel Utterson, nor his to me. Poor Alfred Swain! You do not understand, you see! You never did and I cannot believe you ever will.'

She looked the same to him with the calm pale beauty of a Rossetti model and the incongruously lascivious slant of the eyes. Romana Utterson was now all chestnut hair and nervous beauty. She had changed little in manner but he caught a weariness in her voice. She had lost the edge, the sharpness of its tone. To his surprise, he regretted that.

He sat down opposite to her, on the far side of the round table that served him for dining and reading. Outside in the warm and gritty air, the children were keeping time with gusto as the notes of the barrel-organ clattered their wooden tune.

'Ho, whenever I go out. . . . Yer can 'ear the people shout. . . . '

'And Mr Inspector Swain?' Romana asked. 'What about him? Does he thrive? Do his sketches progress?'

Swain laughed at the supposition.

'Very little. I've been travelling a good deal, on the express railway beween Aldershot and Waterloo. Apprehending military gentlemen who force their attentions upon young ladies.'

Romana gave a sigh of exasperation.

'You are a prig, Fred Swain! And the servant of prigs, which is even worse for you! The dear young ladies would never stand in the least danger from you. One may depend upon that.'

'It was not always so,' he said laconically, 'was it?'

They looked at one another for a moment.

'Show me your sketches,' she said.

He stood up and went across to the plain wooden cupboard at one end of the room.

'There are very few,' he began, apologising as he always seemed to do in Romana Utterson's presence. 'Fewer still that one would care to show.'

'What you sketch interests me, Fred Swain, quite as much as how it is done.'

He fetched the pile of half-completed subjects and set them on the table.

'I shall go and make some tea,' he said quickly.

Least of all did he want to stand over Romana Utterson while she sifted through his sketches and passed comment upon them.

He came back into the room to see that she had left most of the sketches on the table and was sitting in the tall-backed chair so that the light fell full upon her from the lace-curtained window. What she was looking at he could not tell, for the tall back of the chair hid from him all but her head. He put the tray down and walked round. With a quickening beat of the heart he first guessed and then knew what he would find, as he saw the green silk draped before her in discarded flurries.

'The board and pencil, if you please, Fred Swain,' she said imperiously. 'It is evident to me that your subjects of the past few months have left something to be desired.'

But Swain, staring at the pale vision, had no thought of board or pencil.

'You are beautiful, Romana Utterson,' he said, sitting down before her on a stool. 'Quite the most beautiful—'

'Quite the most beautiful beggar maid in the entire kingdom of Cophetua.' Her tone was precise and would tolerate no contradiction.

'If you wish,' he said.

'And I do wish, Inspector Swain. Only think how many gentlemen in your situation would envy you the possession of such a supplicant.'

Before he could say anything else, she slid forward and knelt at his feet. She took his hand and pressed it to her lips to kiss. Swain knew what was about to happen but she held him fast

223

with both hands on his. He gasped as the force of her teeth breaking the flesh brought a start of tears to his eyes. And still the hand was held fast while she slanted her eyes up at him with a look of suggestively unhinged sensuality.

'And now, if you please,' said Romana Utterson softly, 'we will have the real Alfred Swain once more.'